ASSASSIN'S HONOR
Assassins of Landria, Book 1

Gail Z. Martin

Dedication

For my family, and my fandom family.

ASSASSIN'S HONOR

CHAPTER ONE

Roan Destwiler was a dead man, by order of the king. He just didn't know it yet.

Joel Breckenridge, king's assassin, bided his time and hoped his partner got into position to make the shot. If not, the evening would go badly very fast.

The stolen cloak that he had taken off the arms smuggler itched, and Ridge tried not to scratch. He hoped that lice would be the worst of the vermin in the clothes he had stripped off the man he waylaid a few streets over. Ridge did his best to look at ease, accompanying two guards who carried a heavy chest of contraband swords, knives, and war axes Ridge had delivered on an equally stolen wagon.

A third guard opened the doors to the deal maker's opulent office. Destwiler sat behind a wide desk, resplendent in a wine-red brocade frock coat over a deep blue satin vest. He had a broad, plain face with an off-kilter nose, broken too often to ever set right, and a scar through one eyebrow.

"You're late," he snapped, barely favoring Ridge with a glance, which suited the assassin just fine. He kept the arms dealer's stolen hat slouched low to obscure his face.

"Had to get around the king's guards," Ridge lied. "Couldn't have them nosing around." Once he and Rett had nabbed the arms smuggler, it had taken a while to move the weapons into a second chest with a false bottom and with a nasty surprise inside.

"Let's see the cargo," Destwiler said. "It better be what I paid for." He gave a disquieting chuckle. "The buyer is impatient. Then again, now that I've got my 'good luck charm,' we shouldn't have any delays getting the items where they need to go." His gaze fell on the scrawny boy chained to one side of Destwiler's desk, the kidnapped nobleman's son Ridge and Rett had been assigned to rescue.

A small boy, perhaps eight years old, huddled against the desk, trying to make himself invisible. Manacles far too heavy for his spindly arms and legs clanked, practically pinning him in place by their weight. The jacket and knickers he wore were made of fine brocade, sullied and stained by his captivity. The boy's hair hung lank, and his cheeks were hollow so that he looked more like an urchin than an aristocrat's child.

"I promise you, it's everything and more," Ridge replied, opening the chest. As Destwiler's attention went to the box of weapons, Ridge scanned the room. Two guards stood behind him. An iron key hung from a leather strap around Destwiler's neck, and Ridge bet it fit the locks on the boy's chains. Opening up his Sight, Ridge felt no surprise that Destwiler bore the touch of the Witch Lord, a psychic stain like festering rot.

Destwiler had been a worthy target for a long time, escaping punishment for as long as he had only because Burke, King Kristoph's left hand and the commander of the king's assassins, believed the man would eventually lead them to more important criminals.

Then Destwiler got greedy—or stupid—and took the son of a noble hostage to further his schemes, and forbearance ended.

Ridge restrained himself from glancing upward, toward the second-floor windows. Destwiler moved out from behind his desk, and into position.

Breaking glass and the crack of gunfire were Ridge's signal to move, as Destwiler's skull exploded from the matchlock's shot, spattering the crate of weapons with blood and bone. The boy screamed in terror, a thin, shrill sound.

Ridge spun around, grabbing two throwing knives from the top of the stash in the box and had them hilt-deep in each guard's ribs before their swords cleared their scabbards. He dropped the heavy crossbar to lock the door to the office, and dodged back to the box of weapons, reclaiming his own array of swords and knives before teasing out a long fuse from the bottom of the crate. Then he strode over to Destwiler's corpse and pulled the key and its strap around what was left of the man's head.

Ridge removed the warrant from inside his vest and read out the charges as required by law. "Roan Destwiler. By order of King Kristoph of Landria, you stand condemned of crimes against the kingdom and the throne too numerous to note, but most grievously the kidnapping of Kelvin, son of Thad, Lord of Wendover. You are sentenced to death, summary execution, without notice or reprieve."

He rolled the warrant up and tucked it into Destwiler's bloody vest, a formality. Ridge bent down to search Destwiler's pockets, curling his lip at the still-warm blood that soaked the shoulders and sleeves of the man's coat. He found a parchment note tucked beneath the vest and took it to read later, figuring that anything Destwiler found important enough to carry on his person bore looking at closely.

"Are you stealing from him?" Kelvin asked, still eying Ridge with a mixture of fear and awe.

Ridge replied without looking up. "I'm trying to find the keys to those manacles, because I sure as hell don't want to have to carry you and them out of here, and we need to leave." He took the iron key off the strap and then stood and crossed the distance to where Kelvin huddled against the wall.

He stared at Ridge in wide-eyed apprehension, unsure what to make of his terrifying rescuer. His wrists were badly bruised from the weight of the iron, and the mark on his cheek suggested Destwiler or his guard had backhanded the child at least once.

"I'm here to take you back to your father," Ridge said quietly, approaching Kelvin as he would a spooked horse. "I'm not going to hurt you."

"Are you a Shadow Killer?" Kelvin's tone shifted, still frightened but clearly intrigued.

Ridge had always hated that term—he argued that it made it sound like they killed shadows—but it remained what most people outside the palace called the king's elite assassins. "Yes. That's how I managed to get them before they got you—or me," he replied with a tense smile. He'd had very little experience with children since he had left the orphanage, and nothing in his training covered handling jittery child hostages.

"You want out of here? I need to reach the locks." Ridge dangled the heavy iron key from his fingers. "Before someone else comes and makes this a lot harder."

That seemed to decide Kelvin, who thrust his skinny arms and legs toward Ridge. Ridge frowned as he lifted the boy's wrists, wondering how Kelvin managed to move at all, considering the chains probably weighed as much as he did. The fact that cuffs came in a size small enough for Kelvin's thin wrists and ankles made his stomach turn.

The key released the manacles, and the cuffs fell away, banging against the floor. Ridge eyed Kelvin, noting more bruises. He wondered if anyone bothered to feed the boy since Destwiler obviously never intended to give him back. "Can you walk?"

Kelvin nodded. "I think so." His voice still sounded hoarse from screaming, and the attempt at bravado impressed Ridge. Kelvin did his best to haul himself up, leaning on the wall, but his knees buckled, and he would have fallen if Ridge had not darted in to grab him.

"Looks like you skipped a few meals," Ridge said, supporting the boy's weight. "We need to be gone from here, and we need to move fast. So I'm going to carry you, and you're not going to complain about it."

Garrett Kennard stuck his head in the broken window. "Hurry it up!" Rett ordered and dropped a rope down. Ridge gave the rope a good tug, then turned to Kelvin.

"Climb on my back. Now."

Ridge crouched, and Kelvin scrambled on, wrapping his slight arms around Ridge's neck and thin legs around his waist. "You'd better have tied this off to something solid," Ridge muttered at Rett as he started to climb hand-over-hand up the rope.

"Just don't let go. And don't look down," Ridge warned Kelvin.

Rett's anchor held, and he appeared at the top to drag Ridge and Kelvin over the window frame and onto the roof. He gathered up the rope and coiled it over his shoulder.

"Do it," Ridge said to Rett, angling Kelvin so he wouldn't see as Rett used a flicker of forbidden magic to light the fuse beneath the crate.

"Run!" Rett warned, and together they sprinted across the flat roof, came to the edge, and jumped across the gap, landing solidly on the next building. Kelvin gave a soft *oof* at the impact and tightened his arms and legs to hold on.

An explosion tore through Destwiler's office as the fuse ignited the gunpowder hidden in the bottom of the crate. If any of the other guards had succeeded in entering the room, the shrapnel of broken pottery and iron pellets packed with the gunpowder made the threat of pursuit unlikely. A fireball billowed from the first-story windows as glass shattered into the street.

Ridge grinned and sped up to close ranks with Rett. He kept one hand tight on Kelvin's wrists, and had a knife in the other, just in case. The wind that raked through Ridge's black hair was crisp with the promise of autumn. Just enough of the waning moon peeked through the clouds to enable him to follow the path they had laid out earlier across the rooftops, abetted by the smoky lamplight of the questionable lodging houses and pubs below.

Ridge's soft boots let him move silently and sure-footed. Six years of experience made him graceful and fleet. The buildings crowded close together, making it easy for him to jump from rooftop to rooftop. Ridge had long ago lost any sense of vertigo, since he had been doing this kind of work since he was eighteen. If he had ever been afraid of falling, he no longer remembered it.

"He'd damn well better be there," Ridge muttered.

"He'll be there."

They wove a crooked course over the rooftops until they were several blocks north and a couple of streets west of Destwiler's building. Ridge chanced a look over his shoulder and saw the glow from the fire in the distance. With the amount of gunpowder Rett had packed into the crate, the whole building would burn like a pyre.

"Here," Rett said, coming to a stop at the edge of a building with a stout, solidly built chimney. He secured the rope and held it out to Ridge, who grabbed hold, turned, and stepped off into the night.

Kelvin stifled a cry as Ridge rappelled down the side of the building. At the bottom, he stepped away and whistled, Rett's signal to descend. Ridge spun and faced an empty street.

"He's not here," Ridge grated.

"He'll be here," Rett replied, unperturbed.

Racing hoof beats thundered in the night, and a black carriage turned the corner so fast it rose up on two wheels. The wild-eyed black stallion bore down like it meant to trample the three of them, reined in at the last moment by the short, balding, pudgy driver.

"Right on time!" Henri, the driver, exulted. Ridge glowered but said nothing as Rett threw open the door of the carriage, and they climbed inside, Kelvin between them. The carriage started up at a gallop before they had taken their seats, throwing them against the sides.

"Hang on," Ridge advised Kelvin. "The driver is a madman."

Cobblestones at high speed made for a rough and painful trip, and Ridge felt sure the jostling had left him bruised and jarred a few teeth from his head. Kelvin had the glassy-eyed look of a rabbit in thrall, torn between terror and excitement. Rett laughed, bracing himself with one hand on either side of the carriage to keep from being thrown around.

"Nice shot," Ridge said, as the rough ride made his voice hitch.

"Had to make it count, since the matchlock takes so bloody long to reload," Rett replied with a shrug.

Henri slowed the carriage to a more respectable pace. Ridge's heart still hammered in his chest from the fight, the climb, and the escape, and the wild ride did not help. Rett's chestnut hair was wind-rustled, but excitement glinted in his whiskey-brown eyes. "You look like you're having entirely too much fun," Ridge grumbled.

Cobblestones gave way to smooth pavers. The carriage slowed and stopped, as Henri spoke to the palace guards. Then the horse started off again at a stately trot until minutes later the carriage came to rest at the back entrance to the palace.

"Here's where you go find your father," Ridge said, nudging Kelvin's shoulder to get the boy to let go of his death grip on the seat cushion. He climbed out of the carriage and helped Kelvin down, giving a glance and nod as Burke, the officer in charge of the king's assassins, descended from the doorway to take the young man inside.

"Destwiler?" Burke asked.

"Dead."

"And the fire that's been reported in that area?"

Ridge shrugged. "Had to make sure we weren't followed."

Burke fixed him with a glare. "Assassins are supposed to be stealthy, Breckenridge. You keep forgetting."

"Hard to argue with results," Ridge said with a grin, giving Kelvin's shoulder a reassuring squeeze before he climbed back into the carriage. Burke's withering gaze followed them.

"He knew about the fire already?" Rett asked.

"Guards could probably see it from the tower. Good job with the gunpowder, by the way."

Rett grinned, managing to look younger than his twenty-two years. "I'll have to experiment when we have time. Might be a way to blow things up without taking out the building."

"Where's the fun in that?" Ridge asked, giddy with the adrenaline of the fight and the rush of relief that came with surviving another mission.

Before long, the carriage stopped outside the building where they rented the upper floor. Ridge and Rett got out. Henri gave them a nod. "I'll be right there, as soon as I return the carriage to where I stole it." With that, he headed off at a reasonable pace through the darkened streets of Caralocia.

"He does know that when we've got a warrant from the king, it's not really stealing as long as we give it back, right?" Ridge asked as they made their way up the narrow stairs.

"Don't spoil it for him," Rett returned. "I think he enjoys breaking the rules, every once in a while."

The banked fire on the hearth gave them enough light to see as they lit the lanterns, sending a warm glow across the sitting area. Their rooms above an unremarkable pub were hardly luxurious, though they were warm and tidy. Ridge and Rett could afford better, but the part of the capital city of Caralocia they had chosen let them hide among the crowds of shopkeepers and laborers, and lacked the pretentiousness of anything closer to the palace. The king paid his assassins quite well, recognizing the danger and the fact that his elite defenders were unlikely to reach old age. Few made it past thirty, and only a handful made it to forty. Ridge and Rett had plenty of scars to attest to the hazards of their work.

The two friends usually hunted together, a rarity among assassins, who tended to prefer working solo. Their uncanny synchronicity had won over the Shadow Master, and their success record quashed any other objections. They'd been watching each other's backs since the orphanage, close as brothers since Ridge was ten and Rett was eight.

Ridge stood half a head taller and packed a bit more muscle, with crow-black hair, piercing blue eyes, a sharp jawline, and high cheekbones. Rett's brown eyes held flecks of gold in candlelight, as did his chestnut hair, framing delicate features. He might be a bit shorter and less bulky than his partner, but his lean build was whipcord strong, nimble as an acrobat.

"Could you Sight him?" Rett asked as he grabbed a bottle of whiskey from the shelf and Ridge took down three cups.

Ridge nodded. "Destwiler had the Witch Lord's touch on him. He'd definitely given himself over. The others were just regular scum."

The door opened, and both men tensed, then relaxed as Henri stepped inside. The wind made him red-cheeked and mussed what little of his fine blond hair remained. His vest strained over a slightly pudgy middle. "I left coin enough at the livery to compensate the carriage owner since we might have cracked an axle on a turn. Paid the night groom to see that the horse was taken care of." He grinned smugly. "After all, no telling when I'll need to steal him again."

CHAPTER TWO

"Paid one of the beggars down by the waterfront to tell me which ships Destwiler or his men met, and find out where the ships came from or went next," Henri said, digging in the cupboard to put a cold meal of bread, cheese, honey, and dried meat on the table, along with a flagon of ale.

"Can you trust his information?" Ridge asked.

"Yeah, he's a good source. Doesn't miss anything. And it seems that the ships are coming in from Maborne, down on the south coast. Here's the thing—the ships going out, taking the crates of weapons, they're going all over the northlands."

"Which is where the Witch Lord is courting the nobility," Ridge finished.

"Exactly," Henri confirmed. He had come to be Ridge and Rett's valet/squire/manservant by a circuitous route. When his previous employer found himself headed for jail, Henri had no references and nowhere to go. He had begged the two assassins to let him help them, and in the two years since then, had acquired a wide array of skills not usually required of a footman.

Ridge and Rett made an odd pair. Ridge's dark hair and stubble stood out against milk-pale skin. Rett's light olive complexion could turn as golden in the summer as the streaks of blond in his chestnut hair. They might be close as brothers, but no one would mistake them for kin.

Rett didn't remember a lot before he'd been taken to the orphanage. He had been eight, the same age as Kelvin, the boy they'd just saved. If Rett had ever known his parents, they hadn't made much of an impression among the adults he had dodged and feared, fending for himself and staying well clear of the guards. He'd made a mistake and gotten caught—by the monks, not the guards. Inside their quarters at the orphanage, Rett found a new threat in the older, bigger boys who looked at a short, skinny lad and figured he was easy prey. He'd nearly won that fight until too many of the others piled on.

Ridge had waded in and knocked heads together, and the two of them fighting side by side sent the bullies scrambling to get away. From then on, they were inseparable. Ridge taught Rett to read and do sums. Rett taught Ridge how to pick locks and pockets.

"Do you think that's where the box of weapons we stole was heading, to the northlands?" Ridge paused to remove a bit of food from between his teeth. "I didn't have the chance to find out where the drop point was when I waylaid the dealer."

"Your mission wasn't about the weapons; you had to save the boy," Rett said with a shrug.

"Still. If we could prove that the Witch Lord is a threat, maybe someone at the palace, besides Burke, would listen." Ridge drummed his fingers in frustration on the battered table.

"If we could tell them about the Sight—"

Ridge shook his head vehemently. "No. You know we can't. It's not one of the registered magics. And we aren't supposed to have *any* magic. If the king's mages found out, I'm not sure Burke could protect us."

Rett cursed under his breath. "It's a stupid law."

"Doesn't matter—it's still the law. I think they decided assassins shouldn't have magic so we wouldn't get too powerful. That way, the mages have something to use against us that we don't have."

Rett knew all that, but it didn't make the law easier to accept. The secret was another thing they had in common besides friendship. They both had the Sight, a rare ability to see the glimmer of a person's soul and sense whether that person had bound themselves to a mage. The Sight was a quirk of birth; it couldn't be learned or given up. Before she died, Ridge's mother had cautioned him not to tell anyone about his ability, and Rett had already known not to trust most people with secrets, especially not the monks.

"Something else…" Rett said quietly, and his mood grew darker. "I had one of those 'flashes' again. Just as the bells tolled nine. Right after I fired."

Ridge quirked an eyebrow. "What did you see?"

Rett had not only been born with the Sight, but he'd also gotten a little extra magic, glimpses of things that hadn't happened yet. The visions weren't predictable or under his control.

"I saw a man in an expensive coat on a horse in the woods. He was attacked, and someone slit his throat." Rett swallowed hard.

"Shit. Could you tell, has it already happened, or not yet?"

Rett frowned, thinking. "I can't be positive, but I think that it hasn't happened yet. The images are clearer when it's something that's already done, and a little fuzzier when it's yet to be."

"You got the vision right after you shot Destwiler. Maybe he was planning the attack, and it crossed his mind as he died."

"If it hasn't already happened, we need to stop it," Rett said. "There was a feeling of anticipation like it was coming up soon."

"There are too many well-dressed men with horses for us to protect them all, so we've got see if we can narrow it down." Ridge clapped a hand on Rett's shoulder in reassurance, knowing how much the visions upset his friend.

When the glimpses made it possible to avert a tragedy, Rett told himself they were a good thing, although the monks would have thought otherwise. When they didn't, Rett wrestled with guilt, both for not being able to stop the events and for possessing a tainted, erratic "gift." Every time, Ridge was quick to reassure him, but Rett found it difficult to fully believe.

"Destwiler's been a ruffian for a long time, but nothing on the scale of smuggling weapons and kidnapping the nobility. Something made him change his game," Ridge said.

As they talked, Henri went to his room, changed clothes, and went down to the stable across the street to tend to their horses.

"And if he sold his soul to the Witch Lord, that's exactly the kind of thing that could happen," Rett finished the thought.

Rumors circulated throughout Caralocia about Yefim Makary, the wandering mystic whose followers called him the Witch Lord. A handsome, wild-eyed prophet with enough charisma to ingratiate him with the lesser nobility and a silver tongue to sway listeners, he seemed to appear out of nowhere to become the darling of the bored and restless aristocracy. As far as anyone could tell, Makary himself was not of noble birth, and he dressed like a penitent. But rumor had it he was educated and knew courtly manners. King Kristoph and his advisors regarded Makary as a passing fashion, an entertainment that would fade in popularity as new favorites emerged. Privately, Burke agreed with Rett and Ridge, but until the king saw the threat, little could be done officially.

"If we're right about what the Witch Lord does, it's not something the monks would expect," Ridge said. "They're looking for possession cases, evil spirits. But if he promises his loyalists their darkest desires and then he eliminates their conscience and enhances their ruthlessness, it wouldn't look like they were possessed, just the stain we see with the Sight. The monks might not even notice."

Ridge reached inside his jacket for papers and spread them out on the table. "I took these out of the crate when I added your little 'surprise.' They're waybills for more weapons. So along with Henri's informant, we know which ships transported the goods, and we have a name—probably false—of the person who arranged for the shipment. And there's a list of the contents."

He pointed at the sheaf of papers. "There are a dozen waybills, each for a single box. That's a lot of weapons."

"Suspicious, but we don't know who's receiving them and what they want with them," Rett mused. "If we took that to Burke, he'd say that we've got no evidence that there's ill intent. Maybe just some nobles who want to better arm their guards."

Ridge set the waybills aside and began to unfold the note he had taken from Destwiler's coat. His brows furrowed as he read, and he began to curse. "Listen to this. *Fixed for taking care of M. You'll know when it's done.*"

"But who is 'M'?" Rett groaned. "We don't know whether that's a first name or a last name."

Ridge chewed his lip as he thought. "You said the man in your vision was well-dressed, so probably a noble. He'd have to be important for someone to want to kill him. So likely one of the aristocracy who has been a thorn in the foot for the Witch Lord. Does that bring anyone to mind?"

"Lords Moran, Mandroll, and Monthaven," Rett replied.

Ridge shook his head. "Moran doesn't look like the type to ride his horse if he could take a carriage. He's far too fond of comfort. Mandroll barely gets around even with a cane—and he's ancient. Burke said Monthaven disliked the Witch Lord, but the king hadn't listened to him. That could make him a threat if the king ever started to pay attention."

"So Monthaven is likely to be the victim," Rett said. "What's the plan? Having two of the king's assassins turn up on his doorstep asking for him isn't likely to make him feel secure."

"We follow him and intercept whoever Destwiler's contact hired to kill him," Ridge replied.

"So we assassinate the assassins?"

"You've got a better plan?"

"We don't *have* a plan, so I can't have a *better* plan than one that doesn't exist!"

"Gentlemen," Henri interrupted and cleared his throat. "I've taken the liberty of feeding the horses and refreshing your saddlebags with supplies. While I would hope you might get some sleep and leave at dawn, all is ready for your trip." Only the barest hint of a smile touched the corners of the squire's mouth.

"Thank you, Henri," Ridge managed. "Sometimes you're so prepared it's unsettling."

"You're too kind," Henri replied. "And if you're looking for Lord Monthaven, might I suggest the Harvest Festival in Wendover? It begins tomorrow, and it's tradition for him to preside over the opening of the first cask of wine. That usually occurs right before the tug-of-war at fourth bells."

"And you know this because..." Ridge asked, looking at their squire askance.

"I happened to overhear two of the groomsmen talking about the festival while I was in the stable. They expected their masters would want their horses ready early to ride in for the opening pageant, which begins at noon."

"You're sure you're not a spy, Henri?" Rett joked. "I think you missed your calling."

Henri's enigmatic smile seemed out of place on his round, plain face. "Kind of you to say so, Mister Rett, but I'm quite happy to put all my skills to use in the service of you and Mister Ridge."

"And the world is a safer place because of it," Ridge muttered, but there was no heat in his words.

"Thank you, m'lord," Henri replied without a hint of sarcasm. "I'll have trail rations and full wineskins ready for your departure. They'll be on the table near the pantry."

Ridge and Rett exchanged a glance. "We'll leave at dawn," Ridge said with a sigh. "It's a long ride to Wendover, and we need to scout the road between there and Lord Monthaven's manor."

"As you wish, m'lord," Henri said. "And if you'd be so kind as to leave the waybills, my friend on the docks might be able to shed more light on the situation." He gave the barest hint of a bow. "If there's nothing else, I'll be in my room."

Rett watched him go and shook his head. "Most days I thank our stars that Henri's so good at his job, and then sometimes I wonder if Burke planted him here and he really *is* a master spy."

"He's far too ordinary looking to be a spy," Ridge countered, finishing off his drink.

"That makes him even more dangerous. He looks like a clerk. No one would ever suspect him."

"I can hear you," Henri's muffled voice sounded from behind his closed door.

"So we're sticking to the plan we don't have?" Rett asked.

"We have a plan," Ridge defended. "And it'll work. Just wait."

They reached the outskirts of Lord Monthaven's lands by mid-morning. Rett kept a watch on the main road leaving the manor while Ridge went ahead, all the way to Wendover, to scout the road. By the time Ridge returned, two hours remained before the festival began, and the road toward Wendover had already become crowded with travelers eager to attend the event.

"Looks like he's got an entourage," Rett said, with a jerk of his head toward the manor. Across the open lawn, they could see horses and a scramble of retainers getting ready for the lord's departure.

"The road's gotten busy. We'll have to find a way to watch him *and* watch the crowd," Ridge said. "It would have been nice if your vision had included a peek at the killers."

"I don't control it. Wish I did," Rett replied. What he really wished was to be rid of the troublesome premonitions. Having the Sight was one thing; seeing events he had little chance to prevent seemed an unnecessary burden. It wasn't possible to take action on every vision, but when the outcome aligned with their mission as Shadows—in this case, protecting one of the king's advisors from assassination—it eased the weight of his unwanted gift.

They hung back beneath a tree under the pretense of eating until Lord Monthaven's party left the estate and headed onto the road. Monthaven was surrounded by guards and retainers amidst a crowd of other riders heading for the festival. One glance made Rett's stomach plummet as he recognized that the Lord's clothing matched what the man in his vision had been wearing. He gave Ridge a nod, confirming that they were in the right place. He hoped the vision had been merely a warning, something that could be averted, instead of a glimpse of an unchangeable future.

Ridge rode up on one side of the entourage, managing to look bored and distracted while Rett knew his partner constantly scanned the crowd for threat. Rett rode on the other, watching both the travelers and the landscape, alert for potential hiding places that might provide cover for the attackers he had foreseen.

Lord Monthaven joked with the men with him and appeared to be enjoying the ride. The crisp fall air sent colorful leaves wafting down from high branches, while fallen nuts crunched beneath the horses' hooves. People from nearby farms and villages traveled the road on foot, on horseback, or in wagons. Monthaven and his retinue were by far the best dressed. Most of the people had the well-scrubbed look of farmers or townsfolk in worn but carefully mended plain clothing. Rett and Ridge had dressed to blend in, looking the part of merchants who could afford the quality horses they rode. Despite the nice day, Rett felt uncomfortable and irritable.

The half-hour ride was unremarkable—and most notably, entirely safe. The press of the crowd would have kept all but the best-trained assassins at a distance, making it difficult to get close to the target and even harder to get away. So Monthaven rode on, oblivious to the two unexpected additions to his bodyguards, and the travelers around them laughed and talked.

Nothing more dangerous than plodding donkeys or slow cart horses held up the procession. Rett thought that he should have been relieved, but his tension only ratcheted higher in the certainty that the attack was yet to come. He'd had enough visions to know that sometimes he glimpsed the crucial moment itself. Other times he saw a snippet before or after the danger, making the effort to avert the threat even more difficult.

When they reached the Wendover harvest festival, Rett's heart sank. The celebration took place in the open green of the small village, an area bounded by trees, buildings, and stables. Had he been looking for a setting in which to eliminate a target, this would have been a great choice. Someone with a bow or a matchlock could hide almost any-where: rooftops, branches, shadowed doorways, or behind the dozens of large barrels. The crowd made it difficult to trace the movements of any single person, and the converging streets would enable an easy escape.

Since Rett's job today was to *keep* a man from being assassinated, he disliked everything about the location, which only made his task harder. The square bustled with street vendors hawking meat pies and fig tarts, musicians singing and drumming, and children squealing as they played tag.

Lord Monthaven moved through the crowd looking relaxed and comfortable. The guards walked on either side, but Rett could see the men were not on edge. That meant Monthaven had no reason to ex-pect an attack. If Rett's vision was a true sending, then he and Ridge were Monthaven's only real protection.

A glance and a nod of his head gave Ridge all the information nec-essary, silent communication born of long years and plenty of battles. Rett moved to one side, while Ridge went to the other. Both had swords, knives, and throwing daggers beneath their cloaks, but Rett wished for his matchlock. Despite its single shot and annoying reload-ing process, the gun could hit a target at a distance, far beyond the range of anything but a bow. Rett eyed the windows that looked out on the green, perfect for a gunman or an archer. He had already scanned the trees for threats, but the dark windows allowed him no way to see whether anyone lurked in the shadows.

Rett turned his attention back to Monthaven, who stood on a small wooden platform in front of stacked wine barrels. Several men whom Rett assumed were local dignitaries fussed over Monthaven, who ap-peared pleasantly bored. The wine barrels were stacked in a pyramid, and another barrel sat upright on the platform, intended as the first to be tapped for the season. As Monthaven and the others took their places, Rett frowned. He couldn't help but scan and compare the bar-rels; attention to detail often meant the difference between life and death in their business. The top barrel of the pyramid looked wrong.

Ridge glanced his way, and Rett's gaze darted to the stacked barrels directly behind Lord Monthaven's seat on the platform. The mayor rose to speak, and the crowd grudgingly grew quiet, turning their attention toward the guests of honor.

A flaming arrow flew from the second floor of the building nearest to the platform. Rett reacted before most of the crowd made sense of what they saw. The arrow streaked behind Monthaven and the dignitaries and landed in the opened side of the top barrel. Rett plunged through the crowd, leaped onto the dais and tackled Monthaven, taking the stocky lord to the ground and covering him with his body as the top barrel exploded.

Rett held on and rolled, as the blast—it had to have been gunpowder, not wine in that barrel—sent flaming embers down all around and touched off more explosions from other, altered barrels. Screams filled the air, along with the shrieks of children and the cries of the injured.

He lifted his head and saw Ridge running for the archer's building, scaling the outside from sill to drain pipe to chase down the would-be killer. Monthaven jerked free of Rett's grip, and two of the lord's burly guards closed in, grabbing Rett by the arms and pinning him between them.

"Who are you?" Monthaven demanded. "And how did you know that was going to explode?"

"I'm one of King Kristoph's Shadows," Rett said. Monthaven drew back, alarmed. "My partner and I came to protect you, not kill you."

The guard on his left gave Rett a hard shake. "Tell the truth."

Rett raised his head to look at Monthaven. "There's a letter of marque in my vest from King Kristoph, my papers as a Shadow. That should prove who I am. We had a tip from an informant that someone meant you harm, and we came to save you."

Monthaven nodded, and one of the guards reached into Rett's vest to remove the paper, handing it over. The lord frowned as he read the letter of marque, glancing between it and Rett. "That's Kristoph's seal," he acknowledged. Monthaven's clothing bore smudges of dirt, grass, and soot from his narrow escape. He had lost his hat, and his dark hair stuck up in places. Rett had no idea how the others on the stage fared, or how many in the crowd had been injured, but from the wailing and moaning behind him, he knew the attempt had caused casualties.

"Is this what you're looking for?" Ridge's voice cut through the noise. He pushed his way into the small circle around the lord and threw a struggling, bound man onto the ground in front of Monthaven. "There's your archer," Ridge said, handing over the bow to one of the guards. "Any idea why he wanted to kill you?"

"This is my partner," Rett said. "Also a Shadow," he added as Monthaven's gaze narrowed when he looked at Ridge.

Monthaven turned his attention to the man on the ground. Ridge had bound the archer's wrists behind him, but his legs remained free, and he twisted and kicked, trying to get away. Ridge toed him onto his belly and brought his boot down on the man's lower back, pinning him.

"He's a tenant farmer on my lands," Monthaven replied, sounding shaken. "He'd been angry about payments since it's been a bad year for rain. I knew he was displeased, but I never thought he'd try to kill me."

Rett turned his Sight on the prisoner and saw no touch of the Witch Lord. Then he pointedly met Monthaven's gaze and raised an eyebrow. The lord gave a nod, and the soldiers who had kept Rett on his knees grudgingly hauled him to his feet. Monthaven returned Rett's letter of marque, which he tucked back inside his vest.

"I need to make sure that the mayor and the aldermen have the situation under control and have seen to the wounded," Monthaven said. "Then I would very much like to find out why two of the king's assassins rode all the way up here to fend off an attack." His tone made it clear that he issued an order wrapped in the invitation.

Within an hour, they found themselves in Monthaven's sitting room. The lord did not bother excusing himself to change clothing. Instead, he poured himself a drink, then turned to his unexpected guests. "Now I want the real story. Leave nothing out."

Ridge and Rett had already agreed how to explain their sudden appearance without revealing Rett's illegal magic. "We did a job for the king and found a note in the man's pocket. Roan Destwiler. Criminal, smuggler, kidnapper, opium dealer. It sounded like confirmation of a strike Destwiler had arranged, and from what we pieced together, we figured it meant you."

Monthaven paced, pausing now and again to take a sip of his whiskey. "I'm grateful, don't be mistaken. Without your action, I'd have likely been badly hurt or worse. And when you knocked me over, it made the others scramble." He ran a hand through his thinning hair. "Five people died today. More would have, without your help."

"Do you know why Destwiler might have wanted to arrange for you to be killed?" Ridge asked. Rett watched the lord, looking for insights. Monthaven seemed relatively unpretentious for a noble. He had shown genuine concern for those injured at the harvest festival and appeared not to care that he still wore his stained garments, bothering only to smooth his flyaway hair. Rett had been in the presence of other aristocrats whose arrogance made it unremarkable that someone would want to kill them. Monthaven didn't fit the mold.

"None. I've never heard of the man."

"He may have had ties to the Witch Lord, Yefim Makary," Rett added, watching Monthaven closely.

The man's expression shifted, eyes darkening with anger, lips thinning in disdain. "Makary is a liar and a dangerous cheat. He preys on ambitious fools. King Kristoph would do well to take heed and nip his treachery before it grows."

"Opinions like those might have made the Witch Lord decide you were a threat," Rett suggested. "You haven't been quiet about your opposition."

Monthaven let out a disgusted snort. "Not that His Majesty has noticed. He and his advisors still regard Makary as a fraud or a tawdry distraction. I think he's far more dangerous."

"And so do we," Ridge said carefully. "Unofficially."

"What can you do, without a warrant from the king?" Monthaven asked.

Rett shrugged. "Nothing fatal. But Shadows have a good bit of leeway to investigate matters that might pose a danger to the crown.

The difficulty is that the Witch Lord isn't drumming up followers in the town square; he's courting them in the salons and manors of the aristocracy. We could gather more information that might make the king take notice if we could get access…through someone who moves in those circles."

Monthaven's lips curved into a sly smile. "That can be arranged."

CHAPTER THREE

"You're assassins. You're not spies, and you're not bodyguards. And yet you ended up out of the city, in Lord Monthaven's lands, without a warrant." Burke stroked his beard absently, no doubt blaming the liberal sprinkles of gray on the two men standing at attention in front of him.

"We saved his life. If we'd have stopped to get permission, he'd be dead, the king would have one fewer ally, and the Witch Lord one less opponent." Ridge's voice, while respectful, did not back down.

Burke wheeled on Rett. "You went along with him. You're supposed to be the sensible one."

Rett tried not to squirm under the sharp gaze of the Shadow Master. "Seemed like the best way to protect both Monthaven and the king's interests...sir."

Burke turned away, muttering curses. "Someday, one of these little side ventures of yours won't work out well, and there will be a heap of shit raining down on all of us." He shook his head as if there were a lot more he wanted to say. "Fortunately for you, Lord Monthaven sent a courier to let me—and the king—know that you'd saved him from an attack."

"We found a note in Destwiler's vest, and figured it out from that," Ridge said. "So it did come about as a result of official business. We just…took it a little further."

"It's almost certain that if we dig deep enough, we'll find ties to the Witch Lord behind this," Rett added. They dared not mention the Sight or Rett's visions, but enough clues seemed obvious to make a case for continuing to investigate. "Who was Destwiler supplying the weapons to? He never used to be involved in anything big enough to include kidnapping the nobility. And what possible reason could there be for trying to kill Monthaven except for his opposition to the Witch Lord?"

"Very vocal opposition," Ridge put in. "We talked with him afterward. He felt sure the Witch Lord hired the attacker."

Burke let out a frustrated huff. "And you're probably right. But the king has been unwilling to consider the Witch Lord a threat or his supporters a potential danger, and without more evidence, I doubt he'll take Monthaven's word for the source of the attack."

"So what do we do?" Ridge challenged. "Wait until there's a rebellion?"

Burke shook his head. "No. But officially, my hands are tied. We've raised this to King Kristoph. And the nobles who don't trust the Witch Lord have done the same, to no avail. Members of his inner circle are convinced that Makary is at worst a charlatan, perhaps a harmless diversion."

"It makes no sense to allow the Witch Lord's influence to grow until he can do real damage," Rett fumed.

"Of course not. But we have to tread carefully—something neither of you is good at," Burke added with a pointed glare at Ridge. "So I'm going to let you off the leash…to an extent. Track down whoever Destwiler was supplying with those weapons. Gather evidence. Protect yourselves, and trust your judgment on whether you need to kill the ones in charge…unless they're nobility." He shook his head.

"Those will have to be brought to trial, so you'd damn well better have evidence the king and his advisors can't ignore, or you'll be in trouble I can't get you out of."

"Understood," Rett confirmed, with a side glance at Ridge.

"Henri's checking into the waybills," Ridge replied. "I saw an odd symbol on the bills that I've never seen before. It has to mean something, be some type of message. It's not much, but it's all we've got to start with."

Burke nodded. "I'm willing to put you both on 'special assignment' for a month to run this down. No change to your usual monthly stipend." Before they had the chance to be too pleased, he continued. "I expect you to check in with me at two weeks, preferably more often. If it's too big, get out of there. You've had plenty of chances to be heroes. I don't want to lose two of my best assassins fighting a war on their own. Fall back, and I'll find the resources. I do not want to bury either of you over this. Am I clear?"

Rett nodded. Ridge held Burke's gaze for a minute to be stubborn, then also confirmed his agreement. "Thanks for trusting us on this."

"Don't make me sorry," Burke snapped. "I've got a gut feeling that Makary is big trouble. I'd be happy for you to show me wrong, but I'm afraid that's not what's going to happen. So just prove it, so we can take the head off the snake before it strikes. Dismissed."

"You're sure about this?" Rett asked, and for a second, Ridge got a glimpse of the obstinate child he had met back in the orphanage. Rett might have been younger and smaller, but what he lacked in bulk and height, he more than made up for with attitude and a sharp wit. Even back then, he had never blindly followed Ridge, challenging him every step, on everything. Which had probably kept them both alive this far, Ridge had to admit.

"As sure as I am about anything," Ridge said with a shrug.

"Then we're doomed."

Ridge rolled his eyes knowing that Rett's questioning was part validation, part banter, and part bluff. Ridge had hazy memories of his family before the orphanage, mostly of the night that none of them would wake, and he had been taken, crying and terrified, to a large, unfamiliar building run by somber strangers. He had been five then, perhaps a little older. And he had kept largely to himself until five years later when a scrappy new arrival prompted him to wade into a fight. There had been no turning back after that. He and Rett were friends and brothers to the end.

"Don't blame me. Blame Henri. He's the one who tracked the mark to the damn caravan," Ridge said. "And if Henri says they're connected, I believe him. He's rarely wrong."

"Much less often than you are," Rett returned, but a glint of mischief lightened his words.

Ridge responded with a rude gesture.

"They'd better feed us," Rett grumbled. "And I miss my horse." Their own fine black stallions were far too memorable and too valuable to belong to the kind of men who would turn up looking for work at a merchant caravan. Henri had arranged to borrow two ill-tempered cart horses whose best days were long behind them. Ridge had honestly feared that his might expire before they reached the caravan, and if that happened, Rett's had been in no condition to carry both of them.

"Suspicious enough that we *have* horses. Showing up on foot might have been even more believable."

"Looking the part is one thing, but I was not walking halfway across the province just to fit in," Rett objected.

They had arrived a day before, and were hired as tent riggers on the spot. The demands of the job and the sharp eye of their boss had left them scant time to get their bearings.

"Get back to work!" Edels, the crew overseer, yelled. Rett and Ridge went back to the hot, backbreaking work of pounding stakes so tents could be set up for the night.

For a while they said nothing, hammering in the tent poles in rhythm while sneaking glances at the activity going on around them in the camp. Two cooks laid a fire and set up a spit to roast dinner. Merchants rearranged their wares. Stable hands led the horses and mules to pasture.

The caravan traveled from one side of Landria to the other, stopping to buy from and sell to the tradesmen, merchants, and large manors at towns and cities across the kingdom. In addition to supplying hard-to-get and unusual merchandise, the farmers and townsfolk turned out to watch the spectacle of the caravan as it made its way down the road: wagons laden with treasures, painted carts, horses, goats, and donkeys. Some of the traders traveled with a partner, and a few with families, but most of the group were hard-worn men who had spent their lives on the road.

Which is why Ridge paid attention when he saw a child out of the corner of his eye. He glanced over, just in time to see a man hustle the young boy into a tent on the far side of the clearing.

"Did you see that?" he asked quietly.

"The boy?" Rett asked. "Yeah. Makes me wonder what's going on in that tent."

"Nothing they want people to see," Ridge returned. "There are guards around it."

He would have said more, but Rett groaned and went down on one knee, clutching his head.

"Rett?" Ridge called, worried from the way Rett's eyes squinted shut and his mouth tightened. He knew his friend's vision was a strong one.

"What's wrong with him?" Edels barked, making a return pass to assure that all the hired hands were working hard.

"He got bucked off his horse a few days ago. Hit his head," Ridge lied, shifting to make sure he stayed between Rett and Edels. Rett in the grip of a vision was unable to defend himself, and Ridge wanted to make sure Edels didn't get it in his mind to try to slap Rett back to full consciousness.

"Is he going to be able to work? Because if not, he needs to get out."

"He can work. He's been working. Give him a moment," Ridge snapped, squaring his shoulders in an unmistakable effort to get Edels to back off.

"Make sure he does. Or I'll toss the both of you." With that, Edels strode off, already shouting at two men unloading crates.

With Edels gone, Ridge laid a hand on Rett's shoulder. Rett trembled, and his breaths came in hitched sobs. "Rett? What are you seeing?"

Rett gradually stilled, and his breathing slowed, becoming more even. He took a deep, steadying breath and looked up. Ridge could tell from Rett's expression that the vision had left a vicious headache in its wake. "It wasn't a premonition," Rett rasped. Ridge looked around, pulled a flask from his vest, and gave Rett a sip. "It was a message," Rett continued, leaning a little too hard on Ridge as he tried to get back to his feet.

Rett stumbled as he straightened, and his eyes looked glazed. "There was power behind what I saw," Rett explained. "Someone showed me what they wanted me to see, shoved it in front of me, so to speak."

"And?" Ridge kept an eye out. Rett's collapse had drawn notice, and the last thing they wanted was to attract attention.

"I don't know what it means, but it has something to do with that tent," Rett said, with a nod toward where they had seen the boy. He reached for his mallet, but Ridge put out an arm to stop him.

"I'll pound. You tie off the ropes. That way maybe you won't fall down," Ridge added, but his barb hid concern. Whatever touched Rett had hit him hard, and that meant until he recovered, they were vulnerable. He wondered how anyone had known to target Rett's magic. It had to be someone in the caravan. And that someone had to have the same forbidden power, which made Ridge wonder why a person like that was traveling with the caravan. Was it a warning? A cry for help? Or an important clue sent by someone who guessed who they were and why they had come?

Ridge didn't like any of the possibilities. No matter which might be true, it left them open to attack and betrayal. He took cold comfort in the knives and dirks hidden beneath his clothing. Still, he felt naked without his sword, and they had to leave the matchlock and his bow back in the city. Those weapons would have raised far too many questions.

"We need to get into that tent." Rett's voice sounded stronger, though still tight with pain. Headaches could linger for hours after a normal vision, so Ridge knew he should be grateful that this…message…hadn't knocked Rett out cold.

"Tonight," Ridge said. "Can't do it with so many people around. And we're going to have to draw off the guards without waking up the whole camp."

"That's your call." Rett stared across the clearing at the tent. "I'm the one who has to go inside."

"Sard that," Ridge retorted. "The only thing we know about the caravan is that someone here already figured out you have a talent. Maybe the vision is a trap. Just by being able to see it, you identify yourself. Burke might not be able to save you if the monks find out. Shit, Burke might not *want* to save you—we don't know what he'd make of it."

They fell silent as some of the water carriers walked by, balancing heavy pails on yokes across their shoulders. Ridge and Rett had only been with the caravan for a short time, but Ridge already had a good memory for faces and a solid idea of who did what. He and Rett were at the bottom of the heap, along with the stable hands and the men who loaded and unloaded the wagons. Skilled laborers were more valued, the blacksmith and farrier, cooks, healers, coopers, and wheelwrights. The merchants held themselves apart, like erstwhile nobility, leaving the chores to the hired hands while they took care of their ledgers and counted their money.

"Doesn't change things, Ridge," Rett argued, although his voice was tight with pain. "I'm the only one who might recognize either the power or something of what I saw. There were faces, but it was just a flash. Not sure if the images were blurry or whether I couldn't take in everything they were sending."

"I don't like it."

"Still doesn't change things," Rett countered.

Ridge swore under his breath. "All right. Let me see what I can come up with for a distraction."

"We don't have to put the whole camp into chaos," Rett said. "Just pull the guards away from that tent long enough for me to slip in."

"And how are you going to get out?"

"I'll come up with something," Rett promised.

Ridge's expression made it clear he was unhappy with the plan, but he couldn't think of an alternative. While they both had the Sight, only Rett got visions, and it seemed the invitation was directed specifically at him.

They worked for the rest of the afternoon without mishap. Edels seemed to find excuses to walk by and check their work but made no comment. Still, his presence was a silent warning and a threat. Ridge's mood darkened as the day went on, and Rett appeared to be lost in thought.

"I've got an idea for a distraction," Ridge said as they finished the ties for the last tent. "But it won't keep the guards away for long."

"I just need time to get in," Rett replied.

"If the guards go back too quickly, I'll look for another chance to stir something up," Ridge added.

"That's definitely what you're good at. Just don't burn the camp down—yet," Rett said.

CHAPTER FOUR

Rett moved in the shadows once night fell. He and Ridge had purposely chosen civilian clothing in dark shades, both to hide the dirt and to make it easier to blend in.

The guarded tent sat along one end of the camp, out of the main flow of traffic. Any time the caravan stopped, a bustle of activity erupted to feed the travelers and fix anything that had gone wrong on the road, in preparation for their next departure. Tomorrow, the camp would see a steady stream of merchants from nearby villages coming to purchase goods for resale and catch up on gossip from the far corners of the kingdom. A few nosy townsfolk and some of the local boys might try to steal glimpses of the merchants' wares, but they would be sorely disappointed if they expected this caravan to be like the traveling faires that sometimes brought jugglers, exotic animals, unusual food, and wonders that would be the talk of the countryside for months.

Rett sized up the area with the eye of an assassin. Two men

guarded the front of the tent, and one watched the back. He frowned, wondering if that meant the caravan leader feared that someone would break in—or those inside might escape.

If it were just a matter of getting into the tent and then getting away, killing the guards wouldn't have been a challenge. While the men were large and brawny, Rett doubted they could match a trained assassin in a fight. But without any idea of what or who was inside, and how the caravan might have a connection to the waybills in Destwiler's crates of smuggled weapons, Rett couldn't afford to leave a trail of bodies.

As he neared the tent, an explosion from the other side of the camp rumbled like thunder. The guards tensed, and two of them went to investigate. That left one man at the front of the tent and none behind. Rett smiled and jogged closer, already eyeing escape routes.

Just before he reached the back, the presence touched his mind again. "Hide," the voice said, coupled with an image of dropping flat to the ground. Rett took it as a warning and threw himself to the ground, seconds before two men walked past on their way to the front of the tent.

"We've got a buyer," one of the men said. Rett recognized the voice as Edels.

"For which one?" The second man had a gruff manner, and Rett could not place him.

"Doesn't matter, if the skills are right," Edels said.

"They aren't easy to replace," the second man warned. "Can't count on when we'll find another."

"Make enough money off one, and we don't have to 'find' that many. Feeding them cuts into the profits," Edels replied.

Rett heard the rustle of the tent flap, and then the high-pitched voice of a young boy. "Stop! You're hurting me! Don't take me away! Please don't!"

Rett winced as he heard the slap of a hand against skin, and the boy's protests turned to sobs. "Come on. Your new master's waiting. Wipe your face. Think he wants to see you covered in snot?" Edels snapped.

Rett's fists clenched as he heard lighter footsteps join the other two men on their way to the tent's opening, and guessed them to be guards. "No trouble from any of you, or there'll be no supper tomorrow. You hear me?" Edels threatened.

Rett lay still, waiting for the men to leave before he tried to move. Another image hit him, forcing its way into his mind. No words this time, just a picture of someone coming into the tent he shared with Ridge.

Before he could catch his breath, the toe of a boot in his ribs made him gasp. "What are you doing here?" The guard towered over him, and Rett managed his best drunken smile.

"Just goin' back to my tent, mister," Rett said, slurring his words. "Don't know how I got down here. Musta missed a step somewhere."

"Get out of here, before I report you," the guard said. "Lucky for you, I don't want the bother. Now go!"

Rett made a show of unsteadily getting to his feet and swaying once he stood, schooling his features to look as if the idea of walking taxed his capacity. He stumbled off, intentionally going in a direction different than his tent, and kept up the facade until he turned down between two rows of wagons and the guards were out of sight.

He let out a long breath and looked skyward, giving brief thanks to the gods for his escape. The camp had quieted from its earlier hurried preparations, and now most of the merchants had retired either to their tents or their wagons. Ridge waited in their small shelter, and from the impatience on his face, he had beaten Rett back by long enough to warrant worry.

"Well?"

"Nice explosion," Rett said quietly, using a flash of his extra magic to assure that no one was close enough to overhear.

Ridge smirked. "It worked, didn't it? What did you find out?"

Speaking low, Rett filled him in. Ridge frowned, thinking through what Rett said.

"Why would the caravan bother with slaving?"

Rett tensed. He had survived on the streets for a year before the orphanage, and before then, the adults who provided enough to keep body and soul together put their charges to work. Sometimes that meant stealing or hard labor. Other times, darker uses. Ridge had spent his early years in a real family, with people who must have loved him, people he loved in return. Since then, he knew Ridge had seen his share of evil, especially in his time with the king's army, but to a street rat like Rett, his partner could often still be slow to realize possibilities.

Rett shrugged. "Anything for a profit, I imagine."

Ridge had moved quickly from worried to angry. "There's an open warrant against slavers," he mused. "No one could fault us for taking action."

Rett frowned. "I think it's more complicated than that. Let's see if we get a visitor tonight."

Ridge and Rett lay awake, fully clothed, weapons ready. Rett listened for the sounds of footsteps. Few people except, perhaps, master hunters, could sneak up on professional assassins. Sure enough, once the camp fell silent in the darkest hours, Rett heard soft footsteps, too light to be those of an adult, just outside.

A shadow slipped inside their tent and stood still in the doorway. From the silhouette, Rett guessed their visitor to be a young boy, maybe ten at the most, skinny, and from his posture, used to curling in on himself to fend off blows.

"I can feel you in my head," the boy remarked.

Neither Ridge nor Rett moved, though they were both ready to defend themselves.

"I heard you when you called to me," Rett said. "Do you know how you do that?"

The boy nodded. "I felt it when you came into the camp. In my head. And I thought if you could hear me, you could help."

"What help do you need?" Ridge asked in a careful voice as if he soothed a spooked horse.

"They took us," the boy replied. "Because we see things. Know things. Sometimes, things that haven't happened yet."

"So there are others?" Rett thought again about the boy he had seen dragged away.

"Six. There used to be more. Sometimes, they sell us to people who want to make money by having us find things out."

"Like the boy they took today?" Rett questioned.

"Mitchell. He was my friend. He won't come back. They never come back." The world-weariness in the boy's voice reminded Rett too much of his younger self. At least he had found a friend and defender in Ridge, a bond that had grown into brotherhood.

"What's your name?"

"Sofen."

"How did you manage to come to us?" Ridge asked.

"I can make people not pay attention," Sofen replied. "It's hard, and I can't do it long."

"Can any of the others do that?" Rett asked.

"Don't think so. They can tell what people are thinking, or see things that haven't happened yet. That sort of thing."

"And you can do those things, too?" Ridge kept his voice low.

"I can hear thoughts," Sofen replied. "But if I do it too long or there are too many people, my head hurts. I took a chance and thought back at you."

"If you can make people not pay attention, why didn't you run away?" Ridge asked.

Sofen looked down. "They could catch me. And the others wouldn't make it."

"We'll get you out of here," Ridge promised. Rett raised an eyebrow, though the darkness likely hid his surprise. "Do you think your friends could stay on a horse?"

Sofen nodded. "Me and Belan are ten. We're the oldest."

Rett closed his eyes. He didn't have to use much imagination to remember times he had outrun predators in the alleyways, men who wanted him for reasons he hadn't stuck around to figure out. A wrong turn, a twisted ankle, and he could have ended up like the children in the tent. Getting caught by the monks and brought to the orphanage had been a mercy, no matter how unfriendly some of the other residents had been.

As if he guessed Rett's thoughts, Ridge elbowed him. "Here and now," he murmured. Rett nodded.

"You'd better go back," Rett said. "I don't think I can send a message to you, and if you push too hard, your message hurts me. But we'll figure a way to get you out."

"Tomorrow night, after midnight," Ridge said, clearly having already come up with a plan. "Have everyone ready. We'll come with horses, so have your shoes and cloaks and whatever you want to take with you."

"Thank you," Sofen said. "I knew if you could hear me, you'd help."

"Be careful," Rett said. "Don't get caught."

Sofen shot him a lopsided grin. "Don't worry." He vanished, and Rett could barely hear his footsteps.

Rett pushed himself up on his elbows and looked at Ridge. "So we're doing this? Just like that?"

Ridge shrugged. "No time like the present. What if another buyer comes tomorrow?"

Rett sighed. "You're right. But where do we take them? We can't go to Burke. Too many questions and all the wrong answers." Explaining why they had freed the children would lead to having to give the reason for their kidnapping and the value for the slavers. That would not only reveal the children's magic, but also Ridge's and Rett's abilities.

"We'll figure it out once we've got them clear," Ridge said with a vague gesture. Normally, Ridge's penchant for making things up as they went grated on Rett's need for order, although Ridge was right far more often than he was wrong. Now, Rett felt glad he did not have to argue with his partner to get him to save Sofen and the others.

"I wish I knew who the man was with Edels," Rett murmured. "And I wish I could have used my Sight on him."

"Keep an eye out tomorrow," Ridge said. "Listen for the voice. My bet is he's the caravan master."

"We still don't know where the weapons come in." Rett arranged his rucksack so that he could lean back on it. Since they arrived with the caravan, they had taken shifts on watch, unwilling for both of them to sleep at the same time.

Ridge turned over, shifting between the hard ground and his cloak to get comfortable. "We'll find the pieces and put them together. We always do."

The next morning, Edels came by as Ridge and Rett chopped firewood. "I need a hand unloading a wagon," he said. "Come on."

They followed him to the road on the edge of the camp. An empty wagon waited with a driver who was clearly in a hurry to be elsewhere. "There are four crates in the back of that cart," Edels said, pointing toward the merchants' vehicles. "Get them loaded."

Rett risked using his Sight. The driver did not carry the touch of the Witch Lord, but Rett picked up a darkness that limned his aura. Perhaps he had not sold his soul, or maybe the offer had not been made but would have been willingly accepted. Whatever the reason, the driver was not a person to be trusted.

Ridge and Rett headed for the crates. Ridge pulled back the cloth covering the wooden boxes and caught his breath. The same symbol from the waybills marked each one. A glance between them conveyed the question without words. *How do we find out who's in on the smuggling and who's receiving the weapons?*

It took both of them to move each crate. Edels and the wagon driver watched in silence, impatience clear in their faces. Rett looked for any possible clues about where the wagon might be headed. He stole another glance at the driver. The man spoke with a northern accent, and while his clothing looked plain, it did not appear as hard-used as that of most wagon masters. Rett wondered if he might be a servant, sent out on an errand for his master, and not usually a driver.

The crates had no markings on the outside; given their contents, neither the sender nor the receiver would want to be traced. Just the odd sigil, a code revealing the contents to those who were part of the secret.

He paid attention to the merchant's wagon as well, each time they went back for another load. From the way Ridge lingered, just a few seconds each time, he knew his fellow assassin was also scanning for any way to identify whoever had brought the weapons to the rendezvous point.

"That should do it," Ridge said, as they settled the last crate into the second wagon.

"Where're you bound for?" the wagon driver asked Edels.

"We go west from here, on to where the weavers and lace makers live," Edels replied.

"Mind you don't take the Coburn Bridge," the driver warned. "Bad rain last week flooded the river. It's none too steady. Wouldn't risk it."

Edels gave a nod of thanks, and the driver urged his horse into motion as Ridge and Rett headed back toward the firewood.

Ridge glanced over his shoulder to make sure Edels hadn't come up behind them. "I think I know whose wagon brought the crates out here," he murmured. "I've been trying to match faces to wagons, in case we found something. I'll see if I can find out a name."

"Sofen and his friends might know something. We can ask once everything's settled," Rett replied.

Rett's errands took him back and forth across the camp, and any time his path brought him near the tent with Sofen and the children, he scanned the area to assure that the security had not been tightened. One time when he passed, Edels was berating the guard at the rear of the tent, but Rett was too far away to hear what was being said and had no good reason to move closer.

The driver's comment about Coburn Bridge stuck in Rett's mind. He tried to remember who the landholders were on the other side of the river and whether any had been rumored to be enamored of the Witch Lord. Nothing came to him, although he vowed to have a look once they returned to Caralocia and he had access to good maps.

As he walked back toward the firewood, Rett kept his ears open, listening for anything that might be useful.

"...not sure what the hurry is, but Master Kurren seems to be in a rush to get back on the road," a passing merchant said to his companion. "I think he'd have us pulling up stakes tonight if he thought he could get away with it."

"...don't know what's put everyone on edge," complained another man, whom Rett recognized as a rug dealer. "We did a good business yesterday, and again as much today. I wouldn't mind seeing if anyone else comes in tomorrow, but I hear we're moving out."

Did something spook Edels and Caravan Master Kurren to make them rush departure? Are the merchants taking advantage of their customers, so we daren't stay long enough for them to be exposed? Or were they just anxious to be gone, knowing the truth about the weapons they transported and the kidnapped children they brokered like horses? Rett wondered.

Ridge had finished splitting most of the wood by the time Rett got back. "Nice of you to take your time," he drawled.

"Didn't have a choice. Edels seemed to think I didn't have enough to do. Every time I finished and headed back here, he sent me off to fetch water or unload more hay for the horses."

Ridge frowned. "You think he's suspicious of you?" he asked with a glance around to make sure no one else was near.

"I think he's suspicious of everyone," Rett replied, pitching in to finish the last of the wood. "If he had the Sight or abilities like Sofen, he'd have figured us out by now—probably when we first came looking to hire on."

"Maybe," Ridge replied, and his eyes narrowed the way they did when he wasn't convinced. Rett had been watching his friend's expressions for most of his life, and right now, he knew Ridge was already considering alternatives in case their plan went badly. It was a lifelong habit.

Except for two years, when Ridge turned sixteen and was conscripted with the other orphans of his age into the king's army, and Rett was left behind, the two of them had been together since childhood, in circumstances that forced them to depend on one another far more than real siblings. The monks did their best with the orphanage, and at least most of them meant well, but there were too many children from rough beginnings, too few adults who cared, and too little of everything else.

Fights happened daily in the orphanage, over everything from clothing and shoes to food. The oldest, the biggest, or the most ruthless usually won the spoils. Rett had been little and scrappy, willing to bite and claw to hold his own, but he'd learned the hard way early in life that a fighting spirit alone wasn't always enough. But with Ridge on his side, they formed a team to be reckoned with. Still did.

Although the camp wouldn't pull up stakes until the morning, Rett recognized the signs that they were going to move out. Everyone had packed up all they could, to make an early morning departure easier. Even the firewood they cut had been loaded onto a cart since they would not use all of it before the morning.

He and Ridge had brought little with them aside from their rucksacks, cloaks, and the tent, along with horses, tack, and saddles. They'd have to sacrifice the tent—too many questions to be answered if someone noticed it missing in the middle of the night.

That night, neither of them made a pretense of sleeping. "I'll get the horses ready," Ridge said as it neared midnight. "I'll steal better mounts for us and a third one for the older children; you and I will each have to ride with two of the younger ones. If we're quiet about it, maybe we won't need a big distraction." He paused. "I'll have something ready anyhow, just in case."

Rett nodded. "I'll head for the children. Three guards shouldn't be hard to manage since we aren't sticking around."

"You'll have to wait until you hear me coming because someone will definitely notice if there are three dead guards."

"Maybe Sofen will help with his distraction ability. I'd rather not have the guards raise an alarm."

"Wouldn't be the first time we had to fight our way clear," Ridge said. "Probably won't be the last."

Despite the truth in Ridge's words, their odds of survival rose whenever they could minimize confrontation. As Rett frequently reminded Ridge, they were the king's assassins, not his two-man army. Ridge seemed to conveniently forget that point.

When the tower in the distant village sounded second bells, Ridge and Rett slipped from their tent, carrying their rucksacks with weapons hidden for easy reach. Ridge jogged toward the corral for the horses and saddles, while Rett slipped among the shadows toward the tent with Sofen and the others.

Moving silently and seeing in the dark without a light came

naturally to Rett. Long before he became an assassin, they were the skills that kept him alive on the streets. And in the two years that Ridge was gone in the army, they were handy abilities to help him avoid the spite of others in the orphanage who resented that Rett had found an erstwhile brother.

Rett blended with the shadows, pausing at any sound until he was certain the way was clear. The caravan's camp had no need of large public performance space, so it filled a small meadow, with wagons and tents close enough together in most cases for a stone tossed from one to hit another. All except for the tent with Sofen and the enslaved children, which sat near the edge of the camp. Not too close to the forest that verged the clearing, in case any of the children tried to run away. But not among the press of other people, where conversations might be inconveniently overheard.

Rett crouched behind a wagon, confirming that two guards stood outside the front. He circled around, staying low, and timed his approach for the single guard at the rear of the tent. When the man turned, Rett sprinted toward him, crossing the distance in seconds. Before the guard had a chance to react, Rett brought the grip of his knife down hard on the man's head. Moments later, with the guard tied and gagged, Rett pushed the unconscious man beneath the back skirt of the tent.

This time, Sofen's mental touch felt much gentler. Instead of forcing into his mind and dropping Rett to his knees, the contact was like a brush of fingers across Rett's temples, and then he caught the flash of an image, of the guards at the front staring into the distance. Hoping that meant Sofen and his friends had distracted the guards, Rett made his way around the tent, careful not to make any noise.

Two guards meant less chance to end this without violence. Rett did not enjoy killing, but when other options failed, it fell to the king's assassins to do what needed to be done. King Kristoph held a special hatred for slavery. A standing warrant empowered his assassins to kill any slavers they discovered and free their prisoners.

Sofen's distraction might wane at any second. Rett threw two knives in quick succession, and the guards dropped silently.

Hoof beats pounded in his direction, and Rett thrust his head into the tent. "We've got to go. You'd better be ready."

Sofen and another boy his age nodded, and the other children slipped from beneath their blankets fully dressed.

"Bring your blankets; it's cold," Rett said as Ridge stopped the horses a few feet outside the tent. "Hurry—they'll have heard the horses," he urged. A glance told Rett that the horses Ridge had stolen were far better than the plow horses they had brought with them.

Rett handed two of the smallest children up to ride in front of Ridge, then placed two more on his own mount and swung up to the saddle once he helped Sofen and the older boy onto the third horse. Ridge had managed to get their own saddles as well as a stolen third, which would make the ride a little easier.

"Go!" Ridge ordered, and they dug their heels in, urging their mounts forward. Rett maneuvered so that Sofen's horse was between his and Ridge's. He wrapped one arm around the two small children bundled in front of him as they thundered down the road. Behind them, they heard shouting and cursing. Rett hoped that Edels and the caravan master would think twice about firing shots lest they harm their valuable, escaping slaves.

"Sofen—if you and your friends can do anything to slow down or distract people who want to chase us, it would be a big help."

Sofen nodded, although it looked as if he had all he could handle just holding on to the horse. Rett wondered how, with their abilities, the children had been captured in the first place. A threat against their families? Or maybe only Sofen had abilities that could easily be turned to defense. Now that he had seen how young the other children were, he could not imagine how they could be useful to their captors. Perhaps the men who bought them did not need the children to understand, only force their magic on others. Just the thought of it made him sick. A wrong turn, a bit of bad luck, and it might have been him all those years ago.

In the distance, Rett heard the sound of horses behind them. "They're coming!" he shouted. Ridge's muffled curses carried back in response.

"Sofen, can you do something?" Rett asked, trying to figure out how to use his own illegal magic to avoid a fight. It would be almost impossible to protect the children if they had to battle their pursuers.

"I might be able to make them forget us for a little while," Sofen said, his voice barely carrying over the sounds of the horses. "But I've never done it without being able to see who I was aiming for."

"Forgetting would be good, if you don't make all of us forget, too," Rett urged.

"I've always had to see someone to use my magic on them."

"That might not be a good idea," Rett replied. "If they can see us, they might be able to shoot us."

Sofen's brows knit in a scowl. "Don't want the little ones to get hurt."

Rett remembered that look of resolve. He'd seen it on Ridge many times back in the orphanage, a too-old expression on a too-young face. Sofen and the other older boy were about the same age Ridge had been when he became Rett's protector. And while they were both now trained assassins with an impressive kill record to their names, sometimes Rett thought that Ridge had never quite outgrown that old protective streak.

"I'll try," Sofen said. He looked over his shoulder to the boy behind him, a glance that seemed to communicate a silent conversation, and Rett wondered if they could read each other's thoughts. The other boy put his hand on Sofen's shoulder, and they both closed their eyes.

Rett felt a wave of…something…pass over him. He felt a buzz of energy, magic acknowledging magic. The sound of pursuit suddenly stopped.

"Ride harder!" Rett called to Ridge. "I think we've thrown them off for now."

Rett nudged his horse faster, wondering how long they dared ride with their young charges. Had they been the pampered children of merchants or nobles, he doubted they would have made it this far. But these were survivors, toughened by their ordeal, and they depended on one another. Their desperation to escape probably helped, not to mention their magic.

They slowed their pace when their pursuers appeared to have given up the chase, and their horses were at their limit. Ridge led them down side roads and back lanes, finally coming to a stop in a small grove beside a stream.

"We can't stay long, but we should get some rest," Ridge said, climbing down from his horse and stretching. The children practically tumbled off into his arms, and Rett wondered if they had dozed in the saddle. It had been all he could do to avoid drifting off himself, despite the danger.

"Just a couple hours," Ridge warned. "We'll take turns standing guard, so no one sneaks up on us," he told Sofen and the others. "I'll bring up some water from the stream. The horses can drink, too. They can use a rest as well."

Rett walked over to stand beside Ridge. "Where are we going?"

"I figure Sally Anne will take them, at least until we can figure out something else."

Rett's eyebrows rose. "She takes in women who run away from brutish husbands. Not children."

Ridge chuckled. "She's feisty, wealthy, and she owns a damn castle." That much was true. Lady Sally Anne Harrowmont found herself a widow under questionable circumstances, retaining her late husband's wealth, lands, and fortifications. Rid of her drunken monster of a husband, she opened her castle as a sanctuary for others. "Besides, she owes us."

"What about their magic?" Rett pressed, turning to keep one eye on the children. Sofen and Belan, the other older boy, had taken charge and were doing an admirable job of getting the younger ones to rest.

"I wouldn't be surprised if she's protected more than a few women with magic that could get them into trouble," Ridge replied. "Sally Anne doesn't care much for the monks' opinions. Not sure how much she thinks of the king's, for that matter."

CHAPTER FIVE

Provisions were woefully thin for anything resembling breakfast. Ridge searched their packs, coming up with some dried meat and hard cheese. Still, the children accepted the offer gratefully and drank from the cold stream.

"How did the men at the caravan think they were controlling you, to keep you from running away?" Ridge asked as Sofen splashed water on his face.

Sofen dug out an amulet from beneath his shirt and held it up. "They made us wear these," he said. "I 'broke' mine, and we made the others leave theirs back in the tent. Belan and I were stronger, but we didn't run because we needed to look out for the others."

Interesting, Ridge thought. He was about to ask another question when Sofen gave him an odd look.

"Edels and Master Kurren felt strange to my mind," Sofen said.

"Strange, how?"

Sofen chewed his lip for a moment, trying to put thoughts into words. "They had a shadow on their minds, like a stain." He frowned, struggling. "Not all bad men do. Just them."

Ridge nodded. "That's because they've sold their souls to an even worse man," he said. "And I'm afraid that some of that man's followers are the ones who've been buying the other children and taking them away."

Sofen thought about that for a moment. "They didn't hurt us like I thought they would," he said quietly. When he met Ridge's gaze, the boy's eyes were so much older than his years. "They hit us if we didn't listen, or if we struggled, but they didn't...touch."

Ridge felt heat creep to his face. "Good," he said in a rough voice. "That's good. But they shouldn't have taken you." He looked at Sofen. "Do you have families to go back to?"

Sofen shrugged. "Some do. But the bad men will just come back and take us again if we go home. The rest don't have anywhere."

Ridge nodded. "Well, that's going to change," he said. "I've got a friend who will keep you safe if everyone promises to behave."

Sofen grinned. "Will your friend have food?"

Ridge chuckled. "I dare say she will. And if you want, you might even help us get back at Edels and Kurren and the men who took your friends."

Sofen's eyes were wary. "How?"

Ridge clapped a hand on his shoulder. "By doing what you do— from safely inside big stone walls where they can't hurt you."

Sofen's smile widened. "Like a spy? That would be good."

Ridge smiled. "Let's get you a safe place to stay, and then we can talk about the spy part."

To Ridge's relief, the children bore the two-day trip to Harrowmont stoically, making no complaint about empty bellies or sore muscles from the ride. Sofen and Belan called out to the others now and again, trying to jolly them along or asking what they thought of landmarks, plants, or animals they saw along the way. Ridge and Rett snared rabbits or caught fish for their dinner, and together with the bread and cheese they bought from farmers along the way, it was enough to sustain them for the journey.

Ridge rode point, and Rett trailed, bracketing the children between them. That kept the party safe but gave the two assassins no time to talk. When they stopped to rest the horses and let the children relieve themselves and stretch, Rett moved to stand beside Ridge. Never taking his eyes off their new charges, he folded his arms across his chest.

"So what now? We just ride up to Harrowmont with six children and ask to see Lady Sally Anne?"

Ridge shrugged. "You've got a better idea?"

"No. But that doesn't mean I'm convinced it will work."

Ridge let out a long breath. "It doesn't have to be permanent. Just until we figure out this Witch Lord problem. Lady Sally Anne can keep them safe. She's the only one I can think of who wouldn't either turn them in for magic or try to use them for her own ends—Burke included."

Ridge had met Lady Harrowmont during the time he and Rett were separated before Rett was old enough to be conscripted. Ridge was already an assassin by that point, hunting with Noran, the older fighter assigned to be his sponsor.

Promising young soldiers were paired with an older mentor, who was charged with teaching weapons and tactics and keeping the students alive while they learned. Some of the pairings turned into unbreakable friendships, others into more than friendship. And while many of the mentors might have been decent men, Noran abused his power and rank.

When Noran died in a skirmish, Ridge had gained enough of a reputation that King Kristoph offered him his choice of reward. Ridge had asked for first pick of the new crop of recruits to choose a new partner, knowing Rett would be among them. He'd missed his almost-brother, but even more, he wanted to save Rett from what he had endured. Ridge spoke little of his time with Noran, but enough to give Rett an idea of what went unsaid.

One of the few good things Noran had ever done, in Ridge's opinion, was provide an armed escort to a noblewoman and her retinue. Only after they reached Harrowmont did Noran and Ridge finally realize that Lady Sally Anne had spirited the women away from their abusive husbands in disguise, and used the might of the king's soldiers to do it. Ridge had made a favorable impression on Lady Harrowmont, and they had chatted at times throughout the journey, creating a pleasant connection between them. She seemed to see Noran immediately for the kind of man he was and kept a frosty distance, one that only made Noran dislike Ridge even more.

"Please tell me you didn't sleep with Lady Sally Anne."

Ridge grinned. "Would it matter if I did?" When he failed to get a reaction, he shook his head. "No. She was already married and even then, I knew she was way out of reach. Not to mention at least ten years older. Still pretty," he added wistfully.

Back then, Lady Sally Anne had requested another duty of Ridge and Noran before allowing them to go their way, eliminating someone who had threatened her safety, a killer hired by her estranged husband. Ridge and Noran lodged at the manor for a few weeks while they worked the job.

"Sometimes, we'd talk, which surprised the crap out of me, since I didn't think people like her had conversations with people like me. She was nice. Not like most nobles."

"So you're sure she'll remember you? It's been six years."

"My pride hopes so," Ridge replied. "Yes, I'm sure she will. And I'm certain she'll help, especially for something like this."

"If the Witch Lord has a purpose for these children, he'll send someone to take them back," Rett warned.

Ridge gave him a look. "From Lady Sally Anne? Those soldiers will go home with their balls around their necks and their pricks down their throats."

Harrowmont Castle sat gray and forbidding atop a rocky ridge. Ridge had heard stories that it had been built as an outpost by a long-forgotten empire and reworked over generations to suit the needs of its many owners. If true, that meant that the castle was older than the kingdom of Landria itself. If anyone considered trying to wrest control from Lady Sally Anne, her highly proficient, deeply loyal men and women at arms would quickly disabuse them of the notion.

"So that's where we're going?" Sofen's voice squeaked on the last word.

"Look safe enough to you?" Rett joked.

"It's a bloody fortress!" Belan said. The younger children looked up at the high stone walls and commanding towers with expressions of awe and fear.

"Which is why you'll be safe," Ridge said. He rode up to the gate, moving a little ahead of the others.

"I'm here to see the lady of the castle," he announced to the guards. "Captain Joel Breckinridge, from the king's guards."

The soldiers eyed Ridge dubiously, then glanced at Rett and the six children. One of the soldiers opened a small panel within the side door and spoke to someone inside. The portcullis remained closed. Ridge looked up, acutely aware of the murder hole above, where defenders had once greeted unwanted visitors with scalding water, hot oil, or molten lead. Nothing about the castle itself was welcoming, and he hoped that their reception from its mistress would be different.

After a wait, a tap at the panel signaled the soldier to open it and listen to the response. He looked to his comrade and nodded. "They're to be sent in, and wait in the bailey."

Ridge went back to join the others, watching as men winched the heavy portcullis gate open. It hung above the opening like a jaw with sharp teeth, waiting to snap closed. Ridge led the way, and the others followed. He fought the urge to glance overhead as they passed beneath the gate, but could not fully repress a shiver.

Harrowmont's weathered gray stone walls seemed even higher on the inside of the fortress. Within the outer walls sat the dependencies—kitchen, stable, storage rooms, forge—as well as chicken coops, a pigsty, a rabbit hutch, and a pen of sheep and goats. The barracks for the soldiers, like the keep in the center and the large main building where Lady Sally Anne and her "guests" resided were all built of stone. To one side lay a kitchen garden which would be filled with fresh herbs in the summer. Along the far wall were several tilled areas he guessed were gardens, along with a small stand of fruit trees. The smell of smoked meat carried on the wind, and Ridge's stomach growled.

People bustled back and forth across the bailey yard, a mix of servants and the women to whom Lady Sally Anne gave sanctuary. A few paused to look at the newcomers, and Ridge had the distinct impression their interest lay with the children.

"Looks like Lady Sally Anne means for Harrowmont to be self-sufficient," Rett noted under his breath. Their horses nickered and fidgeted as the group waited to be received. Sofen and Belan soothed the younger children in quiet tones, reminding them to be on good behavior.

"It's a big open space, and they've got more use for vegetables than flowers. Still, there's plenty of room to walk around," Ridge noted. "And given the castle's history—and Lady Sally Anne's—I imagine self-sufficiency is worth more than gold."

They dismounted and helped the children down. Ridge and Rett stood in front, while Sofen and Belan organized the others in a neat row. They were dirty from the ride, hair askew, and the children's mismatched clothing showed wear from their captivity. Ridge doubted that he and Rett looked much better. Still, he smoothed his hair and endured a snicker from Rett, but he noticed his partner also brushed dirt from his coat and tried to tame the wild curls of his unruly chestnut hair.

"That must be her," Sofen breathed. Lady Sally Anne of Harrowmont descended the stairs from the living quarters and headed across the green. Ridge guessed that she was probably nearing forty, and the winsomeness of her younger years had given way to a solid attractiveness that suggested character and determination. Lady Harrowmont's blonde hair, shot through with strands of gray, was plaited and wound around the top of her head. Her dress spoke of practicality, not fashion, and had probably been woven here from the wool of their own sheep.

"Captain Breckinridge. This is a surprise."

Ridge gave a deep bow, as did Rett. "M'lady," he said, rising. "May I present my partner, Garret Kennard. And our...charges."

One of the children coughed, and Lady Sally Anne's eyebrows rose. "You've brought me children?"

Ridge cleared his throat. "It's a bit of a special circumstance, and I was hoping for your help," he said. "But if I might impose, we've come a long way, and it's been more than a day since they've eaten much of anything."

Lady Sally Anne motioned for her steward, who lingered a discreet distance away. He stood a bit stiffly, very proper, almost as if at attention, a man in his late middle years, with a balding fringe of gray hair and high, sharp cheekbones. He had a hawk-like gaze, but though the man seemed stern, Ridge thought he saw kindness in his eyes as he looked at the children.

"Harcourt, take our young guests to the kitchen and get them something to eat," she ordered. "Then find them some clothing they might fit into, and have the maids give them a good scrubbing."

Harcourt gestured for the children to come with him. Sofen looked to Ridge, who nodded, and then he and Belan organized the others to follow like ducklings.

"Let's go inside, shall we?" Lady Sally Anne said, then turned, not waiting for a reply, sure of their obedience.

Ridge and Rett walked through an entrance hall and into a small salon. Lady Sally Anne spoke a word to a servant at the door, and the man went to do her bidding.

"Have a seat," she said, sweeping a hand toward the chairs. "I've sent for food and drink. I'm sure you're as hungry as your…charges."

Ridge chose the chair he felt might be least soiled by his dirty clothing, and Rett did likewise, sitting near a small table. Lady Sally Anne's residence, like the woman herself, spoke of breeding and practical wealth without the need to impress. Ridge had been to the palace in Caralocia many times and figured that its ostentatious show of wealth and power was designed to intimidate. These rooms were on a much more human scale, comfortable and expensive without overstatement.

"I don't imagine they're grooming new assassins quite so young," Lady Sally Anne said, taking a seat on a divan where she could see both of them. "So tell me how you came to be in possession of them—and what you're doing here."

Ridge told the story, editing out any mention of Rett's power. He had no way to avoid noting the children's magic, and he knew that even if he warned Sofen not to mention Rett's abilities, such a secret would be difficult to assure. All the more reason he wanted to win Lady Sally Anne's favor.

When he finished, a servant knocked on the door. Lady Sally Anne called for him to enter, and soon two steaming bowls of venison stew sat before Ridge and Rett, along with a crusty loaf of bread.

"Eat," she urged. "I need to think about what you've told me."

It did not take long for them to finish the stew, and by the time they wiped their mouths and washed the food down with tankards of good ale, Lady Sally Anne sat back, eyes fixed on the windows, deep in thought.

"I believe that the Witch Lord is a danger," she said. "He tried to worm his way into my confidence about a year ago. I met him at a dinner at Lord Tannerlyn's manor. He made quite an impression," she recalled. "Unfortunately for him, the impression was negative."

"How so?" Rett probed.

Lady Sally Anne took a deep breath as she considered her words. "He styled himself like a beggar or one of those wandering holy men. Wild hair, unkempt beard, and a robe made out of sackcloth. Bare feet. But he spoke with authority, and he was educated. I didn't care for him," she said with a shrug. "He smelled bad. And I thought he seemed to be playing a part. It wouldn't surprise me if he came from a minor noble house, a bastard, perhaps."

"Others seem to find him quite persuasive," Ridge replied.

She nodded. "He has a way about him when he speaks that draws people in. Most charismatic."

"Magic?" Rett asked.

Lady Sally Anne gave an enigmatic smile. "No. At least, not the way magic is usually used. I know something about these things," she added. "And I always carry charms to detect magic and for protection. My amulets didn't react to him. I think that whatever power he has is more subtle," she said, frowning. "I don't think he forces people to do his will. More like he finds the ones whose desires he can further, and they ally with him to get what he offers."

"We think the two men at the caravan who were brokering the

children intended to spread them among the Witch Lord's loyalists and use their abilities for his ends," Rett said. "Those that could send and receive thoughts would make a valuable, unbreakable, way to communicate in secret."

She nodded. "Yes, they would. And the ones that can glimpse the future would be an unfair advantage in negotiations. What do you think he wants from it?"

Ridge leaned forward, resting his elbows on his knees. "Power. Maybe even the throne. If not for himself, then for one of his loyalists, someone he could control."

She looked as if she debated the idea with herself. "That's quite a stretch from his present means. Most think he's little more than an amusement, or at most a cunning thief. But I fear he's more than that. There was an edge to his words, a way of spreading discontent even as he gathered people to him. I believe that with powerful followers, he could pose a true threat."

"Then we're agreed," Ridge said. "What about the children? Will you give them sanctuary? Their magic makes them valuable—and puts them in danger."

She gave him a shrewd look as if she saw right through him. "I doubt they eat much," she said finally. "And you make a good case. Perhaps once they're properly fed and bathed, I can find out more about their abilities."

"They might also prove to be useful allies, if the Witch Lord is as dangerous as we fear," Rett said.

"Indeed. And what does King Kristoph think of this?"

Ridge fidgeted. "We haven't exactly made an official report about the children," he said, rubbing his neck. "I'd planned to report that the caravan had been kidnapping children and selling them as slaves. The King's Shadows have authorization to stop slavers without a new warrant."

She nodded. "A good approach. We'll call it fostering, and since my lands are fairly close, and we are acquainted, it made sense to bring them here." She shook her head. "You could hardly ride all the way back to the city with them."

"Thank you," Ridge said. "I didn't know where else to go."

Lady Sally Anne smiled. "None of that now. Once my other guests hear about them, they're likely to be mothered more than they can stand. They'll be safe, and if we need to utilize their abilities, if it comes to that, we'll be ready."

"Let's hope it doesn't," Ridge said. "But I fear it will."

CHAPTER SIX

The Black Wolf pub catered to a very particular group of customers. Tucked behind a nondescript butcher shop, across the street from a dodgy rooming house, the Black Wolf had no sign to attract passersby. The name was painted over a battered oaken door, but time and weather had blurred the sharp edges of the letters. Those who needed the Black Wolf knew where to find it, and those who didn't were not welcome.

The Black Wolf existed as a sanctuary for King Kristoph's spies and assassins, dangerous men and women who needed neutral places where they could meet and speak freely. Despite the liquor, none of the Black Wolf's customers ever relaxed. Still, since the entrances were guarded, and entry strictly controlled, patrons could at least be assured that if harm befell them, it would be the betrayal of one of their own, not an outsider bent on vengeance. That passed for reassurance in the crowd that considered the Black Wolf to be their territory.

"Place looks rougher every time I'm here," Rett muttered as he

and Ridge leaned against the bar, taking the measure of the crowd before finding a table.

"Maybe you've just gotten used to a better grade of scum," Ridge
replied.

"Doubtful. I'm with you, aren't I?" Rett's grin took the sting out
of his words.

Two days had passed since their return from Harrowmont Castle.
Burke had listened to their sanitized version of what transpired with
the caravan, taken them to task for recklessness, and then thrown up
his hands, admitting that they had no real choice about freeing the
slaved children. Then he had given them a new mission, to begin in
the morning. But first, Rett steered them to the Black Wolf, to see
what chatter their fellow Shadows might have overheard.

The barkeep eyed them warily. "Breckinridge. Kennard. Surprised
you'd show up here, after the last time."

Rett's gaze flickered to a large part of the back wall that had been
recently repaired. "That wasn't all our fault."

"What part of 'safe haven' don't you understand?"

"Those guys were looking for trouble," Ridge defended. "And
they swung first."

Roland, the barkeep, stood a head taller than Ridge, with a broad
chest and thick arms that strained the seams of his shirt. If an ox could
have been trained to tend bar, Rett imagined it would look a lot like
Roland, who glowered at them as he plunked down their cups of whiskey hard enough to slosh.

"Hey, watch it!" Ridge complained. "Don't waste the whiskey!"

"Just a warning. Last time, you were banned for three months.
Cause trouble again, and I don't have to let you back in—ever."

"We understand," Rett said, stepping on Ridge's foot before he
could open his mouth to argue. "No fighting."

Roland looked doubtful, and his gaze bored into their backs as
they moved to take a table. Rett recognized most of the customers.
The Black Wolf was never crowded; spies and assassins were not that
numerous, and many of them would be on assignment at any given
time. Twenty people made a big night, and Rett guessed that was about

how many people watched them as they moved away from the bar.

Some gave a nod in acknowledgment. Others turned away, pointedly not making eye contact. A few smirked in welcome, while two men leveled a glare that could only be interpreted as a warning.

"Breckinridge. You've got a lot of nerve. What are you doing here?" The speaker looked to be in his early thirties, with a scar that cut down across his skull through his short-cropped hair to where one ear was missing a notch. Rett recognized Skola, a thin, wiry man who had a long history of bad blood with Ridge and seemed to have extended that dislike to Rett.

"Same as everyone else, just here between jobs," Ridge said, not slowing, trying to avoid a confrontation.

Skola looked at Rett. "Better keep an eye on him, or you'll end up dead like his last partner."

"*I'm* not an asshole," Rett replied.

Skola started to rise from his seat. His companion grabbed him by the shoulder and shoved him down, as Rett stepped back. Roland at the bar growled a warning. Skola said nothing more, though the look he gave Ridge spoke volumes.

This is why assassins don't socialize, Rett thought. The nature of the work and the constant threat of danger made for an edginess that never went away. Given that few people from happy upbringings tended to choose to kill or deceive for a living, Rett supposed that everyone in the Black Wolf had plenty of dark memories and troubling dreams. It made for a tinderbox, and slights real or imagined could easily become the spark.

That, and the fact that Ridge had a gift for annoying people.

It didn't help that Ridge and Rett had one of the highest kill records among the Shadows, which only served to wound the pride of people already inclined to handle problems with their fists. At the same time, it served to put their colleagues on notice that any attack was likely to end badly for the attacker. It went without saying that an attempt on one of them earned retribution from both.

Ridge managed to find a table without getting into a fight, and Rett was willing to call that a win. All of the tables at the Black Wolf ringed the walls and were turned at an angle so that no one sat with his back to the door. Ridge settled into his seat, leaning back against the wall and toying with his cup of whiskey. He might have appeared relaxed to others, but Rett read the current of tension beneath the cool facade.

"See anyone you were looking for?" Rett asked as the other customers went back to their conversations or card games.

"A few. Couple of folks I want to talk to, once everyone simmers down."

Rett sipped his drink and made an appraisal of the room's occupants. He recognized the other assassins from the training exercises Burke required periodically. He had no strong feelings one way or the other about most of them, but a few, like Skola, had earned his dislike. Others he mistrusted, and that meant a lot in a business where dangerous dealings sometimes required teamwork.

The spies he knew less about since they stuck close with their own kind and remained even more secretive than the assassins. While they all served King Kristoph, lies, subterfuge, and a healthy amount of distrust meant few people formed friendships rather than alliances. He and Ridge were a notable exception, with a record to silence any detractors. Rett did not want to think about what working the job alone would be like, or what that solitude would do to his soul.

"Only you'd have the balls to walk in here and see what happened." A red-haired man approached their table, hands empty and out to his sides in a gesture of appeasement. Ridge nodded, and the man took the third seat at the table, all of them angled to have a view of the door. Rett had to search his memory for a name, but it finally came to him. Tuvan Rinstead. He was a little older than Ridge, and one of the Shadows who seemed to know the score about Ridge's old mentor. One of the few assassins who didn't look at him and Ridge like they were wondering when the order would come to take the pair of them out.

Ridge faked a cocky smile. "Well, you know me."

Tuvan nodded. "And I'm still here." He glanced from Rett to Ridge. "What do you have?"

Ridge pulled out one of the waybills with the odd sigil. "Ever seen this before?"

Tuvan studied it and then nodded. "Yeah. Thought it was some kind of merchant's mark. Why?"

Ridge leaned forward. "We think it's connected to arms smugglers and slavers. We had a run-in with some of them, and turned up this mark."

"Burke know about this?"

Rett nodded. "He knows. And the open warrant on slavers hasn't changed. The arms smuggler—we're trying to figure out who they're working with, and what they're up to. Can't be anything good."

Tuvan frowned, deliberating. "I saw some crates marked with this a couple of months ago. Trying to remember where." He stared into the distance. "Over at Toad Fred's warehouse—you know the place?"

Rett and Ridge nodded. "Toad" Fred's appearance had earned him the nickname, a short, squat man with double chins and a wide mouth whose unfortunate resemblance to an amphibian was unmistakable.

"At the time, I didn't have a reason to care. Just noticed that it was something I hadn't seen before. I was there for a job taking out an opium dealer, so the crates weren't any of my business. Don't know why it stuck in my mind."

"Can you ask around?" Rett sat back in his chair, still keeping an eye on the patrons around them as much as he watched the door out of long habit. "We keep turning up the boxes of smuggled weapons close to the slavers we've run into," he said, tweaking the truth. "Too often to be a coincidence. Maybe if there were more eyes on the look-out—"

Tuvan nodded. "I'll look into it."

"Keep an eye out for the slavers," Ridge warned. "The caravan we infiltrated was stealing children and selling them off. We got the prisoners out, but that cost us the chance to get more information about the buyers. I know Rett and I aren't the most popular ones with our folks," he said, with a vague gesture to indicate the spies and assassins, here and elsewhere. "But slaving's a death warrant, no questions asked. Clear cut. So no matter what the rest of the Shadows think of us, we've got a mandate from the king—and I can't shake the idea that this is all tied up somehow."

"Told you before, Breckinridge. Not everyone hates you." Tuvan grinned. "And hardly anyone hates Kennard," he said with a nod to Rett. "Thing is, you get the job done. That's all most of them care about. Your smug bastard personality is just a bonus. And you've earned it. You two are good. That rankles with some of them. Those are the kind that keep a kill count, need to prove who's the bigger man."

Rett elbowed Ridge before he could make an off-color comment. "We're not competing," he said in a level voice. "We do the job and walk away. But this job isn't done until we figure out what the slavers and the arms smugglers have to do with each other."

"I heard you two still think that crazy prophet is a threat," Tuvan said.

Ridge's expression grew guarded. "Who's saying that?"

Tuvan shrugged. "No secret that the two of you think the Witch Lord is more than just a clever charlatan, fleecing gullible nobles. And it's also no secret that the king doesn't think he's a danger. But you're not the only ones who don't like the Witch Lord, even if it's just on principle. So you're not as alone as you might think."

Rett managed a wan smile. "Good to know."

Tuvan stood. "I'll see what I can dig up. On the sigil and the Witch Lord. And I'll keep my ears open. I might hear things folks won't say to you." He grinned. "I don't make it my life's work to annoy the fuck out of people."

They left the Black Wolf, and Rett could almost hear Roland sigh in relief that this time their exit didn't involve any fighting or broken chairs. Maybe it would make their jobs easier to be more popular among the other Shadows, but Rett didn't give a flying rat's ass about what the rest of the assassins thought of them.

"Where to now?" he asked as Ridge headed in the opposite direction from their rooms.

"Dockside. I worked a job down by the wharves last year when you were laid up after that son of a bitch carved a hole in you. A former pirate decided he wanted to retire. Gave up his ship, changed his name, started running a thieving ring. Stole from the warehouses and had peddlers who would take the goods inland. Some of the merchants were in on it so that they could cheat on their taxes. Tuvan worked the job with me since you were recovering. Seeing him made me remember."

"Huh? You never mentioned that before. We're going to go see a pirate?"

Ridge shook his head. "No. I had an informant in the warehouse. If he's still around, and if he remembers that I paid him well, maybe he'll know more about the markings."

The city of Caralocia sprawled inland from the harbor, with the palace on a bluff behind a high wall. Ships from all over the kingdom made for a busy port and prosperous shops and marketplaces. Large warehouses near the docks housed shipments from across Landria until they could be sold to the merchants, caravans, and traveling peddlers who would sell the goods from one end of the land to the other.

The warehouses and docks were a long way from the glittering palace or the neat shops and respectable pubs of the main district. The wharves were dark and dodgy, a place for drunks and opium whores, pickpockets, and ruffians. The ships that came into the harbor carried crews assembled from every port in the kingdom, but Rett had also heard tales of men who passed out drunk and woke up at sea, pressed into service. The king's guards patrolled, but they could not be everywhere, and the harbor alleys and side streets formed a dark warren that was almost impossible to fully safeguard. Even assassins knew to be wary walking the waterfront late at night.

Ridge walked like he owned the place, and with Rett in lockstep beside him, others tended to get out of their way. Their weapons could be in hand within seconds, but Rett still scanned the area with every step, looking for danger.

A man dodged from an alley as they passed, lurching toward Ridge. Before the man knew what had happened, Ridge pushed him up against a wall, twisting his arm behind him. "It's not nice to pick pockets," Ridge hissed into the man's ear, earning a curse in response. The thief's left hand twitched, and Ridge slammed the man's wrist against the wall, knocking the shiv from his grip. "You chose the wrong mark." Ridge's punch sent the man reeling, then falling. He'd wake up later if someone else didn't come along and finish the job.

After they had walked a few more blocks, Ridge stopped and nodded toward a two-story building still lit up despite the hours. The large double doors were open, and men moved back and forth between the wagons that carried cargo unloaded from the ships. "That's the place. Assuming he's still there."

Rett and Ridge were dressed much the same as the men unloading the crates. They wandered in, and stood to one side, as Ridge scanned faces for the informant. "There he is," Ridge said, and Rett followed his gaze to a skinny dark-haired man with large ears and a receding jaw. "I called him Twitch because he's as jumpy as a cat in a doghouse."

The man must have sensed their presence, because he looked up and froze, recognizing Ridge. For a second, Rett thought the man might bolt. Then the dockworker slumped, as if accepting the inevitable, and jerked his head toward a side door.

Ridge and Rett slipped out and circled around. Twitch lived up to his name, shuffling from one foot to the other, hands clenching and unclenching at his sides. His gaze skittered side to side, and he led them into the shadows around the corner from the warehouse.

"They'll notice. I can't stay long."

"You've seen this?" Ridge pulled out the same drawing he had shown Tuven at the Black Wolf.

Twitch shook his head, but Rett had seen his eyes widen, giving away the lie. "There's coin in it for you if you tell us what you know," Ridge said, pulling out two bronze from his pocket and holding them up.

"It's marked on special crates," Twitch said, his voice high and rushed. "They come in from all over, not just one place. Maybe once or twice a month, a couple at a time. The boss watches them like they're gold. Maybe they are; I've never seen them open. They're heavy, and they rattle. Those get loaded separate, not with the other stuff. Go out on wagons that come by just for them. Like I said, special."

"Do you know where the wagons go?"

Twitch moved to answer, but his body jerked forward, and his whole form went stiff as his breath ended in a gasp and his eyes went wide. A trickle of blood started from the corner of his mouth, and then Twitch collapsed, a knife hilt-deep in his back.

Ridge ran in the direction the killer must have gone. From the angle of the way the knife hit, it didn't take much to figure out where the thrower had been. Rett knelt next to Twitch. The dockworker was bleeding out fast, but he wasn't dead yet.

"Where do the wagons go?" Rett asked again, leaning down to catch the man's whisper.

"Ranford," Twitch breathed. "Some went..." He slumped in Rett's hold, and his eyes rolled back in his head.

Ridge ran toward them but shook his head as Rett looked up hopefully. "Couldn't find the bastard."

"Cover me."

Before Ridge could ask questions Rett wasn't sure he could answer, he gripped Twitch with hands on either side of the man's temples. Afraid to think too hard about what he was doing, Rett gathered his magic and *pushed*.

He found himself in a dim place filled with images. *Memories*, Rett thought. *Twitch's memories*. Rett had never tried anything like this before, and now he moved on sheer instinct. The images were growing fainter with every second as Twitch's life faded. Rett rummaged through the memories, frantically looking for what he needed, hoping he would recognize it if he found it.

There. Rett thought he heard Twitch's voice, and he saw crates being loaded on a wagon. But unlike the usual plain, battered wagons that hauled cargo to towns inland, this one was painted and in good repair. The driver looked better dressed than the norm, and Rett realized the man wore a livery shirt and pants, minus the jacket. The wagon itself bore no insignia, but Rett caught sight of the jacket on the driver's seat, with a crest on the arm.

Color bled from the images, as they slowed to a crawl. Vivid hues faded to gray, and Rett realized he had grown very cold. *What happens if I'm in his mind when he dies?* Rett thought with horror.

He turned and ran, fighting through the ghostly memories, shivering so hard that breathing became difficult. He could feel his own heart slowing, and his chest felt heavy. Rett tried to pull back, unsure how to let go.

Ridge's voice sounded from a great distance, barely audible, and Rett fixed on it like a beacon. He fought against the torpor that made his movements uncoordinated and sluggish, focused on taking one step and then another, toward the voice that called him.

Pain flared across his face, sharp enough to make him gasp, and then again. It jolted his heart and sparked his anger, and he threw himself toward the source, as another sharp slap cracked against his skin.

Rett came to with a gasp, on his knees over Twitch's corpse, staring into Ridge's frightened face. "Are you back?" Ridge stared at him, pale and wide-eyed as if he had seen a ghost.

"Yeah," Rett managed, fighting to clear his head. His thoughts felt muddy, and his knees almost failed him when he tried to stand.

"We've got to get out of here," Ridge said, hauling Rett up and getting a shoulder under his arm. "Come on. You can tell me what in the name of the gods happened once we're far away from here."

By the time they had gone a block, Rett pulled loose, able to walk for himself. Ridge gave him a skeptical once-over but did not push when Rett kept going. They watched the shadows, wondering if Twitch's killer followed them, or whether he had finished his task when the knife that found its mark in the man's back.

"I saw it," Rett managed, as they neared the place they had left their horses. "The wagon. And the man driving it."

Ridge looked at him, worried and unbelieving. "When? Where? There wasn't anyone else in the alley."

Rett shook his head, his nerves still jangling. "Let's just get inside," he said, refusing to meet Ridge's gaze and swinging up onto his horse.

He avoided Ridge's attempts at conversation on the ride back to their lodging house, trying to figure out for himself exactly what had happened and whether it had been real. Henri met them in the stables with his uncanny ability to predict their arrival, and shooed them inside, promising to see to the horses and assuring them that food awaited.

Ridge could not contain his questions. "You almost died back in that alley." His voice was sharp with worry. "I saw you put your hands on Twitch's temples, and then you just...went away. You didn't hear me; you didn't see me. I thought for sure whoever knifed Twitch was going to come back for us, and you were just...gone."

Ridge began to pace. "And then your whole body went stiff, and your breathing changed, and when I tried to pull you away, you were freezing cold." He blew out a long breath. "I thought you were going to die."

"So did I." Rett turned away as he peeled off his coat and hung it on a hook. Their rooms smelled of warm meat pie, date tarts, and fresh coffee. The food sat on the table, and a cup of what he guessed to be whiskey accompanied each plate, while a pot of coffee boiled in the embers on the hearth.

Ridge watched him, head tilted quizzically as he tried to make sense of what he had seen. "You did something. With your magic."

Rett swallowed hard and nodded. Even now, he didn't feel completely right. His heartbeat had returned to normal, and he could breathe easily once more, but the fog in his head had not completely cleared, and the cold lingered in his bones far more than the temperature of the night would excuse.

"I didn't think about it, I just acted," he said, still avoiding Ridge's eyes as he sat down at the table. Rett fought the urge to down the whiskey in a single gulp. "I knew if Twitch died without telling us what he saw, that we'd hit a blank wall. So I...went in after him."

"In where?" Ridge had not moved, still staring at Rett with a mix of worry and misgiving in his expression.

Rett took a swallow of the whiskey and looked down. "In his mind. Like the Sight except...different."

Ridge stepped to the table, all his focus on Rett. "You went into a dying man's mind? Are you crazy?"

"Maybe," Rett replied with a wan smile. "I told you, I didn't think. There wasn't time. I wondered if I could see what he knew, and so I grabbed him, and I *pushed.*"

Ridge closed his eyes, and from his posture, Rett guessed his friend debated whether to ask more questions or take a swing at him for his stupidity. "Forget the 'how' for a moment. What did you see?"

Rett told him about the wagon and the driver. "I've seen that crest before. One of the minor nobles, I think...out a distance from the city." He paused. "Twitch said 'Ranford' when I asked him where the crates were going."

"Can you remember the crest well enough to draw it?" Ridge asked, and Rett gave a shaky nod. Ridge returned a moment later with a piece of parchment, quill, and ink.

Rett moved his food aside, unsure his stomach at the moment could keep anything down. His hand shook as he took the quill, and he saw that Ridge noticed as well, but his friend said nothing.

"Like this, I think." He sketched out the crest and slid the parchment over to Ridge.

"And he said some of the crates went to Ranford?"

Rett nodded. "That's West of Caralocia. I'm trying to remember which of the nobility have land out there, and who the players are. We don't usually have work that takes us in that direction."

Ridge snorted. "Because the nobles out there rarely draw the king's attention enough to require assassination. Plenty of farms, lots of cows and sheep. Ranford's always had middling power at best to influence the king. Not like the more aggressive nobles who've got their fingers in the shipping trade. You can bet *they've* got King Kristoph's ear."

The door opened, interrupting their conversation. Henri stepped in, managing to look clean and unruffled although he had just come from the stables. Rett privately wondered if their squire stashed extra changes of clothing in various locations. "Is dinner to your liking?"

"Did you cook this?" Ridge asked with his mouth full of food.

A small smile tugged at the corners of Henri's mouth. "I did. Just something to fill the hours while the two of you were away. After I cleaned the tack, polished the boots, sharpened the extra blades…"

"We understand, Henri," Rett said with a laugh. "You're indispensable. Did you eat?"

Henri nodded. "I learned a long time ago to eat when I'm hungry and not wait for the two of you," he observed, raising an eyebrow. "But thanks for asking. Should I retrieve the medical kit? You look undamaged. But there's blood on your jacket," he noted, assessing Rett. "And yours as well," he added with a closer look at Ridge. "Am I missing something?"

Rett rubbed his temple, still feeling off-center from the magic he had used in the alley. "Not our blood, for once," he replied. "One of Ridge's informants was just about to tell us something that someone else really didn't want us to hear."

"I see."

"What do you know about Ranford?" Ridge wiped his mouth with the back of his hand. Rett kicked him, and Henri gave a disapproving look. Ridge muttered something under his breath and reached for a napkin.

Henri took off his coat and hung it on a peg, closing and locking the door behind him. "Funny you ask. I've been making inquiries about that marking you showed me. Some of the people I spoke to remember seeing crates with that mark coming in on ships. None of the boxes had an address for delivery on their paperwork, but one of the serving girls I know overheard a wagon driver say he'd been told to take the boxes to Ranford and meet a man in another wagon who would take them farther."

"What happened?" Rett asked.

"She didn't know. The driver never returned. Killed on the road by highwaymen," Henri replied. "Convenient, isn't it?"

CHAPTER SEVEN

"Her name is Lorella Solens," Burke said. "She claims to be a medium. Talks to dead people. Says the dead talk back." The look on his face gave Ridge and Rett a clear understanding of just what Burke thought of those claims. "Normally, that wouldn't be my business. But we received a tip from one of our spies in Duke Barton's household. He's worried that Solens is exerting an unhealthy influence on the Duke."

"Who does the Duke want to talk to that's dead?" Ridge asked.

"His two children. Boy and a girl, age ten and twelve. Died last year in the fever that went through upcountry. From what I heard, the Duke nearly died as well but recovered. His wife is said to have lost her mind in grief over them. She never leaves her room."

"So you want us to look into it, and if she's taking advantage of the Duke, stop her?" Rett frowned. "It doesn't exactly seem like the kind of thing we usually kill people for. Wouldn't an arrest serve, if she's a fraud?"

Burke shook his head. "Duke Barton's lands lie at an important crossroads, and his holdings include a key bridge and a ferry across the river. Those are strategically important, and cannot be compromised, for the safety of the kingdom."

"How does the Duke wanting to hear from his dead children threaten the bridge and road?" Ridge asked.

"My spy's report suggests that the medium is steering the Duke to make decisions and alliances that may not be in his best interests—and may be harmful to the crown."

"He's asking his dead children to advise him on political matters?" Rett asked, skepticism clear in his voice.

"She's tricky. Never comes out and says what she wants him to do, but the 'children' supposedly pass along information they've heard beyond the Veil, like having an inside source. Barton might even think he's being steered by the gods," Burke replied.

"Is there a connection to the Witch Lord?" Rett asked.

Burke shrugged. "Not that I know about. Doesn't mean there isn't one. Barton would be an asset, given the crossings he controls, if it ever came to a fight."

"How much leeway do we have?" Ridge asked.

Burke looked as if he barely restrained himself from rolling his eyes. "As much as you usually have. That's why I'm giving this assignment to the two of you. If she's not what the spy thinks she is, don't make the kill. Find out everything you can."

"And if she's not dangerous? Can we let her walk away?" Rett pressed.

Burke gave him a cold, level glare. "Yes. But if your assessment turns out to be wrong—"

"We get sent back to make things right," Ridge finished. "We'll figure it out."

"It always rains in the West Country," Rett muttered as they rode toward Ranford.

"Place ought to be an ocean, with how much water comes down," Ridge agreed.

They hunched against the cold rain that beat down on their leather coats and soaked their trousers. Although his hat kept the worst of the weather away from Ridge's face, an icy drop slithered down his neck, under his collar, and ran the length of his spine.

"Not too much farther," Rett said, lifting his head enough to regard the signpost at the next crossroads.

Caralocia and the seaport sprawled across enough territory that many people born there lived their whole lives without traveling elsewhere. Ridge and Rett had seen most of the larger cities in the kingdom as well as its most important castles and manors due to the nature of their work, but the thinly-populated farming regions gave them little reason to visit. The more ambitious nobility, those who sought to advance their visibility and position with King Kristoph, either held lands close to Caralocia or found houses in the city so they could spend their time at court.

Out here, the palace and the harbor seemed a lifetime away. The country nobility might be just as wealthy as their more city-focused peers, but they prized independence from the crown and took their responsibilities as landholders seriously. That didn't mean there weren't schemes and gossip as with the crowd at court, but the maneuvering appeared to be more practical, focused on tangibles like acquiring the best breeding stock or finest horses, or cultivating the most successful harvest.

"That's the Barton manor?" Rett asked, with a tilt of his head toward a massive, stately home on the highest hill in sight. Broadmoor Manor had been in the Barton family for generations, a gift from a grateful king in times long past. Ridge had been surprised to hear Barton's name come up from Burke. While some of the nobility were renowned for their scandals and lack of restraint, the Barton name was mentioned so rarely that Ridge had needed to look up the family in genealogy manuscripts.

"The latest one," Ridge replied. "It's been replaced and added on to over the years. Burned a couple of times, besieged once or twice too."

Rett scanned the fields that stood deep in mud, their main crops for the year harvested, and a sparse seeding of hay struggling to grow in their place. "Seems a bit rural for a siege."

"The Dornan River is just a few miles that direction," Ridge said. "The ferry there is the only way across for fifty miles up or down. And the two main roads that span the kingdom cross just a bit north of here, still in Barton's lands. Not to mention rich farmland, and a kingdom has to eat."

"That 'strategic importance' Burke went on about only matters if someone's challenging control of the kingdom," Rett countered. "Do you think Burke believes the Witch Lord is preparing for a coup?"

Ridge shrugged. "Maybe the potential is there, in the long run. Not immediately. Unless we've all been very wrong about how much support he's got."

Rett shook his head. "I don't think we're that out of touch. Burke's good, and the fact that he's giving us a lot of rope to keep looking into the Witch Lord when Kristoph's dismissed him as a threat proves that Burke doesn't rule out an enemy until he's sure it's not going to be a problem."

The market town of Dolson grew up around Landria's busiest crossroads, the main arteries through the kingdom that carried the lifeblood of trade. Farmers urged their oxen or cart horses on with heavy loads of winter vegetables or ripe apples. Traders from all corners of the land and beyond traveled with wagons full of treasures. Peddlers and their carts vied for room with penitents traveling by foot from one religious shrine to another. Most found some reason to pause in Dolson—for food, lodging, or supplies. By the look of the town, travelers had been very good for business.

The two assassins took a room at the inn and saw to their horses before tramping into the pub soaking wet, chilled through, and overdue for dinner. Rett's stomach growled at the smell of fresh bread and venison stew. Ridge heard and chuckled, though he felt just as hungry.

A tired-looking woman came to their table, a pitcher of ale in one hand and tankards in the other. "You'll be wanting the stew?" she asked, in a voice raw from repeating the same questions, straining to be heard over the rowdy conversations.

"Stew, ale, and bread will do us fine," Ridge replied with a smile that did not seem to register with the harried server.

"Brought the ale," she replied, clunking down the tankards and filling them to the brim. "What brings you this way?"

"We heard tell of a woman hereabouts who can talk to ghosts," Rett replied, managing a soulful look that Ridge guessed had served him well in his younger days as a pickpocket in Caralocia's alleys. "Just lost someone close to us, and well, you can imagine…"

Despite her weariness, the woman favored Rett with a sympathetic glance. "I can. Lost my sister just last year. But I'm not one to chase after the dead when the living have more than their share of problems."

"Have you heard about her? The medium?" Ridge asked.

The server cast a glance over her shoulder as someone gave a shout from the kitchen, and muttered a curse under her breath. "I'm coming," she growled, though the person who shouted couldn't hear her reply above the din. The woman returned her attention to Ridge and Rett.

"I've heard. Mixed things. Some say she can, and some say she can't. Maybe it depends on what someone hoped the dead would say, whether they believe in her or not. But the Duke believes, so I imagine she don't rightly care what the rest of us think!" she added with a raspy laugh.

Rett watched her retreat into the crowd. He took a sip of the ale, and his brows rose in appreciation. "This is actually damn fine."

Ridge chuckled. "Maybe that explains why we almost couldn't get a seat. Hope the food is just as good."

A shouted curse behind them made both men tense. Two of the patrons near the bar got into a shoving match, with the bartender stepping in just after the first blows were struck. Ridge shifted, tempted to give the barkeep a hand, but Rett grabbed him by the arm and pulled him back down. "Not our problem," Rett hissed.

Ridge reminded himself that not drawing attention to themselves would serve them best, but after the long, dull ride he was aching for an outlet. Reluctantly, he turned his attention back to his ale and admired the bowls of rich broth with thick chunks of venison, onions, and potatoes the server brought them.

"You're no fun," he growled at Rett.

Rett rolled his eyes. "Bar fights stopped being 'fun' a long time ago. I don't need any more bruises. The job keeps me well supplied."

"You're just still sore about that bottle."

"The one that left me a scar that looks like a giant bite on one side of my ass?" Rett shot back. "You didn't get an ass full of broken glass. They just hit you over the head—which means it didn't do any damage at all."

Ridge couldn't resist a snicker. "You've got to admit, the guy I hit had it coming."

"Not exactly a fair fight, even if you did let him off easy," Rett retorted.

"Not fair? He had to have been half a head taller and a stone or two heavier!"

"Which goes back to the wisdom of starting a fight," Rett remarked, spearing a chunk of venison with his fork. "I'm still of the opinion that anything short of horse thievery, we overlook. Especially if it's not our horses."

"He cheated me at cards."

"I think what you meant to say is that he cheated you while you were cheating him," Rett replied over a mouthful of food. "Because I know how you play cards. But you're missing the point. If you had taken the man one-on-one, I would have been happy to sit back and charge admission to watch the bloodshed, since I know you can take care of yourself. But no, you had to get me involved, and I ended up picking bits of bottle out of my seat with a long ride the next day."

"I said I was sorry."

"Cold comfort," Rett said, shaking his head.

"Admit it—they're still probably talking about that fight," Ridge prodded, more because he enjoyed annoying his partner than out of pride. Rett was right; he shouldn't have picked a fight with a local, although the brawl had come at the end of their job, with nothing to tie them to either the argument or the disappearance of a corrupt sheriff whose abuses had finally reached the notice of the king.

"I'm sure they are, which might be a problem if we ever have to go back there for a job," Rett replied.

"Not like you didn't take a swing at that man in the town that had the awful beer—the stuff that tasted like puke."

"He was trying to steal my money! And doing it badly, I might add." Rett grinned.

They went quiet for a few minutes, enjoying the stew and the freshly baked bread. Nothing in the pub seemed amiss, and when Ridge opened up his Sight, he saw no traces of the Witch Lord's hold on anyone in the room. Not that he had expected to; the Witch Lord tended to reserve his touch for a more exclusive crowd—the nobles, and aristocracy who could advance his interests. Still, Ridge did not pick up a hint even of the kind of stain he had found on some of the Witch Lord's minions. That let him relax, just a fraction.

The bar fight resolved without the need for anyone but the very large, muscular tavern master's involvement, and the patrons went back to their own affairs. When the woman returned with another pitcher of ale, Rett broke out his best smile.

"Where would we find the woman who talks to ghosts?" he asked. "We've come a long way, and we'd like to see what we think of her for ourselves."

The server frowned. "Suit yourself. But don't blame me if you lose all your coin for a few pretty words." She gave directions, still glowering. "Just remember, I warned you. And mind this—she doesn't open until nine bells, so there's no point running off without breakfast."

Ridge and Rett thanked her and left extra coins with their payment before heading up to the room they had reserved. When Ridge opened the door and lit the lantern from the light in the hallway, he sighed. The room looked cramped and stuffy, with one sagging bed, a chair, and washstand, along with a chamber pot of dubious cleanliness. Still, they had stayed in worse places, and since one of them stood watch while the other slept, the accommodations would suit them fine.

"When I get old, I want my own bed when I travel," Ridge grumbled.

"People like us don't get old," Rett replied, tossing his small bag near the foot of the bed. It held weapons and maps, along with anything they did not dare to leave in their saddlebags. "So enjoy what you have back at our rooms in the city. It'll have to do."

Ridge walked to the window and looked out. By now, the town had grown quiet and sleepy, with the tradespeople, merchants, and farmers waiting for dawn to begin their chores again. "Do you think it's possible?" he asked quietly, staring into the night.

Rett looked up. "Think what's possible? That Lorella is working for the Witch Lord?" He shrugged. "I guess so."

Ridge shook his head. "Not what I meant. Do you think she might really talk to the dead?" He did not turn. It was easier to speak his thoughts aloud without making eye contact.

"Maybe," Rett allowed. "But I'm more in agreement with the serving woman. Let the dead be. We've got enough problems with the living."

Ridge tried to pick out the stars through the wavy glass and the reflection of the lanterns. "It could be nice if it were true," he replied. "Ask questions. Get answers."

Rett leaned against the wall and crossed his arms over his chest. "Then our job would never be over because Burke would have us interrogating corpses. As for anyone else, I'm glad that the people I knew who died are gone. They weren't anything but trouble. Who do you want to talk to?"

Ridge shifted uncomfortably. "My mother, maybe. I was so young when she died; I didn't really understand what was happening. Never got to say goodbye."

Rett nodded. "All right. I can see that. But given what we do, I'd be more afraid we'd get an earful from every mark we killed who would be out to convince us they were really innocent."

Being one of the king's Shadows meant status—and nightmares. To most of the kingdom, the Shadows were a dark legend, used to warn people away from breaking the law. "Be good, or the Shadows will get you," was a warning Ridge had overheard more than once. Yet the average citizen—and even the average lawbreaker—had little to fear from the Shadows, unless their deeds threatened king and kingdom. The king's guards dealt with common criminals. Shadows only emerged to deal with those whose crimes or status became a matter for the crown's concern.

Still, the duties left a mark on those who carried them out. Rett hadn't been kidding about Shadows not having to worry about old age. Few lived long, struck down by a job gone wrong, or just as often, by their own hand. No matter how righteous the kill, dealing out death scarred. Both Ridge and Rett woke in the night, soaked in sweat, remembering the past. The satisfaction Ridge felt in defending King Kristoph seemed hollow at those times, when even the strongest whiskey could not blot away the bloodstains.

"Stop thinking," Rett counseled, gripping Ridge's shoulder. "Let the ghosts go. We have work to do."

Since Lorella didn't open shop until ninth bells in the morning, Ridge and Rett headed over at ten in the evening, easily breaking in through the back door. The old two-story building leaned to the right as if its builders had too much beer the day they raised the walls. The medium's storefront opened onto a side street, around the corner from a cobbler and a bakery.

The sign read, "*Fortunes.*" Curtains covered the windows where another kind of shop would have displayed its wares. The store was dark, but lights glowed in the apartment on its second floor. Ridge wondered whether Lorella lived over her shop, or if not, whether the tenant ever complained of being bothered by ghosts.

Rett lit two candles, handing one to Ridge. They moved carefully through a back room filled with pieces of cast-off furniture, and a few crates of odds and ends. The front room looked like a parlor, comfortable in a shabby way, with a high-backed chair and a small, stiff-looking couch on one side, and a circular table with four wooden chairs on the other.

Ridge opened his Sight but sensed nothing more than a persistent, vague uneasiness as if he were being watched. He recognized the unfocused glaze in his friend's eyes as Rett sought his magic. Rett shook his head, indicating he had learned nothing. So far, Rett's visions had also been absent, meaning they had to uncover whatever was to be learned the hard way.

"Who's there?" a woman called out, her voice angry and defiant. "There's nothing to steal. Get out of my house."

Ridge and Rett remained still. Ridge had drawn his knife, but he hoped he would not have to use it. Footsteps on the stairs told them the speaker edged closer, and Ridge bet she was armed with something. They blew out the candles and set them on a table. Only moonlight lit the room, filtered through the top of the window above the curtains. Out of long practice, Rett went left, and Ridge went right, presenting two targets instead of one.

"I know you're in here," a woman they guessed to be Lorella said. "And if I find you, you're gonna get a beating, so get out!" Anger edged out fear in her voice, but Ridge heard a slight waver.

She moved between them, just as they had hoped. Ridge stepped forward. "We want to talk with you," he said. "It doesn't have to go badly."

Lorella raised a long, thin, dark object defensively. "Leave me alone." She was slender and scarcely as tall as Rett's shoulder, and her black hair hung in loose curls around a heart-shaped face with large, dark eyes. Right now, those eyes looked daggers at them, and her lips curled in a defiant sneer.

"Drop the weapon," Ridge ordered.

Rett moved out of his hiding place along the wall behind Lorella, and the tip of his sword nudged her in the back. "Drop it."

Lorella flung the weapon at Ridge with a curse. She took in their shadowy forms, and the glint of the knives clear in their grip. "I don't have anything to steal. Go away. Don't hurt me."

"Light some lamps. We're going to ask you questions. How it goes after that depends on what you have to say," Ridge said.

"Who are you? Why are you here? I've done nothing wrong." Even facing down two armed men, Lorella remained defiant.

"First, light. Then, we'll talk."

Rett remained close behind Lorella as she went to light two lanterns. They illuminated the cramped space, and Lorella took advantage of the glow to glare at both assassins.

"Now what?" Although she had dropped her weapon, everything about her stance suggested she would not go down without a fight.

"Sit down," Ridge ordered. "We have questions."

Glowering, Lorella sat in the high-backed chair. Rett remained close to one side. He had a glazed look in his eyes, and Ridge guessed he scanned with his Sight. When he blinked, his expression looked puzzled, and the shrug he gave vexed Ridge.

"Tell us about Duke Barton. What does he hear from his children?" Ridge kept his knife down, but it remained in his hand, easy enough for her to see the threat.

"None of your business."

"It's our business now," Rett replied quietly. "And it will go better if you answer us honestly."

"Who are you?"

"Trouble," Ridge said. "Now...tell us about the Duke." He glanced at Rett and gave a subtle hand signal to indicate that Rett should take the lead while he opened his Sight. Turning his magic on the woman who sat ready for a fight, he understood why Rett had looked confused. The touch of the Witch Lord left a stain, yet it was not the taint of those who had sold themselves for profit. Nor did it feel like the wagon driver or the other willing lackeys they had encountered. Lorella bore the Witch Lord's touch, but on her, it felt more like a bruise.

"I don't break confidences," Lorella countered. "What the spirits tell me, what my customers ask...it's private."

Ridge opened his mouth to respond when a crash of glass stole his words. A sturdy pottery jar with a burning fuse rolled across the floor where it landed after breaking the window.

"Run!" Rett yelled, grabbing Lorella by the wrist and pulling her with them. They reached the back room just as the crude bomb exploded, and Ridge got the door most of the way shut in time to block the hail of pottery shards that drove themselves deep into the wood.

"Keep her here!" Ridge hissed and slipped out the door into the alley. He saw two shadowy objects flying toward him, each trailing a tail of fire. He leaped behind a pile of garbage to shield from the blast as they smashed on the cobblestones, bursting into flame and spewing broken bits to strike against the walls. The night stank of gunpowder and sulfur, overlaying the smell of old garbage and piss. Smoke hung in the air, obscuring Ridge's view as he peered warily around the garbage, checking to see if the attacker was waiting to flush him out.

He dodged from cover, throwing knives ready, but the alley was empty. Ridge ran toward the front of the shop. When he reached the street, no one was in sight, and no footsteps pointed him in the direction of the attacker. He turned back to the store and saw flames leaping from the front room, as smoke billowed through the broken window.

Ridge ran back and pulled open the door to find Rett still holding Lorella by the wrist, staring down her murderous glare. "The front's on fire! Let's go."

Lorella struggled to pull free. "I can't leave! Everything I own is upstairs."

"Sorry, but there's a fire between you and the steps," Ridge said, grabbing her other wrist. "We're going now."

Lorella looked at Ridge and lost focus for an instant. When she returned to herself, she paled. "Shadows. Assassins. You came to kill me!"

"We obviously weren't the only one," Ridge shot back. "You have a lot of enemies?"

Lorella threw herself forward, trying to break away from Rett's grip. She fought like a wild thing, twisting and bucking, and striking out with a kick that barely missed Ridge's nuts.

"That does it," Ridge said, yanking a length of rope from beneath his jacket. Lorella's eyes went wide, and she began to scream as he tied her wrists together. Rett clapped a hand over her mouth and swore in pain as she bit down on his palm.

"She sank her teeth into me!" he protested.

Ridge grabbed a rag and stuffed it into her mouth, as Lorella's glare promised him a slow death.

"Yes, we're King's Shadows. But someone else is trying to kill you. So unless you want to be handed over to them, your best bet is with us. Understand?"

Lorella nodded reluctantly. Rett grabbed her bound wrists. "Run or walk with us, or I tie your ankles and throw you over my shoulder," he growled.

Ridge led the way into the darkened alley. Behind them, the old shop went up in flames, and Lorella sobbed through her gag. They began to run, trying to put distance between them and the burning embers that fell around them as the fire burst through the sagging roof.

Neighbors turned out to see what was going on, and the quiet night quickly became chaos. Ridge ducked down a dark ginnel. Dragging a prisoner through the growing crowd seemed certain to attract the wrong kind of attention, and they had no desire to involve the town guards.

"Stay here," Ridge ordered, and Rett responded with a nod, drawing Lorella deeper into the gloom.

Ridge sprinted off, moving through the crowd quickly enough to make haste without looking suspicious. He found what he needed a few blocks away, and returned with a horse and wagon stolen from the stable at the end of the street.

"Get in," he ordered.

Lorella jerked her arm loose from Rett's hold and climbed into the wagon with the imperiousness of a queen, despite her bound hands. The look in her eye that made it clear she blamed them for everything.

"We didn't blow up your shop," Rett said, as Ridge snapped the reins and the wagon jolted away. Ridge couldn't make out her muffled response, but he assumed it cursed them soundly and suggested that their mothers made poor—and possibly illegal—choices in bedmates.

"In fact, we probably just saved your life."

This time, Lorella twisted and managed to dig her knee into Rett's thigh, barely missing his groin.

"Stop kicking for the plums!" he chided, shoving her back with one hand while keeping a firm grip on her arm.

The wagon clattered through the dark streets, a rough ride that sent Rett and Lorella sliding from one side to the other and rattled Ridge's teeth. They didn't dare head back to the inn where they had lodged the night before, not with a captive. And with Lorella's attacker on the loose, that complicated where they might be safe.

Ridge drove to an abandoned barn he had spotted on the outskirts of town. He sighed, thinking about the cold night ahead of them. Steam rose from the horses, and Ridge could see his own breath cloud in the frigid air. He drove them inside the barn, then lit a lantern and got down to take a closer look at their questionable sanctuary. A quick walk of the barn's interior revealed that the previous owners left nothing of value behind. Ridge came around to help Rett with their unwilling guest.

"I'm going to take out the gag, and you're not going to scream," he warned Lorella. "Because there's no one around to hear you, and it annoys the shit out of me. We've got questions. Give us answers, and everything might be all right."

Lorella responded with a grudging nod. Rett removed her gag, being careful to keep his fingers well away from her teeth. He glared at her, and Ridge saw a fresh red bite on Rett's hand.

"Any idea who set your house on fire?" Ridge asked.

Lorella slumped against the back of the wagon as if the fight had gone out of her. Ridge took a good look at the medium. She might have been a few years older than he was. Her face was pretty in a sharp-featured way, and her eyes reflected worry and exhaustion. Soot streaked her cheeks, and a few ashes lodged in her hair. Lorella's nightdress was ripped and stained, and her bare feet looked cold.

"No. No idea," Lorella replied. "Maybe someone who didn't like what the ghosts had to say."

"We're not the town guards. You can be honest with us. Do you really talk to ghosts?" Ridge pressed.

Lorella's glare came back, full force. "I don't care whether you believe or not. It's true."

Ridge let that argument go for the moment. "Tell us about the Duke."

Lorella remained silent, then let out a long breath. "What do you want to know? He lost two children, and it cost his wife her sanity. She shrieks like a mad woman, locked up in a room. The same fever nearly killed Duke Barton, and he wishes he had joined his children instead of recovering."

"Tell us what messages his children give." Rett urged.

A flash of fear and wariness crossed Lorella's face. "The children—Lorn and Betta—pass on wisdom from the other side, as well as their own wishes for their father."

Ridge shook his head. "That's the story the Duke wants to hear. Now tell us the truth."

"Lorn and Betta died when they were small. They miss their parents. They want to come home or have their parents come to them. What did you expect?" Lorella snapped.

"But that's not good enough to keep the Duke coming back again and again," Ridge probed. "What about the 'wisdom from the other side'?"

Lorella looked away. "Sometimes other spirits have messages for the Duke. His children share them."

"I don't think that's how it works," Rett said, earning a glare. "Why don't you tell us who's actually giving you those messages, and what they want with Duke Barton."

Lorella's fear was clear in her eyes. "I can't. They'll kill me."

"We're Shadows," Ridge reminded her. "I have a warrant for you, on suspicion of treason." She flinched at the word and swallowed hard. "The only reason we haven't read it out and done our job is because I think there's more to the story. And someone else just tried to kill you. So...we're your best bet for staying alive."

"You have a warrant," Lorella said bitterly. "It doesn't matter what I say or don't say. I'm already dead."

Ridge shook his head. "That's not the way we work. Help us, and we have some leeway to help you."

She looked at him suspiciously. "Sard it all, guess there's no reason not to," she sighed. "The Duke came to me about a year after his children died. He was desperate to hear from them, to know they had found peace. That's how it started."

"And you actually contacted his children? Or did you make it all up?"

"I've told you. My gift is real. What you believe about it changes nothing. The Duke wanted reassurance. The children wanted to talk to their father."

"Then something changed," Rett nudged.

Lorella swallowed hard and nodded. "The Duke's brother came to me. He wanted me to pass along other messages, advice on business matters, suggestions of who to trust and which friends to let go. He said that he'd report me to the guards for theft, make it look like I was stealing from the Duke if I didn't go along with it. I believed he would do it. He wasn't a nice man."

"So the Duke's brother told you what to say?"

Lorella nodded again, looking down. "If he'd have gone to the guards, lied to the Duke, I'd have been ruined. Jailed, maybe even hanged. I didn't have a choice."

Her confession rang of sincerity, and Rett gave an imperceptible nod, suggesting that he also found her story convincing.

"And you have no idea who tried to kill us back there? Because whoever it was, came around to the back and threw a couple more of those little 'surprises,' waiting for you to go out that way."

"Think about who you've talked with lately," Rett said. "Was someone angry with you?"

Lorella raised her bound wrists to cover her face with her hands. "Let me think," she begged. "There's been too much—"

They stood in silence for a few minutes as she recovered her composure. Lorella lowered her hands and looked up. "I can think of a couple of people. Maybe. A woman wanted to speak to her dead husband. She wanted to know if he'd cheated on her. His spirit refused to come. She cursed me and told me I was a fraud." Lorella gave a harsh laugh. "If I'd been a fraud, I would have pretended her husband's ghost told me whatever she wanted to hear. I can't win."

"And someone else?" Rett nudged.

"A man came to ask the ghost of his mother where she had hidden money. Her spirit did come, but she told him there was no money, that she had spent it long ago, and that she had nothing left. He got angry—with her and then with me. He cursed her and screamed at me, said I was lying, that the ghost had told me where the money was and I meant to steal it from him." She gave a weary shrug. "I told him exactly what the ghost said. He was so angry, I was afraid, and I pulled out the knife I keep under my chair, just in case. Told him to leave and not come back. He left, but he spat on my front step and cursed me."

Ridge met Rett's gaze. "Offhand, I'd say he's a likely suspect."

Lorella looked at Ridge and frowned. "You've lost a daughter…" she murmured, her gaze fixed on something only she could see. Before he could refute her comment, she shook her head. "No. A sister. Young enough that you could have a daughter her age. Long ago. She says the others went on without her, but she stayed because she didn't want you to still be angry with her."

Ridge felt his heart thud but kept his face blank. "Why would I be angry?"

Lorella stared at the empty space, glancing at Ridge now and again as if she were having a silent conversation with someone who mentioned him. "She says the two of you fought before she got sick. She took something you wanted, and you were angry with her. Then she went to sleep. She's sorry."

Ridge knew Rett watched him carefully, questioningly. The incident lingered on the edge of Ridge's memories before he had been dragged off to the orphanage. The last night before everything went to shit was spotty, such a long time ago, but he did remember arguing with Melly over chores, and she had snatched the last of the berries to get back at him. They'd had words, and by morning, Melly and the rest of the family had come down with fever. All but Ridge. And then they were gone.

"Lucky guess," he said, though his throat was tight.

Lorella tilted her head as if to catch a whispered reply. "Melly. Her name was Melly, and she had a rope doll she called Tariann."

Ridge's eyes widened. That bit of information was too spot on, something he had never even confided to Rett, details no one else alive would have known. "She's here? You can talk to her?"

"She's beside you. And just so you know, she says that she's scared for you. You should be more careful." Despite their rocky introduction, Lorella's lips twitched in an almost-smile.

Ridge groaned inwardly. An assassin's life definitely wasn't suitable for his little sister to have a front row seat. "I'll do my best," he replied in a strangled voice. "And tell her I'm not angry. It didn't matter. I'm sorry she went away. And I miss her." He knew a chance existed that Lorella had pried the details from his mind with sly magic, but he doubted it. And if Melly had stuck close all this time, then it was time to make amends and set her free.

"She misses you, too," Lorella replied. "And she's tired, so she says the new brother can watch out for you." Her eyes flickered toward Rett, who chuckled.

"Tell her that he does. We watch out for each other," Ridge replied quietly. "Goodbye, Melly."

Lorella watched the empty space just a bit longer, then looked to Rett, and a little behind him. "You look like her."

"Melly?" Rett countered. "No relation—"

"No, the woman. She's hardly older than a girl. Sister?" Lorella shook her head. "No. Mother. So young." Her head inclined as if listening to whispers. "She died birthing you. Thought the others would take better care. Tries to watch over you. She's sorry she had to leave."

"So am I," Rett said, his voice barely a whisper. Ridge watched his friend struggle to hide the emotions roiled by the medium's words.

If I find out this is all a game, I'll hand her over to the guards, warrant or not, Ridge promised.

"She's glad you found a friend," Lorella continued. "A brother. She just wanted you to know that she didn't want to leave."

"I figured," Rett said, staring off, blinking. "Thought it must have been something like that."

From what little Rett said about his time before the orphanage, Ridge gathered life had been hard and hungry. Whoever had sheltered Rett as an infant had put him out to fend for himself practically as soon as he could hold a cup. If Rett remembered anyone fondly from those years—or much at all about that time—he had never said so to Ridge, not even in the throes of fever or drunk off his ass.

"You've proved your point." Ridge's voice sounded like gravel, but he'd had enough emotional exposure. "Maybe your abilities aren't a sham."

Lorella gave a derisive snort in response. "Would you like me to call up some of the ghosts of the men you've murdered? I imagine they'd like to pass along a message or two."

"No thanks," Ridge replied. "And if it's on the king's orders, it's not murder. Just so you know." The look in her eyes made her opinion clear, but she said nothing.

"We can't stay here," Rett warned. "Whoever blew up her shop is still out there. And we've got a job to do."

Ridge swore under his breath. He turned back to Lorella. "The duke's brother—how does he contact you?"

She sighed as if debating whether to continue her resistance and then gave in. "He would send a messenger to tell me to expect him, and then come by at the end of the day. He'd pass along what I was supposed to tell the duke, and then I'd send a messenger up to the manor, saying the children had spoken to me."

"What do you know about a man people call the Witch Lord?" Rett asked.

Lorella's puzzlement seemed sincere. "A lord of witches? I know a few people with magic, perhaps a bit of ability beyond what the monks permit, but no one of real power. Is there such a person?"

Ridge made a rude noise in response, and Rett glared at him in reproof.

"Not exactly. He's someone who curries favor with powerful people and may not be completely loyal to King Kristoph," Ridge replied, choosing his words carefully.

Lorella shook her head. "I don't know anyone like that. The duke's brother, he says that the duke is stubborn and won't listen to him. That's why he has me say the children pass along wisdom from the Veil."

"If that's all it was, would he need to threaten you?" Rett asked quietly.

Lorella looked from one man to the other. "You think the brother might have something to do with this Witch Lord?"

Ridge shrugged. "Perhaps. Or maybe it's just the brother who's rotten. The advice he's been giving to the duke is drawing the wrong kind of attention. We're here to sort things out."

Lorella paled. "You mean to kill the duke?"

"Actually, we're here to save his life," Rett replied. "If he's being led into treason, then he's a victim. We came to stop the ones taking advantage of his trust."

Lorella's pallor increased as the meaning of Rett's words sank in. "Look, none of this was my idea," she said. "I don't know why the brother doesn't just talk to the duke. But I'm in the middle, and if I stop doing what he tells me, he'll throw me to the guards."

"Help us, and we'll make sure you get safe passage," Ridge bargained.

"What kind of help would that be?" Lorella challenged, feisty despite being the captive of two assassins.

Ridge decided that he liked her spirit. "Help us spring a trap on the duke's brother, and reveal his betrayal to the duke. We'll know whether the duke is loyal or not," he said.

Lorella's eyes narrowed. "You both have magic. More than a lick of it, more than is legal."

"Right now, you need us," Ridge said, his voice low and dangerous. "As I said, we have a warrant for you, and it's up to us whether we exercise it. So I'd be careful about idle speculation."

Lorella held up her bound hands in appeasement. "Hear me out. Can you tell if someone is a witch?"

"Not exactly," Rett replied with care. "You think the duke's brother has magic of his own?"

She shrugged. "No, I don't think so. He wouldn't need me then, would he? He'd just magic the duke into doing whatever he wanted. But if he had a spell on him, if someone compelled him, would you know?"

"We might," Ridge hedged. "There are ways. Is that what you believe?"

Lorella shrugged. "Maybe. Not like I knew the duke's brother before this to compare. But he seems...driven. These messages, they don't seem that important to me, but he's relentless, pushes me to pass them along right away."

"We believe the Witch Lord compels his followers to do his will," Ridge answered. "Getting close to the duke's brother would help us learn more."

"When this is over, what happens to me?" Lorella demanded, raising her chin defiantly. "You make an enemy of the duke's brother—and maybe the duke, if he doesn't trust me anymore—and what becomes of me? I didn't go looking to cause a problem. I had no choice in the matter."

Ridge and Rett exchanged a glance. Ridge knew Rett was thinking the same thing—Lady Sally Anne. "We have a well-placed friend who can assure your safety," he replied. "Make sure no one can harm you, keep you comfortable until this is all sorted out."

"You mean, a prisoner?"

"More like a guest," Rett said. "Enough power to keep anyone from bothering you. We'll make sure you're safe if you help us." It went unsaid that if she didn't, a well-placed caution to the duke could lead to unpleasant complications.

"All right," Lorella said. "I'll help. Don't have a lot of choice, but then again I didn't like the duke's brother putting words in the mouths of the dead. I might shade the truth now and again to save the feelings of the living—angry customers don't pay—but I never used the spirits to lie for my own gain. There's something wrong in that. Disrespectful."

"We'll go to the inn tonight. You'll be safe, I swear to you," Ridge said as she gave them a skeptical look. "Tomorrow, we set you up in the inn's back room doing readings for customers. We'll be your new bodyguards after what happened at your shop. That probably caught the attention of the duke's brother, so he'll want to make sure you can still send his messages. And if the bastard who blew up your shop comes around for another try, we'll set him straight."

Lorella returned a sly smile. "Sounds good." She held up her wrists. "Now can you get me out of these damned ropes?"

Chapter Eight

"It took me a while to find you." The florid-faced man glared at Lorella as if it were her fault someone blew up her shop and apartment.

"I was lucky to escape," she replied. Duke Barton's brother, Fenton, wasn't the kind of man to waste time on pleasantries, especially not with an inferior.

"Did you accidentally blow up the middens?" he retorted.

She fixed him with a cold glare. "No. Someone tried to kill me."

Ridge stood behind Lorella and to her left, positioning himself in the shadows to remain inconspicuous. Rett took up a spot near the entrance, partly for protection and also to keep out any drunks who might open the wrong door. They had managed to obtain different clothing that suggested "ruffian" rather than "assassin." Hiding their identities on a job was not new.

"Hence the hired muscle?" he said, giving Ridge and Rett a dismissive glance. "Best make sure you stay in one piece, woman. I have a job for you."

Lorella regarded Fenton with thinly veiled dislike. It had only taken Rett seconds after the man entered the room to trigger his Sight and validate the Witch Lord's taint. A nod from Ridge told him that his partner had seen the same poison clinging to the man. What happened next depended on Lorella's skill as an actress to draw in the duke's traitorous brother and set him up for a fall.

"I've spoken with Lorn and Betta," Lorella said. "They have tidings to pass along to their father."

"Spare me the dramatics," Fenton snapped. "Save it for the saps that pay coin for your lies. Here's what I need you to have the children tell my brother. A merchant caravan will be passing through his lands very soon. They'll have crates for him, gifts from someone who means him well. He should accept the gifts, and store them in his barn, but not open them until the time is right."

Fenton made no effort to hide his contempt for the medium. "Dress that up in whatever pretty words you want, but make sure he buys it."

"It's an odd request to come from small children," Lorella replied, playing her part well.

"Make it work," Fenton snapped. "Emphasize the 'gift.' My brother's not the smartest of the litter. He didn't earn his title; he got it from being lucky enough to be the first brat my mother dropped."

"And how will he know when the time is right?"

"Your spirit guides will let you know, and you'll be sure to tell him." He leaned forward, looming over her with no subtlety to his intimidation. "Make him believe. Turn on the tears. I don't care what you do, as long as he accepts those damn crates and doesn't open them!"

Rett had no doubt as to the contents or the markings on the crates in question. Fenton might not control the title to his family's valuable lands, but he was clearly getting ready for something big. Something that would require smuggled weapons, and lots of them.

"Yes, m'lord." Lorella dropped her gaze, and her shoulders slumped. Not too much—it wouldn't do for Fenton to doubt her sincerity. Then again, given his bulk and bullish manner, Fenton no doubt expected others to be cowed in his presence and enjoyed making it happen.

"Send a message 'round when it's done," Fenton growled. "Make sure you don't foul it up." With that, he swept from the room like a storm gust.

"Asshole," Ridge muttered. "Is the duke like that, too?"

Lorella shook her head. "The duke has been very gentlemanly. Very much the grieving father. His brother is…not as nice." She looked to her two self-appointed bodyguards. "What's so important about the crates?"

Ridge and Rett exchanged a glance, then came to a silent agreement. "Weapons," Rett replied. "Smuggled, illegal weapons. Which is one of the reasons we think the Witch Lord is up to no good."

Lorella caught her breath. "But the duke doesn't know—"

"And it's likely that's why his brother needs you to manipulate his lordship," Rett pointed out.

Lorella's cheeks colored. "I don't like what he's made me do," she said. "I've been an honest medium and suffered for it. There's plenty more money in lies than in telling the truth. People will pay for pretty lies. When ghosts say something my clients don't want to hear, those clients call me names and leave without paying."

"I believe you," Rett said. "But we're going to have to work together to stop Fenton. We might save the duke's life in the process."

Ridge stayed with Lorella while Rett went down to the common room to bring up supper and ale. He scanned the crowd, alert for the disgruntled client the medium thought might have set fire to her shop. The pub was crowded, loud with voices and drunken song, and seeing through the crush of bodies posed a difficulty. He leaned against the bar, waiting for their food, and caught a glimpse of a man fitting Lorella's description.

The stranger was tall and thin, with long, lank blond hair and a hawk nose. He wore a miserable expression, and the glint in his eyes suggested he intended to share the misery. Rett slipped through the press of tavern-goers, but when he looked again, the man had vanished.

Rett eased out the door, taking a quick look around, but the stranger was nowhere to be seen. Worried and annoyed, he returned just as the server had begun complaining to the barkeep about him skipping out on his order without pay.

"I've got the coin right here," Rett said, holding up the money. "Had to take a piss. Wasn't gone but a minute."

A good tip mollified both the serving girl and the barkeep, and a few coins added to it promised they would keep an eye out for the hawk-nosed man.

"He was downstairs," Rett announced as he returned to their room with the food and ale.

Ridge looked up. "Who?"

"The man Lorella described. The one she thought might have set the fire."

"Tarle Hennessy," Lorella added. "But being here might not have anything to do with us. He drinks anywhere that'll take his money until he's out of coin. Although this inn is a bit above the rat holes he usually frequents."

"If he is the one who tried to kill you, do you think he'd repeat that with the inn?" Ridge asked, moving to look out the windows into the street below.

"Doubt it. He might risk burning me out, but there are too many people about, and the town would string him up if he burned the inn. 'Sides, some of the mayor's guards like to do their drinking here after their shift. Wouldn't be healthy to interrupt their fun."

"Once you expose Fenton to the duke, you won't be able to come back here," Rett said quietly, setting the food on the small table for them to share.

Lorella shrugged as if it didn't matter, but she avoided meeting his gaze. "The shop's gone, and so is everything I owned in my room upstairs. I don't need much to use my gift—just a table and chairs, perhaps some candles to set the mood. But I don't much fancy having to start over. Damn Hennessy and damn Fenton!"

Rett went downstairs an hour later and once again checked both the common room and the area around the inn, but saw no sign of the hawk-nosed man. Perhaps Lorella had been right, and he had landed in the same inn that night by coincidence. Yet experience told Rett that coincidence was far less likely than intent.

"Still nothing," he reported, noting that Ridge also checked the windows, being careful not to frame himself in the lantern's light.

"I agree with Lorella. He's not going to burn down the inn," Ridge replied. "And after tomorrow, it might not matter, since she'll be gone. We'll just keep our eyes open, and stay focused on the bigger issue."

Rett agreed and finished off the last of his ale, but he drifted into an uneasy sleep, and when Ridge woke him for his turn at watch, Rett found himself staring at the shadows beyond the windows, wondering if someone was staring back.

While Rett remained to guard Lorella, Ridge slipped down to the docks early the next morning, returning with a wooden crate and a bag of supplies. By the time Lorella sent a messenger up the hill to Broadmoor Manor, the crate bore a carefully forged sigil just like those Rett and Ridge had intercepted in the caravan. Rocks in the bottom beneath layers of rags gave the box enough heft, and they covered the top layer with some of their extra weapons, then nailed the lid shut.

Duke Barton must have been eagerly awaiting more news from his dead children because Lorella's note yielded an urgent summons to come at once, and a carriage to bring her to the manor.

"Make sure this arrives at Broadmoor Manor in two hours," Rett instructed the man they'd hired from the stable. "Bring the wagon to the front, and ask for the duke, no one else. And this is important. No one must know that you've ever seen me before."

"Understood, m'lord," the hired main replied. The marked crate sat beneath a tarp in the back of the wagon. Ridge and Rett still wore the ruffian/bodyguard outfits from the day before, but their weapons, warrant, and letters of marque identifying them as King's Shadows were hidden.

The crate could be a brilliant stroke—or a dangerous ruse. Rett hoped they could break Fenton's hold over Lorella and alert Duke

Barton to his peril. If all went well, they'd bag a traitor. If it went badly, the day would end awash in blood.

They rode to Broadmoor Manor in silence. Lorella kept her composure, but Rett noticed how she picked at the threads on the hem of her sleeve. He knew Ridge's tells as well, and the way his partner held himself still, with an exaggerated casual slouch told Rett that the other assassin was on edge.

The duke himself met the carriage when they arrived at the manor. He smiled as Lorella alighted, then stepped back warily as Ridge and Rett followed. "Who are they?" he demanded, and Rett could see the resemblance between the duke and his brother.

"My bodyguards," Lorella replied as if the question were trivial. "Someone tried to kill me a few days ago."

Barton gasped, and his manner thawed. "How awful. Were you hurt? I can have my physician tend you."

Lorella gave him a sincere smile, and Rett guessed she had grown genuinely fond of the man. "Thank you, but I was lucky enough to escape without injury," she replied, omitting the role Ridge and Rett had played in accomplishing that feat.

"Please come in," Barton said, focusing solicitously on Lorella and offering her his arm. He paid no further attention to Ridge and Rett, as befitted servants. His steward, however, gave them each a measuring stare of disapproval and followed them in as if to ensure they did not steal the silver.

Barton ushered Lorella into a comfortable parlor. She took a seat on a couch with her back to the wall. Ridge stood to her left, while Rett found a place near the door where he could also watch out the window.

"What have you heard from the children?" Duke Barton asked, almost breathless with excitement. Rett felt a stab of pity at how openly the man wore his grief, how desperate he was for their touch from beyond. Despite his title and wealth, heartbreak had made him an easy mark.

Lorella settled her skirts around her. Rett watched her carefully. Their success depended on the medium's skill as an actress. "The children send their love. They miss you."

"I miss them, too. Very much," Barton replied, his voice tight. "Have they any news?"

Lorella's gaze focused on the middle distance, and while her eyes were open, she did not seem to notice anything in the room. "Lorn was sad that the horse died," she replied. "Betta liked the new kittens in the barn. She wanted to ask if the burn on your arm had healed."

Barton's eyebrows rose, and his right hand went to touch a spot on his left arm beneath his sleeve. "Hot embers from the fire singed my arm," he replied, his voice full of wonder. "Just last night. It hurt, but it's really nothing. Please, tell her that."

A movement outside the window drew Rett's attention, but when he looked more closely, he saw no one. The instinct to investigate warred with the need to be present as Lorella confronted the duke. *Probably just the gardener,* he told himself and returned his attention to the medium.

Lorella nodded and fell silent for a moment. Then she raised her head. "The children are worried. They fear for your safety."

Barton drew back. "My safety? Why?"

Lorella tilted her head as if listening, and perhaps she was, Rett thought. "Someone close to you has fallen in with bad company," she said, hesitating as if she were straining to hear the words before she imparted them. "The children fear you will come to harm."

Barton forced a chuckle to dismiss the warning. "Surely not. I've been busy with the affairs of the manor, not running with cads and rakes."

Lorella frowned. "They see danger and…betrayal…my lord," she reported. "A package will come. It has a strange marking. You must open it, even if others try to stop you. Your life depends on it."

Rett saw the wagon and his hired driver pull up at the front. Minutes later raised voices in the entranceway broke the quiet. The driver put on a good show, arguing loudly that the duke and only the duke must be the one to receive the crate, while Barton's steward pushed back stridently that his lordship was busy and could not be disturbed.

"Bother this," Barton muttered, with an apologetic look at Lorella.

He strode from the room, as Rett and Ridge fell in behind him, hanging back enough so that he would not focus on their presence.

"Blast it—what's the matter?" he challenged.

"This fellow claims he has a delivery for you—and it must come right to you," the steward replied, attempting to maintain his unflappable mien. "We've ordered nothing quite so...personal."

"I was hired to bring the crate here and give it to Duke Barton. No one else," the hired man retorted, and Rett fought a smile at his performance.

"Who hired you?" the steward shot back.

"Some bloke at the docks, but I'm not about to risk losing my pay," the driver said. "Just take the blasted box. It's heavy."

Barton gasped as the man shifted and he saw sigil markings. "Bring it in," he urged, eyes wide. Into my study." He turned to his steward. "Fetch a pry bar."

Another carriage pulled into the entrance road behind the wagon, and Fenton elbowed his way past the wagon driver, who left the box as ordered and hurriedly departed. Rett and Ridge drew back, close enough to hear what was said without drawing attention to themselves.

"What's going on?" Fenton demanded.

"Oh good, you're here," Barton replied, ignoring his brother's sputtered questions. "Just got an odd delivery, and I mean to get to the bottom of it." He turned and headed back to the parlor, leaving Fenton to catch up.

Fenton's eyes widened in alarm, and he hurried after his brother. He came to an abrupt halt as he saw Lorella seated in the chair by the hearth, the marked crate in the center of the room, and when he turned, Ridge and Rett standing sentry at the door.

The steward shouldered between them, an iron crowbar in his hands. "Shall I open it for you, my lord?"

"No!" Fenton's unexpected outburst made Barton turn in surprise. Fenton glared at Lorella, as if prompting her to speak up with the lie he'd given her, but Lorella just gave him a vacant smile. "I mean, if you don't know where it came from, it could be dangerous."

Barton nodded. "Yes, that's what the children warned me about. Danger. That I have to open it."

Fenton stepped between his brother and the crate. "I don't think that's a good idea. Let me handle it for you. Out in the barn, just in case—"

Barton's eyes narrowed. "Step aside, Fenton. The children gave me a warning. I intend to heed it."

Barton took the crowbar from his steward and dug the lip under the lid of the crate. Fenton stepped back, easing himself toward the door. Rett and Ridge closed ranks, blocking the exit with their bodies.

The crate lid gave way with the squeal of nails and cracking wood. Barton stood staring at the array of weapons, and then the odd sigil emblazoned on the crate lid. "What's the meaning of this?"

"I'll see if I can track down that wagon driver," Fenton volunteered.

"I have a message for you," Lorella said, her voice ringing out across the room and freezing Fenton in his tracks. "The ghost of a man with one ear wants to know where you buried his body."

Fenton glared at the medium. "She's crazy. I don't know what she's talking about."

"He brought you crates like this one from a ship, said you'd promised to pay him. But you fought with him. He put a knife scar like lightning on your right shoulder, and you hit him with a rock and killed him."

"I didn't kill anyone. I've never seen a crate like that before." Fenton's tone held privilege and fury, but his skin paled, and a sheen of sweat rose on his forehead.

"It's the crate you told Lorella to say the children wanted Duke Barton to accept, the one you threatened her to lie about." Ridge stepped forward, angry and accusing.

"I don't answer to ruffians," Fenton snapped.

"We're not ruffians." Rett held up his letter of marque. "King's Shadows."

Both Fenton and the duke blanched. "Have you got a warrant?" the duke asked, his voice dry and tight.

"For the man involved in smuggling illegal weapons, a traitor to the crown," Ridge replied. "And all the evidence says that's you, Fenton."

Duke Barton turned toward his brother, his eyes narrowed and appraising. Rett thought that it might be difficult to convince the duke to think the worst of his brother, but apparently, bad blood ran deep. "What have you done?" The duke's voice, low and deep, rumbled with threat and expectations.

"What you're too weak to do," Fenton snapped. "You putter on your precious lands, playing gentleman farmer, ignoring everything else in the kingdom. Open your eyes. Kristoph is a weakling. The other nobles know this, and the smartest ones are making other plans. I wasn't going to let us get left behind because you're bound to an outdated code."

"I took my vows as a liegeman seriously, you horse's ass," Barton growled. "This is just like you. Looking for the easy way out, cutting corners, figuring you'll come out clean because no one will make the charges stick. There are bloody assassins here to kill us. Because of you!"

Barton, Rett, and Ridge closed on Fenton. Fenton wheeled and grabbed the steward, wrapping one arm around the man's chest in a strong grip and producing a small knife from the folds of his cloak and pressing it to the steward's neck.

"I'm leaving," he said, eyes fixed on Barton as if daring his brother to stop him. "Let me go, and I won't skewer your pet."

Ridge met Rett's gaze, and they weighed the chance of being able to wrest the steward from Fenton's grip before the knife slit his throat. They might catch Fenton, but the steward would surely die.

"I will help them hunt you for this," Barton said, his voice hard and cold. "And if you hurt him, I will pay them extra to kill you slowly."

"Have to catch me first. Brother." Fenton moved backward toward the door, dragging the steward with him.

Ridge stayed where Fenton could see him, as Rett slid into the shadows, looking for a way to circle around. As soon as Fenton headed down the hallway with his hostage and was out of sight, Rett bolted down the corridor in the other direction.

Rett burst from the door at the far end of the hallway just in time to see Fenton haul the hapless steward toward the carriage closest to the entrance, the one which had brought Lorella and the assassins from the city.

Fenton kept his grip on the steward as he freed the reins from the hitching post, and he did not let go until he reached the carriage. He threw the steward toward the door to the manor, blocking Ridge's chance to throw a knife, and bounded into the driver's seat.

In the instant before he snapped the reins to send the horses galloping, something small and fiery streaked through the air from the opposite side of the carriage. It broke the window, and then an explosion ripped the carriage apart, sending Fenton flying from his perch. The terrified horses bolted, still dragging the reins and the shafts from the carriage.

Ridge took off like an arrow after a figure on the other side. Rett ran for Fenton, who lay soot-streaked and bloody amid the smoking, broken remains of the carriage. For a moment, Rett thought the man might be dead. His torn clothing provided testimony to the force of the blast. Splinters from the explosion stuck in his skin like quills. The awkward angle of one arm suggested a bad break, and Rett was surprised Fenton hadn't broken his neck as well. Then Fenton groaned, and Rett sighed in resignation, realizing that an easy finish to the mess was not going to happen.

He placed the tip of his sword against the man's throat. "Fenton Barton, you are under arrest by warrant of King Kristoph, under a charge of high treason. Come with me. Answer our questions, and we'll make your death fast and painless—which is more than you deserve."

A muffled explosion in the distance startled Rett, and he looked worriedly in the direction Ridge had chased their mystery attacker. Then he returned his attention to his prisoner, as more of the manor's servants came running to see what had happened. Two of the stable hands helped the steward to his feet, and the older man leaned heavily on them as they made their way back into the house. Duke Barton and Lorella peered out of the large window, taking in the destruction.

Rett called to two of the manservants and tossed them a length of rope from inside his jacket. "Tie his hands, and then haul him back into the parlor. He's got questions to answer."

Fenton's head lolled, and his eyes had an unfocused glaze. Rett wondered how productive questioning him would be, and whether the blast had permanently jarred his senses beyond repair. Still, gleaning anything useful about the Witch Lord would be worthwhile, and if Fenton's injuries did not kill him, then the warrant in Ridge's pocket sealed his death. Best to get the information while they could.

Rett let out a breath he had not realized he was holding as he saw Ridge lope up from the lower lawns, still very much in one piece. As he grew closer, he saw blood on Ridge's coat.

"Damned Hennessy," Ridge muttered as he joined Rett behind the slow procession back into the house. "He must have followed us and thought he'd get another chance at Lorella. Lucky for us, Fenton decided to steal the carriage."

"Is he—?"

Ridge nodded. "Yeah. Tried to throw a second bomb and the damn thing bounced off a branch and came back at him when it blew up. Tore a hole in him no healer could fix, so I put him out of his misery," he said, curling his lip in disgust. "Some kind of divine justice in that, I guess."

The servants deposited Fenton in a chair to face the aftermath. Duke Barton looked up, surprised, as Ridge and Rett followed him into the room.

"He's still alive? I would have thought you'd served his warrant."

"We have some…leeway," Ridge said. "Depending on his cooperation. If he gives up information, we can make it a quick end. Otherwise, there's the public disgrace of a hanging, which I think we'd all like to avoid."

Blood flecked Fenton's lips, but he mustered defiance. "Maybe I'll die and cheat you out of both."

"Who else is part of the smuggling?" Rett pressed. "You've got nothing to lose."

"Just because I'm dying doesn't mean I've changed my mind," Fenton murmured. His labored breathing wheezed, and he had grown pale, suggesting that the blast damaged something inside.

"Why drag your brother into this?" Ridge questioned. "Why try to trick him into storing the weapons?"

A nasty smile twisted Fenton's lips. "Because brother-dear was the last person anyone would suspect. Duke Barton, hopelessly loyal to the crown. Keeps his nose clean. Hates the Witch Lord. And he's at the most important crossroads in the kingdom. A plum ripe for the taking."

"You are no brother of mine," Barton disavowed. "I'd tie your noose with my own hands."

"What of the Witch Lord?" Ridge pressed. "Tell us what you know."

"Go fuck yourself," Fenton rasped.

"Perhaps you should ask the ghosts."

They all turned to look at Lorella. "The closer Fenton grows to death, the more the ghosts gather around him. So many—did you kill them all?"

Fenton gave a harsh, ugly chuckle. "Revolutions have casualties."

"You fancy the Witch Lord leading a revolution?" Duke Barton echoed. "You're dim in the head. He's nothing but a sotting leech."

"I'm afraid he's more dangerous than that, my lord," Rett replied. "Especially since he appears to have won the loyalty of some of the nobility and is gathering weapons for an insurrection."

"The ghosts know," Lorella said, her voice distant as if she spoke in a trance. "Ivan from the docks. Gid who runs the ferry. Tor from the caravan...they accuse you, and they will tell all they know."

"We have weapons you can't dream of," Fenton gloated, then choked, gasping for breath. Blood dripped from the corner of his mouth. "We've already won, before the first shot."

"You're a fool," Duke Barton snapped. "You've always had the morals of a cutpurse. Look where it's got you." He looked from Ridge to Rett. "Anything I can do to set things right, to help you find his accomplices, I am at the disposal of the king."

Rett did not doubt Barton's sincerity, and at the same time, the man's desperation to distance himself from his treasonous brother was plain to see. He itched to get Fenton back to the city, where Burke could put the man in front of the king to validate the threat posed by the Witch Lord. Yet one look at Fenton assured Rett that the man was unlikely to live out the hour, let alone survive a carriage ride. Even if they managed to put him in front of King Kristoph, Fenton would not turn over his associates if he had no desire to make a deathbed confession to heal the rift with his own brother. And while Lorella's discourse with the ghosts might give them valuable information, the king would not rely on her testimony.

"Damn," Ridge muttered, rousing Rett from his thoughts. Rett looked up and saw that Fenton had slumped his chair, breathing labored, skin gray.

"Maybe a healer—"

Ridge shook his head. "Too late."

Rett glanced at Duke Barton. Before his expression shuttered completely, Rett caught glimpses of contradictory emotions: sorrow, anger, disappointment, fear. As if aware of the scrutiny, Barton turned and walked to the window.

"What now?" Duke Barton asked as he stared out at the chaos on his lawn.

"You acted honorably, and your loyalty to the king is not questioned," Ridge replied. "But I'd avoid accepting crates from strangers if I were you."

Barton gave a wan, bitter half-smile and let out a long breath. He turned to Lorella. "Was it all a lie? Something Fenton blackmailed you into doing?"

Lorella shook her head. "No. Lorn and Betta did speak to me, but they spoke as children who miss their parents. No wisdom from the Veil to impart," she said. "I'm truly sorry for misleading you. Fenton threatened me...I was afraid."

Barton snorted. "My brother was good at making people fear him.

Not as good at giving them a reason to like or follow him. I'm sorry he put you in that position." He paused. "I know I need to let the dead stay dead. But...is there anything the children have left to say, or need to hear from me before I let them go?"

Lorella gave him a sad smile, and her gaze went unfocused as she listened across the ether. "Only that they wish they could come home, and they miss you. They are happy to be together, and they'll wait for you and their mother. They love you both."

Barton swallowed hard. "I love them, too. So much. Tell them I'll see them again." Lorella stared blankly for a few seconds until she came back to herself. "Thank you," Barton said. He withdrew coins from his pouch. "This should settle things," he said, handing the money to Lorella. "Now, if you'll excuse me, I have to see to the mess Fenton left behind."

They saw themselves out since the steward was indisposed and the rest of the servants had scattered to clean up the aftermath. Ridge and Rett took back their weapons and loaded the crate into a carriage provided by Barton to take them back to the city. Lorella called to the spirits who had offered to testify against Fenton and relayed their information. While the ghosts confirmed what Ridge and Rett already knew about the sigils and the smuggling, they offered no new leads, other than to further damn Fenton with details of his treachery.

The rest of the ride back to the city passed quietly. When they reached the city, Rett turned to Lorella. "We can get you to that safe house we offered. No one will hurt you there."

Lorella patted his hand. "Thank you. I appreciate the offer. But Hennessy is dead, and Fenton isn't a threat anymore. I'd rather deal with some risk and be free, all things considered."

Rett nodded. "Can't blame you for that. But if you get into trouble, let the barkeep at the Jack and Knave know you're looking for us and where we can find you. We'll help if we can."

"Thank you both," she said as she opened the carriage door and stepped out. "I suspect the spirits may have more to tell you. I believe we'll see each other again."

CHAPTER NINE

"I thought Burke would have been happier about how things worked out," Ridge grumbled. He set his empty glass aside and motioned to the barkeep for another.

The crowd at the Rook's Nest had paid them scant attention when they entered. The roadhouse catered to spies, Shadows, and officers. In its own dissolute way, Rook's served as a waystation for battered souls, a conduit for information, and a neutral zone where men of questionable reputations and even more dubious intentions could negotiate the shady deals that kept Landria running.

"If he wanted 'discreet' we were definitely the wrong ones to put on the job," Rett agreed, sipping his drink. "I imagine that all the explosions were a bit much for him."

"This time, they weren't our fault." Ridge slid his money toward the barkeep for the pour that refilled his drink. "And besides, Burke said we had 'leeway.'"

"I don't think 'leeway' included having two men blow up in front of the duke's house."

"The explosions were Hennessy's fault," Ridge protested. "And it saved us from having to make the kills, or drag their asses back to be hanged."

Rett gave a long-suffering sigh, knowing the uselessness of arguing with Ridge in this sort of mood. "You think Lorella will be safe?"

Ridge grimaced. "I'd have liked it better if she'd gone to Lady Sally Anne, but I guess I can't blame her for not wanting to be stuck inside the fortress if the people threatening her are gone."

"She might be able to help, with the…suspect," Rett replied, not wanting to say the Witch Lord's name where they might be overheard. "After all, the dead have tales to tell."

"Which might help lead us to more evidence, but her witness by itself won't convince the king, or his advisors," Ridge pointed out.

A tall, slender woman sauntered up to their table. Caralin wore a tunic and trews like a man, with her hair in a long, dark braid down her back. If anyone felt inclined to comment on her unconventional attire, the bristle of weapons strapped in plain sight served to dampen conversation. "I hear you almost blew up a duke," she said. "Sorry I didn't get to see the show."

Rett scooted over to give her room to join them. He knew Caralin always seemed to find them amusing, and she'd been a reliable source of information and good backup.

"Shouldn't believe the gossip," Rett countered. "In this case, the truth is far more boring," he added with a grin.

"So Burke didn't send you to muck out the stables?"

Ridge shook his head. "No. Not yet, anyhow."

Caralin leaned forward. "I wanted to warn you. There's been some talk about the two of you—that your results are too good to be just luck and skill. That maybe you've got some kind of extra help. Extra power."

Ridge's eyes narrowed. "What kind of 'power'?"

"Magic. That you've made some kind of deal to gain it yourselves or maybe have a pet witch on your side." Caralin shrugged. "I personally don't believe a word of it. But, people talk. And there are plenty of folks who get jealous when someone shows them up. Sooner or later, if people keep talking, someone important might listen."

Ridge got his temper under control and kept his voice neutral. "Thanks, Caralin. Buy you a drink?"

She shook her head. "Not tonight. Some other time. I've got work to do. Just, keep your ears open. Life would be boring without the two of you." With that, she stood and sauntered away.

Ridge cursed under his breath. "That kind of shit is not what we need right now."

Rett shrugged, trying not to rile Ridge further. "There's always gossip. Outlandish things. She's right. Just someone who lost a pissing contest and wants to take us down a peg."

Rett knew his forced nonchalance did not fool Ridge. Ridge would worry like he always did, that someone would find out about the illicit magic they shared, even though neither of them shied away from using it when circumstances demanded.

Despite Caralin's ominous warning, the next few hours passed without incident. Rett watched as Ridge shoved down his anger and summoned his charm, drawing a crowd of their colleagues to trade stories and bawdy jokes. Rett hung back, listening and observing. The ale flowed, and they spotted a round or two. And if among the jokes and gossip Ridge and Rett tossed out questions about the recent turns of fortune for certain nobles, no one seemed to think anything of it.

Eventually, the crowd thinned. No one in their line of work could risk getting pissing drunk, given the enemies they'd made. A few who courted death a bit too ardently pushed the limits, but Ridge had barely sipped at his ale for the last hour, and Rett was still on his first tankard. Ridge was watching him closely, and Rett suspected that he looked peaked, his brows a bit too furrowed, and the squint in his eyes more from pain than the haze of pipe smoke that filled the tavern.

By this time, their audience had dwindled, and those who remained drifted back to the bar for a fresh draught. Ridge bumped Rett's elbow. "You all right?"

Rett closed his eyes and fought being sick. "No. Not really." He shifted, out of the shadows and into the glow of the lanterns. "Headache coming on." Then he groaned and pitched forward, gripping his temples.

"Shit," Ridge muttered. He glanced around. No one seemed to take note since it wouldn't be the first time someone's intake had caught up with them badly. But after Caralin's warning, both men felt exposed and vulnerable.

"Come on. Let's get you out of here."

Rett panted with the pain. "Can't." He dropped his voice to a whisper. "Vision. The children—"

"Looks like he's had a bit more than he can handle," one of the men at the bar observed. Rett could tell that Ridge barely contained the urge to tell the stranger to fuck off, settling for a glare that conveyed enough malice that the man shut up and turned back to his drink.

"You've got shitty timing," Ridge murmured.

"Didn't pick it," Rett replied, his voice tight.

"Do I need to send a runner to Henri, have him bring a carriage around?"

"No," Rett managed. "Just give me a bit."

"Told you the ale on an empty stomach would catch up to you," Ridge said loudly, for the benefit of those left in the bar. "Should have known your limits."

Rett muttered an obscenity, but whether it was directed toward the headache or Ridge's theatrics remained unclear.

Ridge leaned back, slowly finishing his ale, his sprawl in the seat deceptive as he kept an eye on the rest of the tavern's clientele. The barkeep eyed Rett with weary judgment as if surprised a seasoned assassin would get blind drunk anywhere outside his private chambers with a locked door. Rett didn't expect trouble from the man since the tavern was a safe haven, and Burke would personally mete out consequences if the tavern master did not enforce a peace bond on all who entered.

The two men at the back table were more of a worry. Dell and Slocum were Shadows and had been assassins even longer than Ridge and Rett. They'd made a name for themselves for bloody-mindedness, seeing themselves as grim executioners without regard for what Burke so often called "leeway." Rett suspected that the pair enjoyed the kill, something that even after all these years he did not share. And from the furtive glances in Rett's direction and the men's quiet conversation, it was clear Rett's headache had attracted the wrong kind of speculation.

"We need to get out of here," Ridge said, schooling his expression to make the comment seem casual. "Can you move?"

"I've been worse," Rett said, biting back a groan as he straightened. He blinked as the lantern light hurt his eyes, and his shirt darkened with sweat although the room felt cool. Rett pushed to his feet and stumbled. Ridge steadied him, making sure to grip Rett's left side, leaving Ridge clear to draw his sword if need be.

"Thought he'd have learned to hold his liquor by now," Dell called from across the room, as Slocum snickered.

Ridge ignored them, focused on getting out the door and helping Rett get his balance so they could make a quick exit.

The sound of chairs scraping across the floor warned of trouble. "You too good to answer, Breckinridge? 'Cause your boy doesn't look like he'll make it to the door without heaving up his guts."

"He's not 'my boy,' and he'd as like to rip out your guts as heave his," Ridge growled. "Bugger off. We're not looking for trouble."

"Found it though, didn't you?" Slocum said as the pair moved closer. "Lots of talk going around 'bout the both of you. Wouldn't be surprised to find out most of it's true. Always thought there was something off about you. Did you sell your souls, or give it away?"

Ridge leaned Rett against the wall and drew his sword. A glance at the bar told him the tavern master had vanished, by choice or bad luck.

"I've got no desire to break the truce in here, but that all depends on you. Back away, and leave us be."

"Surely Burke's pet assassins can handle a little skirmish," Dell taunted. "Make you a proper wager. Five silver we can whip your asses."

"Not interested. Stay out of our way, and I won't make you bleed."

"Tough words. Prove it." Slocum challenged.

In the next heartbeat, Rett stood beside him, shoulder to shoulder, sword in hand. "Go away." Rett might barely be able to keep his feet, but he wasn't about to give in, not if he could still hold a weapon.

The sound of a matchlock being cocked rang through the empty tavern. "Move along, all of you," the barkeep warned. "Take it outside, or better yet, shove off and don't come back for a while. We don't want trouble in here."

"We'll be leaving now," Rett said, and nothing in his manner belied his pain. "If it's a fight you want, we'll oblige you, but you won't walk away. Guaranteed."

Slocum's disdain showed clearly in his expression. "We'll have plenty of other chances to prove the point," he said. "Better if you don't see it coming." He and Dell shouldered past and Ridge watched them until they were out of sight, marking their path and figuring a different route home.

"You bloody bastards know how to clear a room," the barkeep said. "Thought I'd have to shoot the sons of bitches, and I didn't want to explain that to Burke." He looked at Rett, who still stood ready for a fight. "Go out the back. Best you don't come round for a bit, let them cool off."

"Don't worry," Ridge said as he stepped out first, checking for threats. "We've got better things to do."

Rett managed to climb the stairs and Henri met them at the door. Once it closed behind them, Rett sagged against the wall.

Henri slipped under his arm without a pause. "Right then. Come along. Get you laid out and I'll fetch tea." He shot a glance at Ridge, looking for injuries. "Brawl?"

"Almost. Ran into a couple of sons of bitches. Dell and Slocum."

"Vision," Rett confessed, easing down on the couch and offering a weak protest as Henri swiveled his legs so he could stretch out. Ridge moved to the window, scanning the street.

"If Dell and Slocum—or any of the others—wanted to come after us, we wouldn't see them. They're Shadows. They know how to hide," Rett pointed out. The altercation in the bar still rankled. Rett knew he should be used to it by now, but being misfits among the other assassins was a bitter pill.

Henri came back with two cups of tea, setting one where Rett could reach it. "I take it the evening went wrong?"

"Just a reminder that we're not well-loved," Ridge answered, closing the shutters with a muffled oath.

"Shall I ready the relocation plan?" Henri asked, bringing out a plate of date bread with butter, dried fruit, and honey.

Ridge sighed. "Probably not a bad idea. We've no doubt annoyed the Witch Lord, who might decide to rid himself of us. If things turn sour, I don't trust the Shadows to have our backs. At least, not some of them."

"Very well, m 'lord," Henri said. "I'll provision the havens." With that, he bustled back into the pantry.

Ridge pulled a chair up near where Rett lay, careful not to scrape across the floor. "Feeling better?"

"It was Sofen again," he replied, speaking quietly because the sound of his own voice hurt his ears. "Like a gong inside my skull. Once he had my attention, I saw images. More children, coming to Harrowmont."

"And now?" Ridge helped him sit up to sip the tea.

"Now it feels like someone's put a spike through my left eye. Sadly, that's an improvement." He sank back down and put an arm across his eyes to block even the dim light of the lanterns. "Damn Dell and Slocum. They saw me double over. There'll be more talk now."

"Couldn't give a flying rat's ass about talk," Ridge replied. "And it'll be *their* asses flying if they come around, sniffing for dirt. Hardly the first time a man's gotten sick in a bar."

Rett gave a bitter chuckle. "Might be believable if I'd puked out my guts, but if there's talk of magic afoot—"

"We'll deal with Dell and Slocum if we need to," Ridge said firmly. "Gods, we could have thrashed them even with you barely on your feet." He grinned. "Good show there, especially since I don't imagine you could see straight."

"Saw two of everything, so I planned to swing wide," Rett replied.

"Seriously, are you going to live? Or should I dig a trench in Potter's Field?" The concern in Ridge's voice softened the words.

"Just a vision," Rett sighed. "I'll live, though I'm not excited about the prospect right now."

"Well, at least we got a warning from Caralin, which says not all of the Shadows are against us. I hope."

"They aren't. Dell and Slocum aren't well liked because they're rat bastards."

"I've heard the same said about us."

"Well, at least about you."

"True enough." Ridge finished off his tea, looked longingly at the pantry as if Henri might magically reappear with the kettle, and then set down his empty cup. "And you picked up on the questions about the nobles?"

"Yeah. Seems like the ones with a streak of bad luck are the most loyal to the king, and the lords seeing a remarkable upswing in their fortunes are those enamored of the Witch Lord."

Ridge nodded. "Think it has something to do with the slave children?"

"How much would it help to know for sure, in advance, which ventures to invest in and which to pass by?" Rett speculated. "Quite an asset, to have someone who can see the future."

"Pity Burke wouldn't think the same of you."

"I opened my Sight while we were in the tavern," Rett confessed. "Before the vision struck. I was afraid maybe some of our people had been compromised. I didn't see anything though, not even a shadow like on Lorella."

"Good to know." Ridge had just started to move to get his tea when Henri reappeared and topped off both their cups and Rett wondered again if their valet/squire didn't have his own bit of foresight. "What about the vision?"

Rett let out a long breath. "Like the last time, the images are jumbled. I don't know if it's Sofen's untrained power or just the nature of the visions, but they're hard to untangle—especially with the way they hit me like a hammer between the eyes."

Ridge walked over to stand by the fire as if still trying to chase away the chill from their trek back from the tavern.

"The more I think about what I saw; I'm convinced Sofen was trying to tell me that they were gathering the other children," Rett said slowly, parsing out the meaning of what he had seen. "No one seemed to be chasing them. I think that somehow he and the others have learned to call to them, to find them before the Witch Lord can."

"So the caravan children are trying to find others like themselves—with magic?" Ridge asked.

"That's how it looked to me. And it makes sense," Rett replied. "Because if they could get the children to Harrowmont, then the slavers couldn't find them and cart them off to the Witch Lord's nobles."

"Why do you think he wanted to tell you badly enough to send a vision? It's got to take a lot out of him."

Rett shrugged. "Maybe he wanted us to know he's found a way to help. If they can keep the children from being taken, the Witch Lord loses out. They're doing their part for a war that hasn't started yet."

"Oh, it's started," Ridge countered. "It's just not the shooting kind of war. Not yet. And if we can get to the bottom of all this, maybe it never will be."

CHAPTER TEN

"I think we need to look at the opium," Henri said as he brought breakfast into the parlor.

Ridge and Rett stared at him. "The what?" Ridge echoed.

Henri placed a plate of sweet cakes, jam, and honey on the small table, and returned with a pot of tea and cups. "Opium," he repeated as if discussing the price of herring. "That man Destwiler was involved with opium as well as smuggling weapons. If the trail has gone cold on the weapons, let's trace the opium."

Ridge gave their squire a reassessing look. With his receding hairline and slightly nearsighted gaze, Henri looked more the part of a clerk than the squire to two infamous assassins. Yet time and again, he managed to stop Ridge flat-footed with his practical courage and a willingness to dive into the dodgiest situations.

"You're bloody brilliant," Rett said, accepting the cup of tea gratefully.

Henri's face flushed. "Just doing my part, m'lord," he replied. "But my mum always said, if you want to know what's really going on, look at who's paying and who's getting paid."

"Then my compliments to your mum," Rett replied with a tired grin.

"You doing any better?" Ridge asked.

Rett shrugged. "A little. Head still hurts, but not as much. I might be able to keep down some tea and a bit of cake. I hope Sofen doesn't make a habit of sending messages like that."

"I'm game to try it Henri's way," Ridge said. "We've figured out the Witch Lord's connection to the smuggled weapons, but without proof, we can't go to the king. So we've got no mandate to go after the lords who've accepted the weapons."

"And unless we can prove they either knew what was in the crates or are holding some of the seer-children hostage—we've got nothing," Rett replied.

"It's as good of a lead as we're going to get until we can find out which nobles are using the children," Ridge mused, in between sips of his tea. "If Sofen ever figures that out and wants to share, that might be worth the inconvenience."

Rett made a face. "I'll let *you* get the vision, in that case."

"So…opium. Destwiler was a dealer, but he had to get his opium from someone. We need to find out who was supplying him, and who's taken over his deals after he died," Ridge thought aloud.

"I've got a friend who's an apothecary," Henri volunteered. "He's the bloke who gives me the tincture I need to take care of you two when you get banged around. And if he doesn't know, I can smoke out some of the others. No one will think much of a manservant looking for some laudanum to ease his master's pain after a bad fall from a horse," he added, and his plain features took on a puppy-like beseeching that no doubt worked well to his advantage.

"Once again, I'm glad you're on our side," Rett said, chuckling. He looked to Ridge. "I say we work the dens and the docks. We've still got some informants down there, and it's been a while since we've had a situation take us to the smoking houses, so no one should be expecting us."

"I won't be surprised to find that Destwiler—and anyone who's taken over for him—was using the opium to pay for the weapons," Ridge said, swallowing a bite of the cake. "We might pick up the trail on the weapons from a different angle."

"Or find out whether the Witch Lord is using the opium for his 'magic,'" Rett suggested. "I imagine there are others like Fenton who take advantage of this situation to climb the ladder a bit higher, grab more power. But we won't know until we do some digging."

"If you have all you need for the moment, m'lords, I'll see to the horses, and then be on my way to roust that apothecary," Henri said.

Ridge nodded. "We'll be fine. But—be careful."

Henri grinned, and his blue eyes held a mischievous glint. "I'm always careful, m'lords." Then with the incline of his head, he went out the door, nabbing his jacket from the peg on the wall on his way.

"I worry about him," Rett said with a sigh. "He's going to get himself killed."

Ridge snorted. "Henri? He's got the survival instincts of an alley cat, and he can fight like a wharf cur. Not that anyone would suspect it, to look at him." He shook his head. "Nobody minds talking to him because he looks so bloody harmless. That's why he always knows all the street gossip. Everyone talks in front of him because they forget he's there."

"And he enjoys every bleeding minute," Rett added, grinning. "I think we've corrupted him."

Ridge's eyebrows rose. "Mate, I think you've got that wrong way around. Or have you forgotten how many horses he's stolen for us when the need struck? Not like he had to learn how or figure it out—he came with the knowledge when he landed on our doorstep. We're just lucky trailing after us amuses him, or we'd find our purse strings cut, and the saddles pawned."

Rett could hear the fondness that took the edge from Ridge's joking accusations. Henri's loyalty had been proven time and again, and in a dangerous business with shifting allegiances, the squire's courage and wit had saved them often.

"Docks first, or dens?" Rett asked.

"Docks," Ridge replied, polishing off the last of his cake as Rett finished the tea. "I want to know who's taken over for Destwiler, so we can start figuring out how to put him down, too, when the time is right. It's like pulling at a knotted ball of yarn. Pick at it long enough, and sooner or later the whole thing falls apart."

The air smelled of flowers, heavy as syrup, sweet and cloying, but the smoke tasted bitter on the back of Ridge's tongue. He glanced at Rett and saw the other man deep in thought. Ridge suspected Rett remembered the thick perfume of opium from his days on the streets when he told Ridge he would pass the dark, crowded rooms and perhaps be sent with a few coins to bring back food for the men who ran the dens. Those days were decades past, but Ridge was sure the scent made Rett remember the dens, and probably also the cramping hunger and the dull ache of the cold that went with those memories.

"Hey." Ridge nudged him with his elbow, intentionally pulling him back to the moment. "You with me?"

Rett nodded, swallowing hard. "Yeah. It's just—"

"I figured." Ridge knew his partner well enough that he didn't need Rett to put everything into words.

Opium taverns skirted the edge of legality in Landria. Its users were rarely violent if one didn't count the thievery done to pay for the next desperately needed smoke. So long as bodies didn't stack up in the streets, the guards ignored them, just as happy to take their bribes in the same potent powder. Since the monks used opium in their religious rituals, tavern owners sketched a few symbols and sigils on their walls and declared their properties to be temples. The tavern owners made a show of offering food and drink to their customers, in addition to cots and pipes. If the most broken men who lingered too often wasted away to nothing because the seductive smoke stole both appetite and energy, no one could fault the providers and their uneaten fare.

"We're looking for Canthis," Ridge said at the door.

Their clothing suggested enough prosperity that they might be suppliers, and their weapons assured they were no one's fools. They had already agreed that Ridge would do the talking, while Rett played bodyguard.

"Maybe he ain't looking for you," the doorman replied. Large, bald, and muscled like an ox, the man's heavy-lidded eyes suggested that sitting in a haze of opium smoke might have dulled his reflexes. But the flash of a blade to stop them from entering put the lie to that assumption.

"Got a shipment of good bricks," Ridge replied, referring to the sticky brown paste in the form most convenient for shipping. "Heard Canthis might be buying."

"How much?" Ox asked.

Ridge named a price, lower than what good opium usually sold for, but not so much of a bargain as to be suspicious.

"I'll give him the message."

Ridge shrugged. "Can't promise we'll still have any left, not at that price. He wants some, needs to get it now."

Ridge had heard that some of the nobility's wastrel sons acquired a weakness for opium, but those who found its oblivion sweetest came from the poorest sections of Caralocia. He suspected that the mother Rett didn't remember had been lost to opium and probably, inevitably, whoring before childbirth finally killed her. Maybe that was why Rett had always instinctively shied away from those dark dens and smoke-wreathed rooms, even in his most desperate days.

The rich could drown their disappointments in brandy, but the broken men and women at the bottom took refuge where they could find it cheaply. Ridge knew that more than a few of the men who looked like famine victims reclining with their pipes had been soldiers once, and what they had seen and done left them unable to live with their nightmares. Rumor had it that over the years, a Shadow or two had found their way to these smoky lairs as well. Ridge did not doubt that. Without each other to rely on, he and Rett might have felt the same pull, to forget, even for just a little while.

"I'll see if he's interested," Ox said, with an expression suggesting that moving annoyed him. He looked toward another man farther inside who lingered near the wall, and with a jerk of his head summoned him to take his place at the door. Ox lumbered off, into the smoke-shrouded darkness, and his replacement looked just as dead-eyed and expressionless.

Ridge stared into the shadowy room. Perhaps the places that catered to those with means might call themselves a parlor, but this sad chamber stank of unwashed bodies and desperation. Rett kept his hand near his weapon. Dens usually hired their own security, thugs to assure that no one would be relieved of their coin before entering, so that the lair's operator could do that once they took their bunks. Still, Ridge did not trust their safety to anyone, certainly not here.

Ox returned after a while, with a thin, stoop-shouldered old man. Canthis's wizened face and bony arms did not fit the outsized reputation for ruthlessness he had among Caralocia's ruffians. When he raised his head, his sharp blue eyes made it clear that neither age nor his chosen product had dulled his wits.

"You have an offer for me?" Canthis asked in a voice like the dry hiss of a snake.

Ridge repeated his terms and brought out a box from beneath his cloak with a small chunk of the dark paste. Canthis touched the tip of his finger to the paste and then to his tongue, silent for a moment as he determined its worth.

"This is very good," Canthis said, giving both Ridge and Rett an appraising glance. "How is it you come by such good paste?"

Ridge's enigmatic smile let Canthis draw his own conclusions. "Some people left the market. That made room for us."

"No one gets shit like this past Rai Gorat," Canthis said, skepticism clear in his voice. "Now that Horan Jarvis is dead, the bastards that killed him make sure Gorat controls everything. Everything—except you?"

That answered one question, Ridge thought. They now knew what became of Destwiler's supplier. Gorat had taken advantage of Destwiler's death to move against his broker, consolidating his power. If Gorat made himself the choke point for opium coming into Landria's biggest harbor, then it stood to reason he had a hand in supplying the Witch Lord's contraband.

"We have friends in high places," Ridge replied with a feral smile. "Gorat's not going to remain the only player."

Canthis snorted. "Many men have been against Gorat. Their blood is in the harbor. Not that a little competition might not make for better prices. But…Gorat won't go quietly. So I'll take your offer, and buy your brick. Come back next week, if you're still alive. I will be surprised to see you, but I will buy if your price is good." He nodded to Ox, who counted out sufficient coin for the rectangular package wrapped in cloth and twine.

"I wish you good luck," Canthis said. "I do not think my wish will come true, but you will need it."

Ox moved forward as Canthis vanished back into the haze of smoke. The big man did not need to say anything. He stood blocking the doorway, hands on hips, his face set in a glower that warned them to move along.

Once they had put several blocks between themselves and the den, Ridge took deep breaths to get the sickeningly sweet smell out of his nose, preferring even the tang of piss and rotting produce to the cloying opium smoke and gave his cloak a flap to air it out. "Well, that went about as well as it could," he remarked.

"Didn't make enough to pay back Henri's apothecary friend," Rett replied.

Ridge made a dismissive gesture. "With how much tincture and laudanum Henri buys to patch us back together, I figure that apothecary has made a fortune." He turned as if simply making conversation, surreptitiously scanned for anyone following them. Rett did the same, careful not to let his gaze linger or move his head too obviously should they be watched. Neither of them saw anyone tailing them, but Ridge could not shake the feeling that they were being watched.

"Canthis is a crafty old bastard, isn't he?" Ridge said. "I wonder what he does with the fortune he makes off those sorry sons of bitches?"

Ridge knew Rett could hear the edge in his voice and would understand it came from the same fear they both felt, that on another day, with the wrong circumstances, life's betrayals could break a man until he craved a dreaming death.

"Don't imagine he'll be happy when he finds out this was a one-time deal," Rett replied.

"Wouldn't be surprised if he didn't set Gorat on us himself," Ridge answered. "I kind of expect it. Might make this next part simpler if we don't have to ferret him out."

"You really want to go up against Gorat's ring, just the two of us?"

Ridge gave him the same cocky, fearless grin that he knew Rett remembered from their more infamous exploits at the orphanage. "That's what keeps life interesting."

"And common sense keeps it long," Rett said. "We don't need to see Gorat. A man named Torson is his lieutenant, and he'll do nicely. By all accounts, he's more brawn than brains. Gorat's likely to make trouble."

"There'll be trouble one way or the other," Ridge replied. "I don't need a vision to tell me that."

Caralocia's bustling seaport drove the fortunes of the palace city and the kingdom. Ridge glanced up at King Kristoph's palace in the distance, high on a hill overlooking the sea. From where he stood on the wharf amidst the bustle of dock workers unloading ships and the jumble of languages from across the sea, the palace seemed impossibly distant. And though Burke summoned Ridge and Rett to the palace regularly, looking up at it from here made that seem like something out of another life.

Gulls swooped and dove, brazenly attempting to steal food out of the hand of a sailor who had just purchased a meat pie from one of the vendors along the waterfront. The smell of pickled herring, roasted cabbage, spiced meat pasties, and candied nuts warred with the less pleasant odors of the seaweed, bilge water, and dead fish.

Ridge wondered if he or Rett might have ever been tempted to go to sea, had they not been sent to the army and from there, conscripted to the Shadows. He had no illusions about how hard life was aboard one of the ships, though their own lives were hardly free of danger or likely to be long. Ridge rather fancied dry ground beneath his feet, glad that he had never been faced with the choice between staying in Landria and sailing for distant ports.

"You think Torson will be here?" Rett asked in a low voice.

Ridge shrugged. "He's here most days, from what my informant said. And if the deal is good enough, I imagine he'll come if he isn't here already."

The warehouse loomed over a stretch of the wharf, its wide doors like an open maw. Men hurried to unload wagons from the ships and load others bound inland. Crates bearing the markings of Landria's many trading partners were stacked higher than even Ridge's head. The workers shouted to each other in the common trading language, albeit strongly accented from their port of origin. They cursed in their native tongues, at each other, at the horses, at the wind.

Ridge sniffed the air as they entered. He caught a hint of coffee from the southern realms, tea from more moderate climates, and the smoky-dark spices of dried meats from the northern lands, but not a hint of opium's floral scent. Then again, wrapped in enough silk, or perhaps sealed in wax, even such a pungent smell might be covered.

This time, having sent word ahead that hirelings of Lord Tremont had come to broker a supply for their master, they faced a much warmer reception than at Canthis's den. Torson and his bodyguard came to meet them with a forced friendliness barely covering their greed.

Ridge smiled. He had never cared for the highhanded and arrogant Lord Tremont, so the possibility of besmirching his reputation with rumors of a fondness for opium was hardly reason for pause.

"Good sirs," Torson said, and both his voice and manner suggested an eagerness to take their supposed lord's money. "I understand you come to do business for your master."

Ridge managed a somber expression, which Rett matched from long experience. "He's had difficulty sleeping these past few weeks," Ridge replied as if obtaining more opium than the apothecary would dispense were a matter of life or death.

"Of course, of course. So many responsibilities. Hardly a surprise it weighs on one's shoulders," Torson commiserated. "How can I help?"

Ridge did the talking while Rett stayed a step back, on guard. Ridge opened his Sight and felt bitter satisfaction to note not just a shadow, but the taint that confirmed Torson had sold himself to serve the Witch Lord. He came back to himself, catching the conversation in the middle.

"...a dose for an adult or a child?" Torson asked.

Ridge covered his lapse of attention well. "It's for the lord," he replied. "His wife is most concerned about his...condition."

"Ah," Torson said as if a code had been passed. "I see. Does she wish for him to sleep or just drowse?"

Ridge understood the intent behind the question, and out of the corner of his eye, he saw Rett flinch. Years of dangerous living meant both Shadows hid their thoughts and emotions well, but Ridge knew his partner's tells. He felt his own temper flare and tamped it down as he saw the subtle shifts that signaled Rett moving from astonishment to disgust to fury, hidden behind a cold mask.

"Drowsy, for now," Ridge replied without pausing. "So much easier that way."

"I understand," Torson said. "I have exactly what you need." He left his bodyguard and disappeared into the warehouse without inviting them to step inside.

Ridge felt exposed framed in the warehouse doorway, even with Rett backing him up. He shifted to put his back to the door, but the sense of danger only grew stronger. Rett rubbed his forehead as if he felt a headache coming on. Ridge's eyes narrowed as he caught the gesture, asking a silent question in his gaze and getting a shrug in response.

Rett suddenly moved forward. Ridge stepped toward him, worried but still maintaining their roles. Ridge knew that no matter what Rett's vision showed, they dared not be suspected of being anything but the messengers of a bothersome lord. Yet in every fiber, he knew they needed to move...now.

Torson strode toward them, carrying a small package. As he

reached the doorway, a shot rang out. Torson's head exploded. Rett was already in motion, diving to knock Ridge out of the opening and into the shadows. Rett rolled to get out of the marksman's sights, as the bodyguard cursed and took off running to find the sharpshooter.

The warehouse workers fled except for Torson's overseers. "What happened?" The speaker was stout with a thick neck and massive arms. He took in the spatter where the bullet had shattered Torson's head, and then looked to Ridge and Rett, who had regained their feet.

"Don't know," Ridge replied, his confusion sincere even if the note of panic in his voice was a performance for the benefit of the overseer. "One minute he was walking toward us and then—" He and Rett stepped closer to the body, and Ridge saw the package lying near Torson's outstretched hand.

"Gods, I think I'm going to be sick," Rett groaned, falling to his knees next to the body so that his coat covered the motion as he slipped the package beneath it.

"Get him out of here," the overseer growled. "Where's Torson's guard?"

"He went after the shooter," Ridge replied, pointing in the direction where the bullet most likely came, the rooftop of the building across the street.

Rett got to his feet, and both he and Ridge stepped back inside the doorway and out of sight, unwilling to stay exposed in the doorway now that the marksman had time to reload his matchlock.

Torson's bodyguard hurried up the street, face flushed and winded from his run. "I got to the roof," he huffed. "But whoever shot him was already gone."

Ridge dug out payment and pushed the coins into the bodyguard's hand with the urgency of a messenger unaccustomed to bloody death. "Take the money," he snapped, with a believable edge of panic in his voice. "We're getting out of here."

Ridge grabbed Rett's arm and nearly dragged him out the back of the warehouse, moving too quickly for the stunned overseer and guard to react.

They did not stop running until they were out of sight of the warehouse. Ridge dropped his grip on Rett's wrist, and both men drew long knives.

"Was that shot meant for Torson...or us?" Ridge's voice had an undercurrent of steel.

"Maybe both," Rett replied as they circled back around to approach the marksman's position from the other side, out of sight of the warehouse. "Torson had the Witch Lord's mark. I figured you saw that, too. But if the Witch Lord thinks we've figured him for a threat, then maybe he's going to make sure his people know it's dangerous to talk to us."

They scaled the old building easily, careful to keep out of sight of the warehouse. To their disgust, the marksman left no evidence behind to identify him.

"Something's burning," Rett said, pointing to the column of smoke rising in the distance.

Ridge squinted, raising a hand to shade his eyes. "That's in the direction of the opium house." He and Rett exchanged a look. "You don't think—"

Rett nodded. "I bet."

"Shit," Ridge sighed. "Going to be hard to get information out of people now."

They climbed down, dropping to the alley and glancing around to assure no one lurked to finish the job.

"Did you get the same impression from what Torson said that I did?" Rett asked. Returning to more crowded streets gave them a measure of protection, and while they sheathed their knives, neither man relaxed.

"That somebody's been using the opium to drug children...and other people?"

"Yeah. That's what I took from it, too," Rett agreed. "Now it might be a sudden outbreak of colic and teething. But I'm betting those children are the ones sold off from the caravan. The opium's being used to keep them under control," he added, anger clear in his voice.

"And it makes me wonder if the Witch Lord is drugging some of his so-called supporters as well," Ridge mused.

They took a roundabout route back to their rooms, watchful to assure that they were not being followed. The marksman who killed Torson and the arson at the opium lair made them extra wary.

That was an effective warning to anyone connected to the Witch Lord not to talk. And an equally effective threat to let Rett and him know they were being watched? Or to back off before the bullets aimed at them? Ridge wondered.

"You're too quiet," Ridge prompted as they hurried up the stairs to their rooms. "That's always a bad sign."

Rett shrugged. "The marksman worries me. If he got Torson, he could have taken either of us."

"But killing one of the King's Shadows isn't just a death sentence, it's almost as bad as killing the king himself," Ridge pointed out. "Hanged, drawn, quartered, burned, and gibbeted. Maybe the Witch Lord isn't quite ready to make that big of a move." He peeled off his coat and hung it on the peg. "After all, right now King Kristoph doesn't believe the threat. Kill us, and he might think someone meant business."

Rett hung his coat up and took a deep breath, as if he were enjoying the smell of rich curry, something Henri must have brought back for their dinner. "We wouldn't be the first Shadows to die on the job. All they have to do is make it look like an accident."

"You're usually the one reminding me not to worry," Ridge said. "Take your own advice. Let's eat before it goes cold; whatever Henri brought smells amazing."

Henri had just begun to ladle out a thick, orange stew into bowls of rice and looked up. "Glad to see you're back safely," he said. "Eat. Then I have some news that may be good."

Ridge and Rett sat and tucked in. Ridge's stomach grumbled, and he felt the night's chill down to his bones, but the hot meal and the spicy curry quickly warmed his blood.

When they pushed back from the table and their empty bowls, washing down the meal with tankards of ale, Rett looked up at their smug squire. "You look fit to burst. What did you find out?"

Henri grinned. "I discovered that a few of the noble houses are using a lot of laudanum, more than usual, and managed to get the names after we got to the bottom of a bottle of whiskey," he added with a smirk. "But...I also found out that Yefim Makary, the mystic, will be a guest at Lord Rondin's manor in three days, and the lord is gathering his closest friends to listen to the man speak." His smile grew wider. "And since Lord Rondin is in need of extra help for the party, I've taken the liberty of hiring myself out as temporary labor to afford us access. In other words—I can get us in, and I've got an idea of how to make it work."

CHAPTER ELEVEN

"This will never work." Ridge walked away from the table and paced. "It's too dangerous."

Henri and Rett remained seated. Three amulets lay on the table, and even with his limited magic, Ridge felt them like an itch in his bones.

"We can't get close," Rett said. "Regardless of whether the marksman was aiming at Torson or us, we were intended to get a message. The Witch Lord and some of his people might already suspect we're after them. And they know what we look like."

"If they've followed us, then they might recognize Henri as well," Ridge protested. These arguments were nothing new. They had been part of the fabric of his relationship with Rett since their days in the orphanage. Rett remained the careful pickpocket, while Ridge took big risks. Every job meant both men went all in, but Ridge seemed to enjoy tempting fate, while Rett eased his jitters with precise planning, even if in the end, their risk-taking pushed the bounds of sanity.

"I don't see another way," Rett argued. "Henri can get in, close enough to overhear what the Witch Lord is saying to his devoted followers. So far, we haven't been able to be on the inside, and I can't imagine that we'll get another chance."

"We have to be close enough to get him out if things go wrong," Ridge insisted.

"We'd have to be that close anyhow. The amulets can only project what Henri sees over a short distance," Rett replied.

Ridge knew his partner understood how he thought, how he had to work his head around a plan. It wouldn't be the first time Rett had worn him down, eliminating objections one by one. Ridge often wondered if Rett realized that in doing so, the plan took shape.

"What if the Witch Lord senses the magic in the amulets?" Ridge countered.

"We don't know what kind of magic the Witch Lord has," Henri pointed out. "It might be minimal, perhaps nothing at all. He seems to be a master of appearances."

Could that be possible? Ridge wondered. He had assumed that Makary had magic—strong magic—to earn him the name of "Witch Lord." *What if it's just him talking big about himself, spinning tales to make himself sound more intimidating?* He shook his head. "The children in the caravan—they had ability."

"And maybe the Witch Lord does, too," Rett agreed. "But it may be less than he leads his followers to believe. If he were all-knowing or all-powerful, he'd have squashed us by now. So he must have limitations, and I'm betting more of them than he'd want us to know."

"Maybe," Ridge allowed, as he processed Rett's argument. Henri would rarely argue directly, although his demeanor as an "obedient servant" was largely a pretense. Instead, Henri usually primed Rett or him—whichever was predisposed to be most amenable—with the points to argue the side he favored.

"And perhaps the Witch Lord will favor his audience with a demonstration of his magic, and we'll see what he can do," Rett added. "At the very least, we'll know more about who's following him—and who's sniffing at his heels. Then we can keep an eye on those nobles, both for signs of treason, and to find more of those slaved children."

Ridge had no counterpoint to that, and grimaced in frustration, huffing out a breath as the corners of Rett's lips twitched in triumph. "All right," he grated. "We'll do it. But how do we know these amulets will even work?"

Henri's expression grew serious. "I received them from a person I trust, one who keeps to the shadows because her power would attract the wrong kind of attention. We've done each other good turns, and she owed me a favor."

He picked up one of the amulets, just a clay disk with runes scratched into it hanging from a thin leather strap. "This one is for me," he said. "When I wear it, the people who wear the other two amulets will see what I see, for several hours at least. She couldn't say for how long—it varies by person and by the distance between the sender and the receiver."

"Do we have to do anything to activate the magic?" Ridge asked, skepticism clear in his voice. He came back to the table and peered at the runes. The etchings on the necklace Henri held were different from those on the other two clay disks. "No drop of blood? Incantation? Spit and sweat?"

Henri shook his head. "No. Just your body heat and your energy. I asked most specifically about any consequences or effects. She assured me there were none, and she has reasons to desire my future cooperation," he added. "Every reason to make certain I am satisfied and remain healthy."

"I don't want to know the details," Rett said, holding up a hand. "That's between you and your lady-friend."

"She is hardly a 'lady-friend,'" Henri protested, a flush creeping to his ears. "We are colleagues who sometimes can do one another favors."

"What do you need?" Rett asked. "An outfit to blend in with the servants? You'll take weapons, of course—just in case something goes wrong."

"Of course," Henri replied. "Although if I'm suitably invisible—as a good servant should be—they'll be none the wiser, and I'll walk out with a night's pay in my pocket."

"If anything goes wrong—anything you can't handle—we'll move," Ridge promised.

Henri grew serious. "I know you will," he said. "That's how I have the nerve to go in. But I'll do everything I can to avoid needing help. I'm afraid that if it reached that point, things would end...badly."

Ridge couldn't argue with that. The Witch Lord was likely to have his own guards, as would the visiting nobles. And if Makary did have magic, countering him could be difficult. Not to mention the consequences. Burke had given them leeway, but he could ignore their unauthorized forays only so far. An incident involving several well-placed nobles would inevitably bring the king's notice, and without proof of the Witch Lord's treachery, it would not go well.

"We'll have to make sure it doesn't come to that," Ridge replied, with a smile that made it clear he relished the challenge.

Lord Rondin's manor Bleakscarp sat high on a cliff overlooking the sea, its dark stone walls reminding Ridge of a dangerous old man, stooped with years but still deadly. The square, thick-walled central section had been built onto over generations, with more of an eye to defense than opulence. It belonged to an age before Landria knew the peace of a settled monarchy, when King Kristoph's ancestors battled renegade nobles for control and fought off would-be invaders, or forced the nobility to take sides in the many dynastic wars.

Even now, from a distance, Ridge saw the lingering damage of those old conflicts. Scars on the stone from the pounding of a battering ram, soot streaks from old fires, broken crenellations along the tower's ridge. Landria had been at peace with a stable line of succession for a hundred years, and the kingdom had prospered. Despite the benefits, Ridge guessed that a new generation of nobles itched for the so-called excitement of wilder days when the strong took what they pleased without the rule of law. Perhaps that explained the Witch Lord's appeal, the fantasy of a return to a rough-and-tumble past whose reality delivered far less than promised.

"Gonna be a real bitch to break into," Rett muttered as they reconnoitered the estate. Henri had reported for duty just after dawn, leaving

Ridge and Rett free to get a feel for the area before the evening's event.

"I'm hoping that's not going to be necessary," Ridge replied, though his thoughts echoed the same concern. "Henri's got a knack for espionage."

Rett's hand went to rest on his chest where the amulet hung beneath his shirt. "Can you feel anything yet?"

Ridge shook his head. "I think one of us should open up the Sight when it's time, while the other stands guard. I'm worried that if we're both overwhelmed by the link to Henri, we'll be vulnerable."

"I'll do it," Rett said, as Ridge had known he would. "Maybe it'll trigger with my extra magic."

"You don't have to if you'd rather I do it," Ridge offered, although he agreed with Rett's reasoning. Still, they usually shared tasks and risk, and he didn't like to push too hard on Rett's magic for fear of unforeseen consequences.

Rett gave him a look that said he might as well have heard Ridge thinking aloud. "Thanks, but I've got more experience being knocked for a loop by magic I'm not supposed to have," he added with a dry chuckle.

Henri's friend had warned him about the range for the amulets, so as Ridge and Rett scouted the estate in the pre-dawn dark, they looked for a place that hid them from the watchful eyes of the patrolling guards, but enabled them to keep a spyglass on the manor house and see through Henri's eyes inside. They found a stand of trees on the hillside with enough underbrush to afford a hiding place.

Ridge pulled his amulet out so that it did not hang against his bare skin. "I've got it if I need it, but I don't want to be distracted while you're in a trance."

Rett settled in against the fallen trunk of a large tree. "Might as well sit down before I fall down. I don't exactly know what the connection is going to be like."

Ridge's gaze grew distant for a moment. "I can't sense individuals from here, but I'm picking up both stain and full taint from the Sight."

"I haven't tried to look yet," Rett replied. "I suspect that once the amulet starts working, Henri and I will both feel a drain."

Ridge found a place to sit in the crook of a tree close enough to the ground that he could jump down if needed to protect Rett, but which afforded him a good view of the manor with the spyglass and a clear view of the lawn should guards decide to investigate.

By the time the bells in the tower tolled the tenth hour, Rett had begun to feel the amulet's effects. "It's like seeing two scenes at once," he recounted, quietly enough that Ridge had to strain to hear him. "I'm here—but I'm also in the kitchen. The food looks good."

"Pity we won't get to eat any. Is Henri helping serve the guests?"

"Just carrying out tea and cakes now," Rett replied quietly. Ridge knew he would have to wait for the full report until they were somewhere they did not have to risk being overheard. Now, he trusted Rett to give him the most important details. "Nice house," he added. "But a little past its prime."

If Lord Rondin were indeed beset by financial trouble, it might provide a weakness the Witch Lord could exploit, Ridge mused. "What else?" he asked quietly.

"A lot of guards. Can't tell who they belong to."

"What's Henri doing?" Ridge asked, straining to see into the house with the spyglass.

"He's taking out a pot of something. Oops, he tripped," Rett said, then scowled. "Only I don't think it was an accident. Whatever he's carrying poured all over the walkway and he threw the rest out on the lawn."

"What's he playing at?"

"It's Henri. Face of an innocent, mind of a card sharp. He's got something planned." Rett fell silent, watching the images shared in his mind. "He's waving off one of the guards, playing the fool. They believe him because he's 'only' a servant." He barked a laugh. "The guard cursed him and walked away."

That left Ridge wondering whether each of the visiting nobles had felt the need to bring bodyguards, or whether those were for the mystic who, despite his ragged robes and bare feet, appeared to be far savvier than an innocent from the backwater.

"He's going into the room. I see...Earl Kinney...Duke

Farnston...Lady Millworth...Lord Rondin...Lord Penwort..."

Ridge committed the names to memory. Some, like Farnston and Penwort, he and Rett had suspected of being among those enamored of Makary. Millworth and Kinney he had not thought so easily duped, and he wondered what had become of Lord Millworth that only his wife attended such an important meeting.

"Two more...I don't recognize them," Rett continued. "Definitely wealthy. I'd assume noble, since the others treat them as equals. A sharp-featured man with crow-black hair and a crooked, hawk-beaked nose."

"Probably Lord Talmudge," Ridge muttered. "He's the kind of son of a bitch who would like Makary."

"The other man is blond and young—probably not yet thirty. Pretty more than handsome. Bit of a cruel look in his eyes."

"Sounds like Lord Sandicott's son. Don't remember his name, but he's quite taken with himself."

Rett fell silent, and Ridge scanned in all directions, then lifted the spyglass to view the house. Two men whose posture and bearing suggested a military background stood sentry by the front door, with a man at each corner as well. Their post was up a rise from the manicured grounds, in an area left to nature to preserve the estate's privacy from the road nearby. On the lower lawn, more guards patrolled, posing a real problem if Henri needed to escape. Ridge had a few distractions in mind and hoped he did not have to use them.

"They're talking," Rett said, breaking the silence. "Polite chatter. Wait—Lord Rondin's gone to fetch Makary. Everyone's abuzz."

"Can you see him yet?"

"Door's opening. Rondin's putting on quite a show." Distaste colored Rett's voice. "There he is. Bloody bollocks. Skinny man with a hermit's beard and long hair. Looks like he's been sleeping in the woods. Tattered monk's robe that past due for washing. Bare feet. But..."

"What?"

"Power," Rett said, rubbing his temples. "I can feel it."

"So he really is a witch?"

"Or something," Rett replied. "Gods, they're fawning all over him. Even Henri feels the pull. Maybe that's his magic, some kind of influence…"

Ridge gestured for Rett to be quiet, and neither man moved until the guards down the slope had passed by on their rounds. Ridge didn't know how sound carried here and had no desire to find out. "All clear."

"He…makes you want to look at him," Rett said, sounding puzzled. "He's not handsome, but he's…interesting. Compelling. His accent's from the foothills, but I don't think it's real. And his eyes…he's sharp. Sizing them up."

"What else?"

"They all rose to shake his hand…now they're sitting down again. He's got the seat of honor. Rondin's standing behind him like a proud papa."

"Glad I can't see."

Rett went silent for a while, and Ridge fought the urge to prod for details. They had agreed to keep conversation minimal, so repeating conversation word-for-word was not an option. That meant giving Rett time to digest what was said and convey the gist, while not missing the next comments.

"He's got the accent of a poor farmer, and chooses his words like a scholar," Rett finally continued. "I think the 'farmer' part is an act. He might not have money, but he's been around it. He's not distracted enough by the jewels and fancy surroundings."

Rett had come from the streets, and Ridge's family had been poor. Ridge remembered being struck wordless in astonishment the first time they had been summoned to the palace amid the casual opulence of the truly wealthy. Makary's ease with the powerful men and women who would have been his "betters" and his acceptance of the luxury around him suggested that regardless of his beginnings, he was now no stranger to wealth and privilege.

"It's like he has them under a spell, but I don't think it's actually magic," Rett reported. "Like those actors at the theater, he's one of those people who pulls you in." He went silent again, listening. "He doesn't say anything outright treasonous, but his arguments make you feel discontented. He praises the nobles, says what a shame it is they aren't appreciated more…should have more input…should be more involved in the governing…"

"So he doesn't attack the king, but he damns with faint praise," Ridge grumbled. "Stokes their vanity, leaves them feeling unappreciated, even if they didn't before."

"Henri has to step out to fetch something," Rett said. "Back with the servants in the kitchen. There are whispers. The maids don't like the way Makary looks at them. They say he raises their hackles. They don't trust him. There's talk of curses for those who cross him, bad luck. Someone says their mistress claims he brings good fortune." He paused. "Henri is going back. Makary's still talking."

"That kind likes to hear their own voice. What now?"

Rett tilted his head as if he were listening in person, straining to hear a faint voice. "Spinning a tale about how things might be if the nobles could be heard more. Everyone richer, more trade, take a firm hand with the rabble," he added, making a face. "They liked that part. Rid of the beggars and the lepers. Says there are ways to keep blight away from the crops and locusts out of the fields."

"And they believe him?" Ridge asked, incredulous.

"They're eating it up, practically drooling," Rett said. "Starting to talk amongst themselves now, embroidering on his ideas. Going farther. Ah…now there's veiled criticism of the king, swearing the others to secrecy."

"And I bet Makary is loving every minute."

"Smiling proudly," Rett replied. "He doesn't have to say anything dodgy, and they'll protect each other. Seems to have hit a nerve about not being appreciated. Talmudge and Sandicott's son, especially. The king doesn't take their advice, doesn't ask for their opinions, doesn't recognize their value. King's too cloistered with his council—"

"That part might actually be true," Ridge replied. "Old blood, old ways of thinking. They all echo each other. Like how he hasn't taken Makary seriously."

"Talk of a petition to make the king change his council."

"Good luck with that," Ridge muttered. "Can't imagine a petition going over well."

"Ah…now the tempers rise. Farnston and Penwort talking about taxes being too high, not enough patrols on the roads to keep down highwaymen. More complaints about everything wrong in the kingdom. No one's saying it, but the impression is that Kristoph could fix it if he wanted to."

"Figures," Ridge said. "He gets them worked up, points them in the right direction, and lets them go. Then he just sits back, and they think he's a prophet."

"Uh oh," Rett said, his expression wary.

"What?"

"He's warning them that not everyone shares his views…some would like to see him silenced…his servants have been beaten and killed…he fears for his life."

"Damn right," Ridge muttered. Rett gestured for him to be silent.

"There's outcry…of course they're pushing to find out who might be behind it. He doesn't name the king outright. Oh, gods. Says he's being pursued by assassins. Shadows. Which throws blame on the king anyhow. They're angry. Makary's the vulnerable victim, a misunderstood wiseman." Rett practically choked on his outrage.

"Time to get Henri out of there," Ridge said. "Time for us to be gone, too."

Rett doubled over, and his hands cradled his head. "A warning. From Sofen. Need to go."

Ridge reached down and helped Rett to his feet, moving carefully to avoid making any noise that might attract the attention of the guards patrolling the yard.

"Can you warn Henri?" Ridge asked.

Rett clasped his hand around the amulet and closed his eyes. "I think so," Rett gasped, his face tightening in concentration as he tried to marshal his power. "Just a word—"

His knees buckled, and Ridge kept him upright. "That's it. We're heading for the horses." Rett went rigid in his grasp, back arching and hands closing into fists. Ridge's hold on his arm tightened as his alarm grew. "Rett?"

"Henri," he gasped. "They're on to him."

"Sard," Ridge muttered. "All right. I'll get you to the horses, and go back for Henri."

"Go. I'll make it there."

"Gonna crawl? Because you sure as the Pit can't walk," Ridge snapped. "Come on. The faster I drag your ass to the horses, the sooner I can pull Henri's ass out of the fire."

As if on cue, the sound of an explosion and the roar of flames broke through the quiet afternoon. Ridge turned, staring across the lawn toward the manor house to see a wall of fire rising between the woods and the grand home, and a man running toward the carriages that were fastened in front.

"Cooking oil," Ridge muttered. "That wasn't water. That had to be cooking oil. And one of our bombs. We really ought to increase his wages. That's sarding brilliant."

Before the guards could catch him, Henri had untethered a carriage and its horses and thrown himself into the driver's seat, snapping the reins as he dragged himself up. The toes of his shoes slewed through the gravel as the horses bolted, spooked by the fire. The carriage almost rolled up onto two wheels as Henri crawled onto the floor by the driver's bench, keeping low to stay out of the hail of arrows raining down from the manor's highest towers.

"Halt!"

Ridge froze, then felt anger surge. "Shit," he muttered. Rett shifted, taking his own weight through sheer dint of will. Ridge raised his hands, turning slowly to see two guards dressed in Lord Rondin's livery with their swords drawn.

"The

"The lord's going to want to know what you're doing, trespassing on his land," the taller of the two guards warned. The shorter man gave an amused snort.

"I bet he would," Ridge growled.

Training and practice meant Ridge and Rett moved in synchronicity without the need for words or even a shared glance. Rett groaned loudly and listed to one side, drawing the guards' attention as he stumbled. That distraction provided all Ridge needed to drop throwing daggers from his wrist sheaths and hurls the knives, burying the blades deep in the chests of the two unlucky guards.

Ridge managed to catch Rett before he hit the ground since the collapse had been more real than not. "They'll have friends," Ridge muttered, getting his shoulder under Rett's arm and nearly dragging him along.

Voices shouted from behind them, warning them to stop, threatening consequences. Unless the men had bows and could shoot while running, Ridge felt sure they could reach their mounts before the men could catch them.

Branches and bushes tore at their skin and yanked their hair as they ran through the underbrush. Rett stumbled, nearly taking them down, but Ridge had a grip on the younger man that would probably bruise. "Nearly there," he panted, putting on a final burst of speed to afford them a few extra seconds to mount their horses.

Ridge helped Rett up to his horse, then swung into his saddle, and the two urged their mounts to a gallop. The angry guards shouted and cursed behind them, but without bows, there was nothing they could do to stop the fleeing trespassers.

After they had traveled a few miles without pursuit, once Ridge assured himself that the guards had not followed, he slowed. Their horses were flecked with sweat and Rett had a dazed look as if he only barely hung on to his seat. Ridge climbed down and led his horse to a stream to drink as Rett did the same.

"Now what?" Rett asked, leaning against a tree. He looked spent from the magic and the unexpected vision. After a moment, Rett let himself slide down to sit on the ground as they watched their horses. Ridge stood nearby, where he could still keep an eye out for danger.

"Don't know," Ridge confessed. "That went better—and much worse—than I expected. If the Witch Lord was able to read anything at all from Henri, we sure as the gods can't go home. I'm glad Henri provisioned the safe houses. We'll go to the first one and hope he meets us there."

"Think he got away?"

Ridge pushed aside the worry that had gnawed at him since he'd seen Henri's catastrophic exit. "Yeah. I'm sure he did," he replied, forcing himself to sound more certain than he felt for Rett's sake.

He looked at his partner, taking in how utterly spent Rett looked, leaning against the tree as if he could fall asleep on the spot. "We're either going to have to figure how to build up your stamina or do without magic," Ridge said. "It's not worth it if it kicks your ass every time. If it's a choice between magic or you being able to fight, I'd rather you have my back."

"I won't always be able to choose," Rett said. "We needed to see what happened in the house."

"Henri could have just reported what—and who—he saw," Ridge argued. "The Witch Lord probably picked up on the magic from the amulet. That made it more risky, not less."

"There's no guarantee that someone wouldn't have gotten suspicious of Henri no matter how we did it, and since we saw what he did, if he'd gotten into real trouble, we would have known."

Ridge dug through his pack and tossed some dried meat to Rett. "Eat something. We've still got a long ride, and I don't want to have to tie you to your saddle."

"Not funny," Rett muttered, but he ate the food quickly, and Ridge guessed that channeling the magic had stoked his appetite.

"I'm not against using magic," Ridge said, choosing his words with care. "I never held with what the monks said—you know that. We both have the Sight, and it hasn't been a problem. But we don't really know anything about what else you can do, except what pops out at the damnedest times."

"Which has saved our asses more than once," Rett pointed out through a mouthful.

"Granted. And I don't know of anyone safe to ask, someone who could teach you. I'm just afraid that one of these times, you're going to try to do something, and it's gonna come back on you somehow, bad." Ridge paced as he spoke. "Maybe something I can't fix. And I really don't like to think about that."

Ridge knew that the rest of the Shadows worked solo. Even when the assassins met up in neutral territory like the Black Wolf, it reminded him of predators circling each other, competing to find out who topped the pecking order. Maybe the idea of being beholden to no one, dependent on nobody held an allure for the others. Then again, given the number of Shadows who died young and badly, either from strikes gone wrong, by their own hand, or at the bottom of a bottle of whiskey or the dregs of an opium pipe suggested that the solitary life had its own perils.

"We'll figure it out," Rett said, pushing himself up to stand as the horses finished drinking. "We'd better get moving. No use letting them catch up."

"They won't," Ridge assured him, squeezing Rett's shoulder to see if he was steady on his feet. "I just hope Henri has plenty of food and ale stocked for us since I don't imagine showing our faces in the pub is a good idea right now."

CHAPTER TWELVE

They chose a roundabout way to the city, sticking to back roads, wary of other travelers. Once they reached Caralocia, they had several bolt holes, and beyond the city even more. The sanctuaries were smaller and had fewer comforts than their previous rooms, but far surpassed sleeping outside or finding shelter in abandoned hovels—both of which Ridge and Rett had done more often than they liked to recall. Rented under false names, maintained anonymously for months without being used, the rooms gave them a place to fall back and recover where even Burke would have trouble locating them.

By the time Henri caught up, Ridge and Rett were well along in altering their appearance. Cropping his black hair short made a stark initial change for Ridge. Growing a beard and slouching to hide his height would further the transformation, as well as switching out their usual dark clothing for the rough homespun and woolen garments of a laborer. Rett sat near the fire, letting warmth and vinegar lighten his chestnut hair, which he had also cut shorter.

Both men rose, weapons ready, when a key sounded in the door. Henri entered, hair windblown and face reddened by the cold.

"Thank the gods," their squire huffed. "I didn't know if you'd gotten away."

"We saw your grand exit," Ridge said, managing a tired grin. "A bit memorable, wasn't it?"

Henri averted his eyes, but Ridge thought he looked rather proud of himself. "It worked. Everything I know, I've learned from the two of you."

Rett chuckled. "He's got you there."

"What did you do with the carriage?" Ridge hurried to get a cup of hot tea for Henri, who looked half-frozen.

"I should be fussing over you, not the other way around," Henri chided.

"You look like something the cat dragged in," Ridge countered.

"I left the carriage down an alley a mile or so away," Henri replied as he sank into a chair by the fire. "I suspect the horses will be fine— given the crest on the rig, no one would dare harm them."

"You didn't mind stealing them."

"I'm a bit less intimidated by nobility than your average ruffian."

"Because we're above-average ruffians?" Rett asked, and Henri spared them an exhausted smile.

"Quite."

Ridge and Rett had already scrounged a cold supper for themselves from the supplies, augmented by a loaf of bread Rett insisted on buying from a street vendor on the way back. A chicken, along with potatoes and onions, had been a purchase from another stall, and the combination stewed in a pot at the front of the fire, filling the small haven with the smell of roasting meat.

"We saw a lot," Ridge said once Henri had eaten. He relayed the scenes he'd glimpsed of the gathering. "Was there anything else we might not have noticed? And how did they figure you?"

"I suspect I paid more attention than a servant should have," Henri replied ruefully. "Sorry about that. Or maybe Makary picked up on the amulet after a while. I guess we won't ever know."

Henri pushed his chair back and sighed. "I'm thinking that if I shaved my head and my beard, it might do the trick." He glanced at their altered appearance and giving a wan smile. "Sorry. My thoughts wandered." After a moment and a few swallows of tea, he looked up once more.

"As for what you might not have seen, I don't think I had the amulet active all of the time I was in the kitchen. There's always gossip, but I didn't know how much the spell would drain us, and I wanted to save it for the Witch Lord himself, so I muted the amulet a few times. I had forgotten how much the staff talk among themselves! None of them liked Makary; they said he made their skin crawl," Henri confided.

"Then they're smarter than their masters," Rett replied. "Anything else?"

Henri nodded. "One of the Talmadge maids said something that made me think perhaps her master has a slave child from the caravan. Mentioned 'the boy they brought' and how he keeps to his room."

"That's good—we know where to find one of them," Ridge said. "What about the others?"

"The Sandicotts' maid said something about how the lord himself was too sick to come and sent his son in his stead," Henri replied. "Whatever the ailment, it came on slowly and has the man bedridden."

Ridge and Rett shared a look. "Interesting," Ridge replied. "I've met Lord Sandicott, not that he'd remember me. Hale and hearty. Didn't look like the sickly sort. And a staunch loyalist. Seeing his son there, fawning over the Witch Lord, surprised me."

"They're all snakes," Henri said darkly. "And Makary is the worst. All he had to do was nudge them a bit, and they were quick to list off all their disappointments with the king. He's poison."

"Agreed," Ridge said. "But I'm afraid that the tale that gets back to Burke and the king about today will make it harder than ever to convince Kristoph about the danger. They'll tell it to their advantage, like we're the menace."

"If they recognized—or suspected—us as Shadows," Rett put in. "Makary might have picked up on the magic without knowing who

Henri is. After all, he didn't go in under his own name. And the guards who came after us are dead."

Ridge raised an eyebrow. "And if a tale comes back to the king about two assassins without a warrant skulking around Rondin's manor and killing his guards, do you think for a moment Kristoph—or Burke—will have to wonder who it was?"

"Shit," Rett muttered, turning back to the fire, rubbing his hair where the vinegar itched. "We'll be summoned, sequestered—Burke won't let us out of his sight."

"We've already gone dark," Ridge said. "Burke doesn't know about our bolt holes. So by the rules, we're rogue."

"Do you think he'll send someone to hunt us?" Rett asked quietly, and Ridge heard sorrow and fear in his voice. Over the years, a few of their fellow assassins had broken ranks, either to defect or in violation of orders. Each time, other Shadows whose loyalty remained unquestioned had been sent to bring them back or put them down. Once, the task had fallen to Ridge and Rett when the assassin in question had gone over to the side of a traitorous lord.

Most of the time, the nature of their work did not bother Ridge. He believed in the process that led to issuing a warrant, and he'd known enough about the marks they killed to believe the execution to be as righteous as slaying the enemy in battle. Now he wondered which of their comrades would draw the task of hunting them to ground, whether it would be a reluctant friend or an enemy glad for the chance to end their winning streak.

"Maybe," Ridge replied. "Burke'll be angry, no doubt about that. We weren't supposed to be noticed. And if the king forces his hand, he won't have any choice. But if he has discretion, maybe he'll read what happened for what it was." He sighed. "Until we can prove that the Witch Lord is going against the king—with evidence that can't be denied—we're going to have to manage on our own."

After a couple of days lying low, they ventured out. Rett headed down to the docks to see what news he could find about the caravans and the opium traders, or whether more of the sigil-marked crates had come into port recently. Henri went to meet with some of his sources, brushing aside repeated cautions and assuring that he would be careful.

Ridge had his own agenda. In a broad-brimmed hat pulled low and a scarf wrapped high, his first stop was a busy market. Rett had told him about his own days on the streets, lingering near the marketplace in the hopes of cadging a meal from a sympathetic passer-by or perhaps earning a few coins with an odd job. He saw a young boy loitering at the edge of the tangle of booths, carts, and stalls, far enough away to not be chased off by the merchants, near enough to be able to size up the crowd.

"You there," Ridge said, slouching to make his height unremarkable and roughening his voice. "Deliver a message for me, and I've got coin for you."

The boy gave him a mistrustful look. "Where do I gotta take it?" His threadbare coat was thin for the weather, and from the scrapes on his cheek and the growing bruise on his temple, he'd had a rough go of it.

Ridge named an address, one of Burke's delivery points, someplace he dared not go near himself. "Go straight there, and when someone answers the door, give them this. Then run, and don't go back."

"They ain't gonna grab me, are they?"

Ridge hid a wry smile behind the scarf. "Not if you run fast." He held up two coins and saw the boy's eyes widen. "Just hand off the note and leave. Got that?"

The boy nodded. "Aye."

Ridge gave the boy a hard stare. "Make sure you do just as I've said. I'll know if you don't. That would be bad."

"I keep my word," the boy retorted, sounding offended. "You can be sure of that."

Ridge handed off the folded, sealed note he'd written to Burke. The code would mean nothing should the boy lose it, but Burke would know what to make of it. "Go straight there," he repeated before he handed over the coins.

"Done." With that, the boy took off, and Ridge watched until he vanished into the crowd.

Ridge kept his head down, hands in his pockets, invisible in the press of the marketplace. He listened to the buzz of conversation around him as tinkers and peddlers hawked their wares, alongside the butcher, baker, and fishmonger. The smell of freshly slaughtered chickens mingled with the spice of cooked meat and the perfume of spiced cider. Others might think him oblivious to his surroundings, but Ridge kept a sharp eye out beneath the hat that hid his features, and his hands closed around dirks in both pockets, ready for an attack if it came.

"...more rain. As if we haven't already nearly drowned!"

"...what do you expect? Always trouble on the docks."

"...those prices! Feels like my pocket's been picked."

Ridge meandered through the crowd, picking up what he could from overheard conversations. He did not expect to learn any news about rogue assassins or barefoot mystics; such things were not the concern of the people he dodged and who jostled him. Yet Ridge learned long ago that the talk on the street offered the best indicator of the health of the kingdom. Griping over petty inconveniences augured well; it meant people had nothing more pressing to fuel their complaints.

As kings went, Kristoph ruled with an even hand. He might not be remembered for daring military exploits or for conquering territory to win wars, but he had presided over a time of peaceful prosperity that would have been the envy of his forebears. Harvests had been good, trade favorable. For the most part, his guards permitted the people to go on about their business without interference.

But for the nobles who thronged around the Witch Lord, that wasn't enough, Ridge thought and tamped down his anger. Lack of real problems had given them time to feel aggrieved, unappreciated, and to covet even more wealth and power than they already possessed. Imagined slights and exaggerated snubs fed old jealousies, and the steady hand that governed began to look weak compared to the fist of a tyrant. Ridge had paid attention as the monks droned on about history. It was an old pattern, too oft repeated, but cautionary. And the peace from which so many benefitted would be compromised unless he and Rett and Henri could secure sufficient proof to convince a king whose basic honesty sometimes blinded him to the perfidy of others.

His route took him near the harbor, and more conversations cut through his thoughts.

"Cut down like sheep to the slaughter," a man in sailor's clothing said to his companion as they passed down. "Throats slit like they knew what they were doing. A dozen men and they never stood a chance."

"Thieves aren't so bold," the other man replied.

The sailor gave a harsh laugh. "Wasn't thieves, I hear. A pair of assassins, gone bad. Some of the king's own, if you believe the stories. Got the guards looking for them, and a reward that ought to flush them out. But I hear they can be like ghosts when they need to be. No big surprise, once a man kills for pay he's going to go wrong."

Ridge's thoughts spun as the men moved on, and he hung back to let them pass. Someone had murdered—slaughtered—twelve men and pinned the blame on him and Rett.

Gods above and below, we can never go back, he thought, fighting down panic. Yes, he and Rett had gone rogue, but Burke believed them about the Witch Lord, and if he had to play politics and give in to pressure to call them to heel, Ridge had felt sure their master would tacitly understand their disappearance. *Burke couldn't forgive this, even if he wanted to. If they catch us, we'll hang. And there's no way to prove anything, not about the killings at the docks and not about the Witch Lord.*

As he passed the mouth of a narrow alley, a woman's startled shout forced him from his dark thoughts. Ridge hesitated, torn between the instinct to help and the need to avoid a brush with the guards. Yet no soldiers rushed to aid, and Ridge heard sounds of a scuffle. Making a split-second decision, he slipped down the alleyway, keeping his back to the wall and drawing one of his knives.

What he saw made him hesitate to be sure his eyes were not playing tricks on him. One woman struggled with two larger, more solidly-built assailants. What appeared to be half a dozen ghostly figures swarmed to fight off the attackers, and Ridge was surprised that he could see the spirits.

The ghosts tore at the men's coats, sometimes able to pull at the cloth, and other times passing through like mist. Yet even then, the ghosts' touch caused the attackers to pause as if their grip carried the chill of the grave. Beneath the press of men and ghosts, the victim put up a mighty struggle, kicking and twisting. As more ghosts massed, the temperature in the alley plummeted, and the spirits kept up the defense until the attackers shivered violently.

Cursing under his breath, Ridge closed the distance. "Get away!" he shouted, brandishing his knife. "Run, before I thrash you!" He had no desire to dive into a fight and leave behind tales of a memorable rescue.

To his relief, the two men ran off, unwilling to take on yet another opponent. Ridge saw the nearly-transparent shades fall back, lingering in the waning light. As he neared, the victim rose to her feet. As soon as he saw the fall of dark hair across her shoulders, Ridge knew.

"Lorella?"

The medium raised her right hand warily, and he saw she gripped a small dirk. The ghosts moved closer, gathering to protect her. Their presence dropped the temperature still more, and Ridge could see his breath fog. Lorella eyed him, trying to identify the person hidden beneath the hat and scarf.

"It's me," he said in a low voice, not wanting her to call out his name. He pulled the scarf away enough to show his features, and Lorella relaxed, just a bit.

She tilted her head, assessing. "Guess it's true, what the spirits said. We need to talk, but not here."

"Second thoughts about that safe haven we offered you?"

Lorella snorted. "Nowhere's safe. Thought you of anyone would know that." She gave him an appraising look. "Someone's trying to kill you. They're after me, too. The ghosts...know things."

Ridge weighed his options. He could take her back to the bolt hole and risk compromising their position. Or they could go to a tavern and chance being spotted. Ridge knew just how many eyes and ears were for hire, how quickly word of a sighting could be passed along if a reward hung in the balance.

He took another look at Lorella. A bruise darkened one cheek, and her cloak looked stained and dirty. Wherever she'd been staying hadn't been clean or comfortable. They were both being hunted, probably by the same people. "I can take you somewhere safe, but if you come with me, then you stay with us. We can't risk exposure."

"Fine with me."

"Come on," Ridge said. "Let's get out of the street." Lorella followed him in silence as they wove through the alleyways, taking a roundabout route in case they were followed. Ridge braced himself for arguments from Rett and Henri as he went to unlock the door.

"You've changed locations. Smart," Lorella observed.

Ridge grimaced. "Long story. I'll tell you inside," he added, pushing the door open.

"About time," Rett said, looking up from where he sat at the table, playing cards with Henri, who appeared to be winning from the big smile on his face.

"We've got a new lodger," Ridge said, taking another step into the room so Lorella could enter. "She got jumped by a couple of ruffians—and had a dozen ghosts come to the rescue."

"Can't be sure you're safer here, but welcome," Rett said. He caught Ridge's eye, a look that suggested a conversation later. Ridge introduced Lorella and Henri.

"I'll see what we have to make up another bed," Henri said. "We're a bit cramped, but nothing that can't be worked around," he added, bustling off to rearrange their provisions.

"I'm sorry to impose, but I don't have anywhere else to go." Lorella sat in the chair Henri vacated, and in the lantern light, Ridge could see how much the past few weeks had worn on her. When they had first met, Lorella looked well-rested and well-fed, clean and prosperous. Now her face looked thin, and her torn, dirty clothing seemed to hang on her too-thin frame. Dark circles shadowed her eyes, evidence of worry and troubled dreams. A bruise on her cheek had begun to purple. The set of her chin and the stubborn pride in her eyes forbade him from mentioning it.

"What happened?" Rett asked, rising to pour her a cup of tea from the pot simmering in the fireplace. Lorella accepted the cup gratefully, wrapping her hands around it to warm herself.

"Nothing good," she said with a sigh. "Maybe I should have accepted your help after we left Duke Barton's manor, but I thought it would be over, with Fenton and Hennessy taken care of." She shook her head. "It wasn't. I hadn't wanted to be locked up somewhere for my protection—"

"It wouldn't have been liked that," Ridge interrupted. He settled for a seat on the floor, stretching out his long legs. "Our contact would have kept you safe, but it wasn't a prison—"

"She couldn't have left," Rett countered. "Not a prison, but not free. I think I understand."

Lorella gave a grateful smile. "Maybe I was wrong. I didn't expect to be followed the way I have been. Tonight wasn't the first time. The other times, I was faster. I saw those ruffians coming. They ambushed me tonight. I'm not used to hiding."

"We can hide you, but it's going to mean staying hidden," Ridge warned. "If it's any consolation, we're holed up, too. We've become a little too famous lately."

"What he means is, you're in good company. People are trying to kill us, too," Rett added.

Ridge caught his breath. "Yeah, about that. Maybe a few more than before." He recounted what he had heard near the docks, about the murders and the set-up. "We're on our own for sure now," he said. "Burke can't help us even if he doesn't believe we did it. The king will force his hand. And the Witch Lord will maneuver his people so that we don't have a chance to prove our innocence."

Rett paled. "Shit. The rest of the Shadows will be after us, even if they weren't before."

Ridge nodded. "Some of them—the ones who don't trust the Witch Lord—might have given us a pass for what happened at Rondin's manor, keeping tabs on a noble after a tip that something suspicious might be going on. But this…it looks like we've gone on a mad killing spree." He ran a hand over his face. "We're dead men walking unless we can prove the Witch Lord is behind it."

"I might be able to help." They all looked at Lorella.

"You said the ghosts knew things," Ridge said. "And you had already known that people were after us. What have you heard?"

Henri bustled behind them, rearranging the bedding to make room for a fourth person, with a little privacy for Lorella. He returned with a bottle of whiskey and then took up a seat near the fire to stir a pot of soup. Ridge knew that despite their squire's apparent preoccupation, he listened to every word.

"Ever since the…incident…at Duke Barton's, the spirits have been seeking me out," Lorella replied. "They won't leave me alone, actually. The Witch Lord has a lot of enemies among the dead. They come to me—in my sleep and when I'm awake, even when I'm not trying to channel them—and they want to bear witness."

"He killed them?" Rett asked, leaning forward to rest his elbows on his knees. Lorella stood much shorter than both of the assassins. With Rett bent forward and Ridge sitting on the floor, they were nearly on eye level with the medium.

"Some of them," Lorella answered. "And his followers killed the rest. Some for power, others for silence. It's bigger than maybe you realize. Certainly more than King Kristoph knows, or he'd surely have raised an army by now."

"And once again, the evidence isn't something we can bring to him, even if we hadn't gone rogue," Ridge said. "Back in the alley, when you were being attacked, the ghosts were visible. Did you do that?"

Lorella shook her head. "No. The ghosts might be able to draw on strong emotion to make themselves visible, but I've never been able to force them to show themselves."

"Even if you could make the ghosts visible and let him hear them accuse the Witch Lord, the king'd still wonder whether you somehow just made the whole thing up," Rett said.

"I know," Lorella replied. "Doesn't change the information they provide from being true."

"Who have the Witch Lord's followers killed?" Rett asked.

"Servants who knew too much. The arms smugglers kill anyone

who gets in their way or might threaten their operation. Some of the Witch Lord's followers have killed family members to keep them from going to the king."

"Shit," Ridge muttered. "Although given what we saw from Fenton, I shouldn't be surprised."

"A new ghost showed up last night. Lord Sandicott's valet," Lorella said. "He fears for his lord's safety. Sandicott's son and wife are drugging him, and the ghost said the lord is half dead with it."

"Opium," Rett muttered.

"The maid," Henri said, looking up from his spot by the fire. "She said Lord Sandicott was unwell."

"And apparently, he had help getting that way," Ridge fumed. "He's always been one of the king's staunchest supporters."

"His son was very much an admirer of the Witch Lord at the gathering," Henri added.

"The ghost brought a warning," Lorella said. "In a fortnight, there's to be a big feast at Lord Sandicott's manor. The king will be in attendance. It's been planned for over a year. Some kind of liege obligation," she added, with a gesture that said she didn't quite grasp the details. "Sandicott is drugged to the gills, barely alive. The wife and son are planning something big at the feast. The ghost feared they mean to kill the king and somehow blame Lord Sandicott."

Rett let out a whistle. "It just might work."

"Kristoph's guard will be down," Ridge said, pacing in the small room. He rubbed the back of his neck as he thought aloud. "He'll feel safe in Sandicott's manor because the man was one of his top generals. They fought together in the last war. There are all kinds of stories about Sandicott saving the king's life. He'll have bodyguards, but they won't be expecting a threat from the lord or his family; they'll be watching for an attack from outside."

"For us," Rett said, meeting Ridge's gaze. "They'll be watching for assassins. The Witch Lord set us up. If anyone sees us, they'll think we mean to kill the king. And if Sandicott's son succeeds, they'll spin a tale that we were working with his father, who's so addled by opium that he's gone mad."

"I'm afraid that's quite possible," Henri agreed. He pulled the pot of soup from the fire and filled four bowls, which he handed out along with spoons and chunks of fresh bread.

Henri gave a self-deprecating smile. "My apologies for such poor fare."

Lorella lifted the bowl and savored the aroma. "No apologies needed. This smells wonderful."

"Henri cooks the best food any wanted men could ever hope for," Ridge replied.

They ate in silence. After she finished, Lorella pushed her empty bowl aside and sighed in contentment. "Thank you. I was getting desperate when you found me. I might have come looking for you, but I didn't know how to locate you."

"Good thing you didn't, or you might have been caught by the guards as an accomplice," Rett said. He gave Lorella a searching look. "Have any of the ghosts who've come to you about the Witch Lord been children? Perhaps with a very strong resonance?"

Lorella frowned. "Magic?"

Rett nodded. "We found out that the Witch Lord is kidnapping children with abilities and enslaving them, selling them to his followers to use for their own gain. We managed to free several from a caravan, but there were others who had already been sold. We don't know who has them, but they're being used as an unfair advantage to gain more wealth and power for the Witch Lord's disciples."

Lorella closed her eyes. "Damn. This is even bigger than I thought." She took a few deep breaths. "No. I haven't seen any child ghosts. That doesn't mean the Witch Lord's people haven't killed any children; they just might not have made their way to me. I'd notice a child with power. That's something that lasts beyond life."

"Truly?" Rett asked. "And the gods permit it?"

Ridge felt a stab of sadness at the open need in Rett's face. The monks at the orphanage had been adamant about the evil of unsanctioned magic. Not that anyone seemed to be holding that against Makary, who wore the title of Witch Lord as an honorific. But for two poor orphans—or even two of the King's Shadows—a touch of magic meant shame, taint, fear of discovery. They had only ever been able to confide in each other, and then in Henri when the secret couldn't be kept from him. Ridge had made his peace long ago with the Sight, figuring that whatever gods gave them their abilities had no right to judge them for those same powers. But the stigma had always bothered Rett more, which seemed odd since he had so little conscience about his thieving past.

Then again, Rett had stolen to survive in those early years. Thieving was something he did, not something he was. Rett had the Sight, and a dollop more of magic they had yet to fully understand. Before the present disaster, Ridge had hoped that if their abilities ever came to light, Burke would somehow overlook it as another kind of weapon in the service of the king. Now, if they were caught, it would be another nail in their coffins.

Lorella's expression told Ridge she had picked up on the unspoken plea in Rett's voice. "*What* we are is how the gods made us," she replied. "Who are men to judge that the gods made us wrong? With everything we're given, we do no harm."

Rett nodded, and stood, gathering their empty bowls for want of something to do. "Glad you think so," he said in a tight voice.

"I'll take those," Henri said, rising and relieving Rett of the bowls. He washed them in a bucket and set them to dry. "Not elegant, but functional," he said of the arrangement. "I'll go get more water." With that, he grabbed the bucket and went downstairs.

"What now?" Lorella looked from Rett to Ridge.

"We can't stay in hiding forever. Sooner or later, the other Shadows will track us down. If not the Shadows, then the Witch Lord's people," Rett replied.

"We have to stop the Witch Lord, save the king, and convince Kristoph to believe us," Ridge replied.

Lorella gave a snort of disbelief. "Is that all? How are the three of us going to manage that?"

"Four." They looked up to see Henri in the doorway. "There are four of us. Strength in numbers."

"Don't discount Henri," Ridge said with a smile. "He thrashes people—very politely."

"What can we use?" Rett walked over to check the street below, staying hidden by the curtains from prying eyes. He looked back at Ridge. "You and I have our…abilities. Not sure how they can help, other than recognizing who's completely sold out to the Witch Lord."

"You can do that?" Lorella asked sharply.

"And we've got Lorella's connection to the spirits," Ridge continued, not answering her question. "They may be our best informants if they can be gathered," he added with a questioning look to Lorella.

"I think so. I'll try."

"I have sources as well," Henri volunteered. "They know me under other names, and they don't know about my employ with you. So I should be able to continue getting some information that way." He paused. "What I heard today suggests more people missing—probably showing up as Miss Lorella's ghosts."

"Be careful," Ridge said. "People have the damnedest way of figuring things out when you don't want them to. You'd make a tempting hostage."

Henri seemed to pluck a small dagger from thin air and twirled it through his fingers, then sent it flying to stick in the wood above the hearth. "I'm always cautious," he said with a slight smile. "And you've taught me well."

"All anyone wanted to talk about near the docks were the murders," Rett said. "As soon as I figured out what was being said, I left. But I did find out two important things. The dead men were killed assassin-style, and definitely by a pair of assassins. No doubt that it was meant to put the blame on us. And the second—the trade in opium's better than ever. Likely thanks to the Witch Lord and his followers."

"I sent a message to Burke," Ridge replied. "Coded," he added as Rett moved to argue. "And this was before I heard about the killings. I told him not to believe what he hears, warned him that the king is in danger." He sighed. "Doesn't mean he'll listen."

"Do you think Caralin—" Rett began.

Ridge shook his head. "Too dangerous. For her and us. She has to follow orders, or end up like us. I think we have to count the Shadows out. Too many of them would love to see us brought down a peg or two, and the rest won't risk their necks against something this big. Even if they believe in the Witch Lord, they believe in the Code more. We broke it when we went rogue. Burke, he might agree about Makary, but with the rest—we've gone too far. He'll send them after us, and he'll mean it."

CHAPTER THIRTEEN

Rett woke to the sound of muted screams and plaintive whimpers. For a second, he didn't recognize where he was until the desperate events of the past few days caught up with his sleep-addled mind. Outlaws. Hunted. Hiding.

Ridge awoke more quickly, rising from his spot on the floor to join Rett in bending over their newest houseguest. Lorella twitched and trembled, caught in vivid nightmares.

Rett knelt beside her, gently lifting her hand. Lorella did not rouse.

"Come on, wake up," Rett urged, patting her face. He had more than his share of troubled dreams, given everything he had seen, and the things he'd done that rested uneasy on his soul. He was no stranger to waking in a cold sweat, breath heaving, trembling with the adrenaline of the fight, or the imagined loss of a battle gone wrong. He knew that Henri had learned early to call out to him from a safe distance, or poke with a broomstick rather than risk a fist to the jaw.

This felt different. Rett gripped Lorella's shoulder and shook her gently, careful to block her hands to keep her from swinging at him. She didn't even try, and somehow that seemed worse. "I don't know why she isn't waking up."

"Room's cold," Ridge observed.

Henri padded up behind the couch where Lorella had been sleeping, looking like a stranger shorn of his hair and beard. Rett wondered if the disguise bothered Henri. He hadn't felt like himself since he'd cut his hair and changed its color. Bad enough to hide from people who wanted to kill them; worse to feel like he no longer recognized his own face. "Could it be something to do with the ghosts?"

Rett stroked a hand over Lorella's face. Her skin felt clammy, and beneath her eyelids, her eyes flicked back and forth quickly. She cried out, a muffled, desperate sound. "Maybe. Whatever's happening, it's not good."

Lorella gasped, eyes opening and wide with pain. She stiffened, practically coming off the couch, and Rett grabbed her shoulders to steady her.

"Gods. Look!" Ridge pointed. Blood beaded from three fresh red gashes across Lorella's chest, as if claws had torn across her flesh.

"What—"

"Something's attacking in her dreams. And the cold—either the spirits are coming to see what's happening, or whatever's doing this to her *is* a ghost."

"Let me try," Rett murmured, unsure of just what he intended to do. He laid the palm of his hand over Lorella's eyes and called to his Sight, but it revealed nothing. This was one of the few times he wished he could have a vision when he needed it.

And yet…something stirred. Rett had no training with his magic; to even seek such a thing would have meant disaster. He had only experimented when dire circumstances forced his hand, and then only to save Ridge's life or his own when all else failed. So now, the best he could do was blunder toward something elusive that his gut told him he had to find.

Rett pulled harder on his errant magic, making this up as he went. If he could somehow enter Lorella's dreams—impossible as that sounded—perhaps he could guide her back, help her escape the torment that locked her into unconsciousness.

Or maybe get trapped himself.

Suddenly Rett's world went black.

Complete darkness gave him no way to find his bearings. Rett thought of catacombs, and they appeared around him. He looked for a stairway, and the carved stone steps stretched down into the depths. He thought of light and found himself holding a torch. Just as easily, an iron knife felt real and solid in his other hand.

Torn between feeling ridiculous and being completely terrified, Rett pushed on, and as he moved through the darkened passageways, Lorella's screams grew louder. The air around him chilled Rett to the bone, enough to make his teeth chatter. He wondered whether the medium always felt like this, halfway between living and dead, or whether it was a trick of the nightmare.

Up ahead, around a corner, Rett caught a glimpse of light. He moved cautiously, remembering that whatever injured Lorella in the dream world had left physical wounds in the waking world. He had no desire to discover whether death was final in both.

He turned the corner, and Fenton looked up from where he had Lorella pinned against the rough stone wall. "You," the ghostly traitor snarled. "You're not supposed to be here."

Lorella's head lolled to one side, her lip split, one eye swelling shut and a darkening bruise on her cheek. The ghost attacker had been busy; those marks weren't on her when Rett began his journey. Maybe they were real, or perhaps they were only in the dream world. But the bloody gashes were seeping rivulets, staining Lorella's shirt.

"Let her go," Rett challenged.

"You have no power here." Fenton sneered at him.

"Are you sure about that?"

Fenton let go of Lorella, and she slid to the floor. The duke's dead brother turned on Rett, teeth bared, fists clenched. "She lied!" he roared. "We had a deal. She betrayed me to my idiot brother, got me killed. I owe her."

"You betrayed your brother—and your king," Rett returned,

keeping both torch and knife ready for an attack. "It's not her fault it caught up to you. If you want to be specific, Hennessy—the crazy man with the bomb—killed you."

"She's the one who opened her mouth and ruined everything," Fenton growled. "Without her, even if I'd died, my brother would have accepted the crates. The revolution would have gone on. Now, she's compromised the plan."

"That's what brings you back from the dead for vengeance? The Witch Lord's stupid 'revolution'?" Rett knew he had to keep Fenton talking. Already the ghost had mirrored Rett's movements, unintentionally stepping farther from Lorella.

"He's brilliant!" Fenton shouted. "Much better than that weakling king."

"How is it you have the power to be here?" Rett asked, shifting a half-step at a time to draw Fenton off from his intended victim. "How are you here in her dreams and the other ghosts aren't?"

"Maybe I had more of a reason."

"Maybe the others didn't have someone to open the door," Rett replied.

His dream-self sprang forward, slashing at Fenton's ghost with his iron knife and swinging at the apparition with his torch. Fenton's image broke apart, splintering like shattered glass, vanishing for an instant. Rett knew he would be back, and he knew what he had to do.

Rett cast his magic back along the path that brought him here, back to the anchoring feel of his hand on Lorella's forehead, and the grip of Ridge's hand on his shoulder.

In the next breath, he called to the ghosts that had been worriedly hovering around Lorella's prone form and felt an onslaught of spirits surge through him like a bridge. Their dead chill froze him to the marrow, and the unrelenting cold constricted his chest and tightened his throat. He labored to draw air and feared he might lose consciousness.

If I pass out here, can I ever get back? Will Lorella and I both die, tangled up in a nightmare that never ends?

As suddenly as his breath left him, the tightness vanished, and he sucked in a deep, desperate gulp of air. In the pause between dispelling

Fenton's spirit and summoning the ghosts, the duke's faithless brother returned, his expression even more malevolent than before. This time he closed on Rett, hands clenched into claws, not even needing a weapon. He swung at Rett, who had not completely shaken off the disorientation of the ghosts' passage.

The clawed fingers raked across Rett's face, and he reeled back as warm blood oozed from the wounds. Instinct and training had his body reacting, jabbing with the torch and slashing with his knife. The iron blew apart the revenant, but Fenton formed behind him, and this time the slashes ripped through his shirt, digging into his back.

Rett wheeled, stabbing with the knife, only to send Fenton elsewhere in the next breath. Fenton was already dead; he could keep this up forever. Rett and Lorella couldn't last. Already, Rett felt himself waning, and Lorella had been Fenton's prisoner even longer.

Fenton's nails cut across Rett's shoulder, staggering him. Rett had never used this much magic, hardly more than a touch or a small surge, nothing this sustained. The drain went soul deep, taking energy and life with it to maintain the connection, leaving him dry and cold.

He heard voices shouting in the distance. Henri, worried to the point of panic. Ridge, barking commands, frightened and angry. Rett knew he needed to let go, to come back to himself, or what remained of him. But he couldn't. Not yet. Not without freeing Lorella.

Fenton closed again, and Rett knew this time the mad ghost would rip out his throat. The feral gleam in Fenton's eyes gave away his intention. Rett's spent torch guttered, flickering. Once it went out, there would be only darkness.

Fenton lunged. Rett dodged and stumbled toward Lorella, landing on his knees beside her. Ghosts surged between him and their attacker and began tearing into Fenton, whose screams echoed as loudly as Lorella's had. Rett wrapped his arms around Lorella, folding her against his chest. Blood soaked his shirt and smeared his cheek, and Lorella felt small and too still in his grip. If they were ever going to get back, they couldn't wait any longer.

Still making it up as he went, Rett closed his eyes. He held onto Lorella, and let go of everything else.

They fell.

Rett felt hands on him, tearing Lorella from his grasp although he tried to hang on. The floor beneath him was wood, not the cold stone of Lorella's dream, and the air felt warm, though the chill still froze him bone deep.

"Wake up," a voice commanded, edged sharp. "Come on, wake up, dammit!" Ridge sounded worried. "Why is there so much blood? Gods, what happened to you?"

Rett wanted to answer, and he tried to open his eyes. His body lacked the energy, and his exhausted mind lacked the will. Instead, he floated, no longer falling, not yet landed. Adrift on a warm current, mostly numb to the injuries Fenton had inflicted, or maybe beyond caring.

"Any luck?" Ridge asked, his voice a note higher than usual with apprehension.

"She's warming up. Altar and athame, I never saw such a thing."

"Ghosts," Ridge said, and his tone settled into an angry, rough rasp. "Must have come for her in her sleep. And Rett…he found a way to go in after her."

"Magic?"

"What do you think?" Ridge's footsteps receded, then came back, and he eased off Rett's ruined, blood-soaked shirt. A warm, wet cloth gently wiped at Rett's cheek, shoulder, and chest.

Lorella groaned, and Rett heard shuffling behind him, then Lorella's murmured questions and Henri's quiet answers.

"I don't know what you did, or how you did it," Ridge said, "but you saved Lorella. You're both beat to shit, and I figure there's a story behind that, but you're here, and you're breathing. Now you've got to wake up. Come on. I can't save the kingdom by myself."

Rett clung to the familiar voice and pulled himself toward sound and light, more by instinct than intent. With one final leap toward consciousness, he found the strength to open his eyes. Ridge sat next to him, weary and relieved, his back against the couch where Lorella lay.

"Good to have you back," Ridge said. "I was afraid you wouldn't find your way."

Rett allowed himself to relax, now that he was finally safe. "I wasn't sure I would," he admitted. "Fenton's ghost attacked Lorella in her dreams. He was angry because we fouled up the Witch Lord's plans. Can you believe that?" His voice sounded weak, even to him. "He had her down. I tried to stop him, but I couldn't by myself. I helped some other ghosts cross over, and they fought Fenton back."

Ridge raised an eyebrow at that but remained quiet, and Rett figured his partner was saving the questions for another time. "It worked?"

Rett managed a shrug. "Guess so. Is Lorella all right?"

Ridge glanced at the still figure on the couch, and at Henri's concerned expression. "Seems to be. You're both breathing and talking. And bleeding. Looks like you went a couple of rounds with a wildcat."

"Felt like it," Rett replied. "Fenton was as much of a son of a bitch as a ghost as he was when he was alive."

A few minutes later, Henri hunched next to the couch with a cup of hot tea for Lorella and handed off a second cup for Rett. Ridge helped him sit, and steadied the cup while he drank. "So the ghosts followed you over?"

"I called out to them for help, and they used me for a bridge," Rett replied with a rueful tone. "Went right fucking through me. I think that's why I'm taking longer to bounce back."

"Did they get stuck there, in her head?"

Rett took a sip and let the tea's soothing aroma ease his tension. "Don't know. Ask her. They were fighting off Fenton to give us a chance to get clear."

Later, when he had all his wits about him, Rett would need to think about what had just happened, what kind of risk he had taken, and whether more could be made of this newfound ability. Now, he just wanted the pounding in his head and the chill in his bones to go away.

"I'll bring you something to eat," Henri promised. "My gran always said food grounds you. You look like you could use an anchor. Then maybe some whiskey to go with it, and a good night's sleep."

"Sleep? I don't know about that." The fog in Rett's head cleared enough to remind him where they were, and the dangers of their changed circumstances. "We need to stop the Witch Lord. We don't have time for this," he murmured.

"Unless you're planning to stop him by collapsing on him, you need to rest," Ridge said, fixing Rett with a look. "Saving the kingdom can wait until tomorrow."

"I have an idea." Lorella's voice sounded tired and strained, but beneath it lay steel. "I think I've got an inside man who can help."

"What do you mean, we have to get him out?" Ridge glared at Lorella, and Rett felt uneasy.

The medium looked up from the candles and cards she had used as a focus point as she called to the spirits. "The ghost I called felt adamant about the danger. The ghost was a butler to the father and grandfather of the current lord, loyal to the bone to the Sandicott family—at least, to the rightful holder of the title," she added. "And he believes the wife and son aren't content with keeping Sandicott drugged. He says they've discussed killing the lord so the son can take the title—and side with the Witch Lord."

"No surprise about whose side the son's on," Rett mused. "We've seen his true colors."

"Also no surprise he'd get impatient about wanting more power, especially if Lord Sandicott remained a threat," Ridge mused. "If his father ever got free, he could take down the whole house of cards."

"That's why you need to free Sandicott," Henri said, putting away the dishes from dinner. "Get him out, sober him up, and have him tell his story to the king. Kristoph might not believe Burke or the two of you, but Sandicott's another matter."

Rett and Ridge exchanged a glance, and Ridge shrugged. "It might work. Assuming we could get into Sandicott's manor and get the lord out. If he's drugged senseless, I don't relish trying to rappel down a wall with dead weight."

Lorella shook her head. "He's not unconscious. Oliver—that's the butler—has been checking on him, trying to take care of him as best he can given that, well, Oliver's dead."

Rett remembered just how dangerous and solid the ghosts in

Lorella's nightmare had been and repressed a shudder. "Does Oliver have access to the whole house? And more importantly—do Sandicott's son and his wife know about the ghost?"

"Yes, he has access. No, he's sure they don't know," Lorella answered. "He's painfully polite, but he's tremendously disappointed in the wife and son, and says they are completely wrapped up in their own schemes."

"It's easy for Oliver to suggest we kidnap the old man," Ridge said, pacing once more. He rubbed his hand over the beard that still seemed like it should belong to someone else. "He can walk through walls. Does he have any brilliant ideas on how living people could do it?"

"Actually, yes." Lorella grinned. "Seems Oliver has been thinking about this a lot since he couldn't do much else. Then one of my other spirit contacts led him to me, and he realized we could save his master. Oliver's willing to help us map out the house—"

"How?" Rett asked, intrigued. He'd spent a lot of time since being part of the nightmare dreamscape thinking about ghosts and their energies, and how they were similar and different to magic. More importantly, he'd been trying to figure out how his power had enabled him to do what he had done, and how they might use that magic as an asset. More troubling, he had also wondered about the personal cost. The lesson that nothing came for free had been beaten into him early in life.

"Through me," Lorella answered his question. "I don't just talk to the spirits; they can possess me. That's part of being a medium. So Oliver takes me over and draws the house plans."

"Could he answer questions when he's…wearing you?" Ridge asked.

Lorella bit her lip. "Yes. But I can only share my body with him for a very short time. That kind of connection takes a huge amount of energy—from him and me. That's one reason I'm not afraid to allow the possession. He can't stay long. On the other hand, information passes much more quickly. If he thinks it, I know it, so the transfer is easier than trying to put everything into words."

"Huh," Ridge replied. "That has to be strange, having someone else in your head."

Lorella shrugged. "I've been doing it long enough; I don't think about it that much anymore." She looked at Rett. "How did it feel to you?"

Rett struggled for words to wrap around what he had experienced. "I was still me, but I saw you, and I saw the ghosts," he replied slowly. "I could feel the ghosts using my power to cross into your dream, but they weren't in my mind."

"Because all of you were in mine—including Fenton's spirit," Lorella added, grimacing in distaste.

"Has Fenton shown up again?" Rett asked.

"No. And I hope he doesn't. I'm not sure what the other ghosts did to him, but if his energy survived the fight, I don't think he'll risk coming back soon."

"Survived?" Ridge questioned, stopping as he tracked back and forth across the small room. "Can a ghost be any deader?"

Lorella chuckled. "Ghosts can be banished, and they can also be dispelled. There are rituals to release their hold here and send them on to...whatever comes next."

Rett stared at the flickering candles. Despite being raised by the monks at the orphanage, neither he nor Ridge had ever been particularly religious, other than making the sacrifices for good luck in the hunt that were more superstitious ritual than observant. Given their profession, it didn't do to dwell too much on death. He hoped that some of the sorry sons of bitches the two of them had killed got what they had coming to them. He feared the same would be true for him when his luck ran out. And he refused to think about "death" and "Ridge" in the same sentence.

"You talk to the dead," Ridge said sharply. "What does come next?"

Lorella looked at Ridge for a moment before answering, and her gaze made him uncomfortable because he shifted and turned away. "Something. What, I can't say."

"Can't or won't?" Ridge's voice had an edge Rett recognized, but was surprised to hear directed at the medium. Then again, Ridge remembered his family enough to miss them. Rett didn't.

"Can't," Lorella replied. "And the ghosts don't know, either. Not until they choose to pass over."

Whatever darkened Ridge's mood, he seemed to pull himself out of it. "So Oliver can give us the floor plans. Can he do anything else? Throw vases, break crockery, set things on fire?"

"I don't know. He's extremely proud of his position as butler; I can't imagine him breaking anything on purpose."

"Might come in handy in a pinch," Rett observed. "Any other helpful family ghosts he could muster to the cause? I'm with Ridge on this—getting in and out isn't going to be easy, and we're already in enough trouble. We get caught, we'll hang."

"Remember what I said about getting caught?" Rett muttered as he and Ridge hunkered in the darkness outside Bleakscarp, the Sandicott ancestral home. Unlike the Barton castle, Bleakscarp was a newer, more elegant home built after the wars for control of the crown were over, when power began to concentrate into the hands of those whose lands had been gifts from the king.

Despite its ominous name, Bleakscarp's handsome symmetry and measured proportions had the look of an aristocrat of fine breeding. The location, however, lived up to expectations, a windy rise above a sheer, rocky cliff overlooking the sea.

"So the Sandicott forebears were pirates?" Rett said, taking in the lay of the land.

"More like wreckers and smugglers, from what Lorella could prise out of old Oliver," Ridge replied. "And far too recently for it to be covered over and forgotten. Apparently, they were still at it during the reign of Kristoph's grandfather."

"So smuggling some weapons for the cause of a usurper isn't too far afield," Rett mused.

"Obviously not."

Lorella remained hidden on the beach below the cliffs, where she could still see the house. Having the manor in her line of sight would strengthen her connection to the ghosts. "Glad Oliver could come up with a few more loyal retainers. I still think this is one of our dumber moves," Rett said and glanced up at the mansion, concern clear on his face.

"What's one more in a long line?" Ridge replied with a grin.

Henri waited in a boat in the cove near Lorella, below the smugglers' caverns that Oliver planned to use for their escape. The ghost had assured them that the last Sandicott to use the caves had been the current lord's grandfather, and he could recall no further mention of them after the old man died. For all their sakes, Rett hoped the ghost had a good memory.

Getting in proved easy enough. Oliver had enough power to flick open the latch on a back door, while other, more lively ghosts sent a wind through the house, knocking over breakables to send the staff scurrying and focus attention away from them.

Ridge and Rett, clad in all black, slipped through the doorway into the large kitchen and quickly made their way to the servants' stairs to take them up to the floor where Lord Sandicott was imprisoned in his rooms. Thanks to the restless ghosts, none of the servants were in sight.

They peered anxiously around the corner and found the hallway empty as well. Both assassins had committed the floorplan to memory, and much as Rett would have liked to appreciate the fine artworks and priceless trinkets that decorated the manor, he dared not spare the attention.

Ridge counted the doorways under his breath while Rett remained alert for anyone coming up behind them. When Ridge stopped, Rett moved to cover him as Ridge bent to pick the lock. He glanced at Rett.

"Is it spelled? Can you tell?"

Rett concentrated on the doorway, hoping his magic would respond. Consciously using more than just his Sight was still new and felt dangerously untried. He dared not use too heavy a touch, or else someone else nearby who could also do magic might notice. He felt the power heed his summons, and then with a thrill of victory, a frisson of energy sizzled through his nerves.

"No spells inside," he whispered in warning. "Doesn't mean no traps."

Ridge nodded and eased the door open. The room inside smelled of sweat and sickness. Ridge swept the room for trip wires or other alarms and found nothing. Sandicott's traitorous wife and son apparently felt no need for anything beyond the poison they used to control the manor's lord.

On the far side of the room, they saw a man lying in a huge four-poster bed. He didn't stir as they approached soundlessly, weapons ready but concealed to avoid panicking Lord Sandicott.

"If you're here to kill me, you're almost too late," a raspy voice said as they reached the bed. "My son and my wife have my murder well under way." Sandicott slurred his words slightly, but Rett heard steel beneath the man's weak voice.

"We're Shadows. We've come to rescue you because you're loyal to King Kristoph," Ridge said. "But we've got to hurry."

"Gonna have a hard time sneaking me out the door," Sandicott wheezed. "Whatever they've given me has taken the starch right out of me."

"Opium," Rett murmured as he and Ridge bent to help Sandicott out of bed. "They're poisoning you with opium."

"Shit. That's what I thought. I wasn't sure I'd live long enough to worry about it, but I've tried. No wonder it hurt so damned much." Sandicott tried to help, but the drugs made his movement uncoordinated.

"I'll hold you up," Rett promised. "And if necessary, I'll carry you. But we've got to go before people come back." Outside, they heard the sound of more broken glass, and Rett figured the ghosts were still putting up a lively distraction.

Ridge checked the hallway, as Rett half-carried, half-dragged Sandicott in his stained nightshirt and robe. They had managed to get slippers onto the lord's feet to protect him when they reached the caves.

"Go," Ridge hissed. They headed into the corridor, with Ridge taking the lead and Rett helping Sandicott stumble his way toward freedom.

"In there," Rett directed, and Ridge led the way into a small room at the end of the corridor, a place for servants to store linens and supplies. It hid a door to secret passageways that led down to the caves beneath the manor; an escape route built when the Sandicotts still earned their fortune from looting unlucky ships driven ashore on the rocks. Without Oliver's ghostly help, they never would have found the well-hidden door. Ridge removed a small lantern from his pack and lit it, holding it aloft so they could see in the lightless tunnel, and made sure to close the door behind them.

"How did you know?" Sandicott asked, trying and failing to take more of his own weight so he and Rett could navigate the narrow steps more easily.

"A ghost told us," Rett replied. "One who's very worried about you."

To Rett's surprise, Sandicott began to chuckle. "Oliver?"

"You know about the ghost?"

Sandicott nodded and then seized in a coughing fit. "Oh, yes. He's haunted the mansion for many years. Doesn't show himself to just anyone. My wife never saw him, nor my son. Curse their souls. But my father spoke to him often, and as the years went on, Oliver must have decided I was acceptable because he started to turn up, now and again. Didn't expect him to engineer a rescue."

"He had a little help," Ridge replied as he led the way through the cobwebbed passage. Clearly, no one had been this way in a long time. Rett dared to hope that extracting Sandicott from his captors might go smoothly.

"What's the plan?" Sandicott wheezed. "Beyond getting me out of that death trap."

"We know that your son and wife are loyal to the Witch Lord," Rett replied. "And we have some idea how dangerous Makary is."

"Damn right he's dangerous. Wily like a fox, and a traitor to the core," Sandicott returned, with a fire that told Rett not to count the old man out yet.

"King Kristoph doesn't understand the danger," Rett continued. "Some of his advisors think Makary's a fool."

"He plays one, but he's not," Sandicott said. "He's a snake."

"The king will listen to you," Rett urged. "You can change his mind about the Witch Lord. We have to get him to understand. And soon, because when he attends a dinner at Bleakscarp, your son and your wife intend to kill him."

Sandicott stiffened against Rett, taking his own full weight for the first time. "Kill the king? We can't let that happen."

Rett chuckled. "That's why we're here, m'lord. You might just be the most important man in the kingdom right now."

The pitch black of the passageway threatened to close in around Rett. Dust filled his nose and threatened to constrict his lungs. Sandicott tried to hold himself up, but he had been too weakened by the opium to have the strength necessary to completely bear his own weight, and the extra ballast made Rett unsteady on the stairs. Rett fought the growing claustrophobia, the feeling of being buried alive, and felt his heart pounding in his chest.

Behind them in the distance, they heard shouts and curses, and then the thud of footsteps as their passageway was discovered. Crashes and bangs accompanied the pursuit, giving Rett to believe that Oliver and his rowdy spirits had not yet spent their anger.

Ridge had already reached the bottom of the hewn rock steps and shoved open a heavy door at the bottom. The lantern's glow revealed a room that might have begun as a natural cave, but from the marks of picks and chisels on the walls, had later been expanded. Rocks littered the cave floor. Just a few dozen steps and they would be on the riverbank, where Henri and the boat waited for their getaway.

"Come on!" Ridge urged as the footsteps grew closer.

Rett nearly dragged Sandicott clear of the doorway. He and Ridge put their shoulders into shutting the door, but there was no latch and nothing to use to block it. They hurried to put distance between themselves and the passageway. From the other side, they heard a surprised yelp, more thuds and crashes, and a string of muted profanity.

"We're not alone," Ridge said, eying movement in the darkness.

Just then, the door flew open, and four large men appeared, dressed in the livery of Sandicott's estate.

"Let go of Lord Sandicott and stand aside!" The first man through the doorway ordered. From the bruise darkening on his cheek, Rett wondered if the man had been caught in the tumble down the stairs.

"So you can go back to poisoning him?" Ridge snapped. He stepped between the newcomers and Rett, who still half-carried the elderly lord, and set the lantern down carefully, never taking his eyes off the men. Ridge held a long knife in one hand, a match to the wicked blades held by the estate guards.

"You're a liar," the guard shot back. The three men stepped to flank him, presenting a solid wall of well-armed muscle.

Rett eased Sandicott to the floor and stood in front of him, guarding the man with his body. He had a knife of his own drawn from the sheath on his belt, and a dagger in his left hand. "No lies," Rett said, ready to fight. "You're not taking him back there to die."

The four guards surged forward, blades flashing in the lantern light, moving with training and skill. They were good, but they weren't Shadows. Still, close quarters and brute force strength made for dangerous combat, and Rett knew better than to underestimate the danger of a brawl.

Two men went for Rett, while the other two closed on Ridge. Sandicott scooted backward to get out of the way. Ridge's opponents launched themselves at the same time, slashing with their knives and thrusting with daggers to close him in and back him against the rough stone wall.

Ridge pivoted, dropped, and rolled, coming up to one side, close enough to sink his dagger deep into the nearest man's side and land a kick to the knee that sent the bleeding guard to the floor, writhing in pain.

Rett faced down his attackers, mindful of the injured old man on the cave floor behind him. One man ran at him while the other tried to circle to get to Lord Sandicott. Rett lunged at the closer man, meeting the man's blade with his own, feeling the strike of steel on steel reverberate in his bones. Rett had skill, but the other man had sheer strength. The guard broke off the clash of knives and thrust with his dagger, but Rett sidestepped; the blade tore his tunic but did not cut his skin.

A flurry of feints and thrusts kept Rett's attention on his opponent, while Ridge battled his remaining attacker. Rett knew that one of the guards headed for Lord Sandicott, who was cursing fluently and with more vigor than Rett expected. From the clatter, he was also throwing rocks, with enough force to make the guard cry out in pain as some of the missiles connected.

The temperature in the cave plummeted, and an unlikely rescue party of ghosts streamed down the steps. Oliver led the way, grim-faced and determined. Behind him came stable boys and gardeners, scullery maids and kitchen helpers, all of them angry and looking for someone on whom to take out their pent-up fury.

The ghosts swarmed around the guard who battled Sandicott, as Ridge and Rett dispatched the other three men who cried out in fear at the specters' attack. Rett's breath fogged and frost crept over the damp cave walls.

Ridge and Rett backed away, leaving the ghosts to their vengeance, watching in horror as the angry spirits pressed smotheringly close around the remaining guard until the man could no longer be seen, and only his muffled, panicked cries remained.

Then, silence.

The vengeful ghosts turned to acknowledge Sandicott, who stood on shaky legs partially supported by Rett. Oliver's spirit came to the fore and inclined his head. Then the ghosts vanished, leaving four dead bodies.

Rett started to move for the cave mouth, but Ridge thrust out his arm, blocking his way. "Wait. It's not over yet." He turned toward the deeper shadows of the cave. "Is it?" he asked the darkness.

Caralin stepped out, into the glow of the lantern. She had knives in both hands, but kept the weapons at her sides, pointed toward the ground. "Nice show," she said.

"Why are you here?" Ridge asked, his voice a low, angry rumble. "You intend to take us in? We're not going to go quietly."

"Leave them alone," Lord Sandicott spoke up, pulling away from Rett and managing to stand on his own, defiant and determined. "They came to rescue me. So help or get out of the way."

Caralin raised an eyebrow. "Interesting." She glanced from Ridge to Rett. "Kidnapping?"

"Protective custody," Rett snapped. "His wife and son want him dead to take over the title. There's more going on than you know, Caralin. Don't get involved."

"You're lucky I *am* involved," Caralin replied, slowly moving toward them, blades still lowered. "Lady Sandicott got word that the 'rogue assassins' were out to kill her husband. Burke sent me to 'defend' her."

"She and my no-good son are trying to kill me," Sandicott stormed. "Get your facts straight."

Caralin gave a dangerous smile. "Burke got your note," she said, looking to Ridge. "He believes you, but you can't come in yet. Too dangerous. I'm not the only Shadow who agrees with you, but I'm not sure who's solidly on your side."

"So we're still out in the cold," Rett replied, his patience wearing thin.

"For now," Caralin replied. "You need help getting Lord Sandicott somewhere safe?"

Ridge shook his head, unwilling to trust. "No thanks. We've got it figured out."

"I hope so," Caralin said. "I'll tell Lady Sandicott that I found the caves too late to stop you. Watch your backs. She knows if he reaches the king first, her plans all go to nothing. That'll make her even more dangerous. She's got nothing to lose."

Ridge jerked his head toward the cave opening, indicating for Rett to help Sandicott out to the boat. Ridge kept his weapons in hand and his eyes on Caralin. "Stay inside until we're out of sight," he warned as he reached the beach. Behind him, Henri had brought the boat to shore with Lorella already seated, and he and Rett helped the shaky older man aboard.

"I'm not your enemy," Caralin replied, remaining inside the cave. "And unofficially, I hope you win this. I'll help you where I can."

"Right now, anything you can do to buy us time would be great," Ridge said as he climbed into the boat, still wary. "And Caralin? Thanks."

Henri shoved off and clambered aboard, then he and Rett leaned into the oars, taking them out from shore and down the coast.

CHAPTER FOURTEEN

"Take me into the city." Lord Sandicott wore his dirty nightshirt with the poise of a man dressed for court. Ridge didn't doubt that the opium still affected Sandicott, but its grip had eased enough for his iron will to come to the fore.

"We'd best get you cleaned up and have a plan before we try to take you to the king," Ridge warned.

"Not the king. Not yet," Sandicott answered. "Lord Kronath will be at his residence in Caralocia. He never misses the social season," he added with a grumble that held a trace of fondness. "He's a good friend of mine. No fan of the Witch Lord's, either. And he's got the king's ear. My wife will make certain her lies reach the king. Kronath can intervene until we're ready to play our hand."

"How certain are you of his loyalty?" Ridge asked, trying to assess how clearly Sandicott was thinking. "We've broken some rules trying to get the evidence we need to turn the king against the Witch Lord. Right now, we're officially unwelcome."

"Gathered that from the chat in the cave," Sandicott snapped. "And I'm well aware that anyone loyal to the Witch Lord will see killing me as a way to curry favor, to shut me up before I can wreck their plans. But Kronath can help. I trust him."

Ridge looked over to Lorella, who sat quietly on the carriage seat beside Rett. She had barely spoken since they left the river. He wanted to ask what the ghosts had revealed to her and what she had seen of Oliver and his friends wreaking havoc at Bleakscarp, but he decided those questions could wait until they could speak privately.

"Can you ask the spirits to vouch for Kronath?" he asked.

Lorella looked up. Remaining an open channel to the spirits at the manor had taken a toll. She looked haggard, and she drooped in her seat. "Doubtful," she replied. "What we just did took almost everything I had. I don't have the energy to search for a spirit and compel it to talk to me."

"That won't be necessary," Sandicott replied. "I trust Kronath."

Ridge's eyes narrowed. "My lord," he began, trying to keep the stress from showing in his voice. "The fate of the kingdom may rest on your shoulders. We have to be careful."

"I was planning battles before you could walk," Sandicott grumbled. "I'm well aware of the risks. But we need Kronath. If I show up to tell my tale, Kristoph may be swayed by advisors who doubt me. But if Kronath supports us, Kristoph will be more likely to come to his own conclusions."

Ridge heard the exhaustion in the old man's voice, and while he had rallied for the fight, his words were beginning to slur once more. Henri had already made certain to have enough tincture of opium to help wean Sandicott off of the drug. The mixture awaited them with their hastily packed supplies and satchels in yet another bolthole apartment.

"Surely you'd like a chance to get cleaned up—" Ridge started.

"No." Sandicott cut him off. "Let him see me like this, see what they did to me. All the better to testify."

Ridge and Rett exchanged a look, and Ridge shrugged in surrender. He looked to Lorella. "You and Henri, head back to the new place.

We'll join you when we can. See what you can learn from the ghosts in the meantime."

Lorella nodded, taking his meaning. If things went badly with Kronath, Ridge hoped that she and Henri could work out something with the help of Oliver and the other ghosts to save the king.

Ridge looked at Lord Sandicott as Henri pulled the carriage up in front of the darkened residence. "You're sure about this, m'lord?"

"Yes. Now get out of my way before these damn shakes make this harder," Sandicott replied, and as he reached for the door, Ridge saw the way the man's hands trembled as the opium demanded its due.

Despite the cold, Sandicott shrugged off the blanket they had wrapped around him, heading for the door of his friend's imposing residence clad only in a nightshirt and slippers. He looked older than his years, hollow-cheeked and unshaven, and the shock of gray hair on his head stood out at all angles. Yet his blue eyes glinted with purpose, and he held his head high, squaring his too-thin shoulders as he slammed the knocker against the door.

A servant came to the door and eyed him with disdain, then attempted to shut the door. Sandicott's hand came up, blocking the door open with a stiff arm. "Lord Sandicott to see Lord Kronath," he barked in a tone used to being obeyed.

The servant's gaze went from Sandicott's ragged appearance to the two imposing, black-clad men behind him. "He's not to be disturbed."

"I'm disturbing him," Sandicott said. "He'll see me. This is a matter of security for the kingdom, dammit!" He threw his weight against the door, catching the servant off-balance, and stumbled into the entrance hall. "Beck!" he shouted at the top of his lungs. "Beck!"

Two other servants came running as Ridge and Rett muscled their way into the house to keep Sandicott from behind thrown out. "Beck! Get your ass down here. I need to talk to you!"

"Sir, if you would—"

"Sir, you need to—"

"That is entirely enough—"

The servants rushed to keep Sandicott at bay, but he slapped their hands and leveled such a lethal glare that all but the two boldest hung back. Finally, as Sandicott continued to shout, a man Ridge guessed to be the butler and another man each grabbed him by the arms and began to push him back toward the door, as Ridge and Rett blocked the exit.

"Let go of him!"

The butler and his helper dropped Sandicott's arms and took several steps back as a large man in a dressing gown lumbered down the steps. Beck Kronath looked to be at least a decade younger than Sandicott, in his middle years with graying temples and fierce, dark eyebrows.

"Cael?" Kronath gasped, taking one look at the disheveled man in his foyer. His eyes flickered to Ridge and Rett, and he caught his breath. "Are those Shadows? What are Shadows doing here?"

"Saving my ass from my no-good wife and son," Sandicott replied. "We need to talk."

A few minutes later, Sandicott and Kronath sat in front of a hastily stoked fire in a comfortable parlor, while Ridge and Rett hung back to guard the door and keep a watchful eye on the street outside the windows. The apologetic butler fetched hot coffee as well as a clean robe for Sandicott, then left them alone after Kronath instructed that no servants were to leave the house and that no one was to know of his visitors.

Ridge fidgeted as Sandicott spilled out his story. Kronath listened in silence to Sandicott's tale of betrayal, how the dosages had begun small and been increased until he could barely function, resulting in him being locked up his room, a prisoner in his own house.

"I ate as little as I could," Sandicott finished, "but if I didn't eat, they'd force that damned poison into my mouth." He yawned, fighting his body to remain awake. The tremor in his hands made holding his cup impossible. "I tried to wean myself off it, but I couldn't, not completely, damn it all."

Going without the drug for several hours was clearly taking its toll. Kronath sent his butler to fetch laudanum and waited while Sandicott took a dose. The tremors eased, but not the sweat that beaded his forehead or the restless tracking of his dilated eyes.

"And you believe it's all on account of Makary—the so-called Witch Lord?" Kronath asked, still looking a bit stunned at the story.

"My miserable excuse for a son is taken with the bastard," Sandicott growled. "Loves the idea that he might get to traipse around the palace, being 'important.'" Derision soured his tone. "And my wife cares far more for her position than she ever did for me. So yes, if this Witch Lord dangles the opportunity to become influential at court, to mingle with the hangers-on they see as important, they'd do anything to win that chance."

"Including kill the king," Ridge spoke up. Kronath's head snapped up. "We learned of a plot after an incident at Lord Rondin's—"

"I heard about that," Kronath replied, giving Ridge an appraising look. "I'd also heard someone made an attempt on his life."

"The only lives in danger were ours," Ridge replied. "We were able to observe a number of aristocrats in a private gathering with the Witch Lord. Lord Sandicott's son was one of them."

"And you believe Makary means to kill the king? For what purpose? To take his place?" Kronath's brow furrowed, as Ridge felt relief as he realized the man was taking their allegations seriously.

"We're not sure," Rett responded. "Makary himself may not want the visibility of being on the throne. He strikes me as the kind who would rather put his puppet there, and rule from the shadows."

His choice of words made Kronath's eyes narrow. "Speaking of 'shadows,' how is it the two of you are involved?"

Ridge drew a long breath. "We've suspected for a while now that Makary was more dangerous than many people—including the king—believed. We investigated, outside of official channels—"

"You're the two who went rogue."

Ridge found no reason to deny the truth. "Yes. To save the king. Because the Witch Lord's people will stop at nothing until they get what they want."

Kronath turned his attention back to Sandicott. "Damn. You've dropped quite a mess in my lap." He rubbed his neck, then stroked thumb and forefinger across his temples as if to ease pain. "What do you want me to do?"

"Talk to the king," Sandicott urged. "He listens to you."

Kronath moved to disagree, but Sandicott shook his head. "It's true. You know it is," Sandicott pressed. "We believe that my son and wife plan to kill the king at a party at Bleakscarp. We need to get a warning to Kristoph."

"We can't," Kronath replied, dropping back against the cushions. "He's gone hunting. No idea where. I believe he intended to come back to the Sandicott event before returning to the palace."

Ridge muttered a curse under his breath. "Are you invited to the party?" he asked.

Kronath nodded. "I had been looking forward to it. Been too long since we'd had a chat," he said, with a smile directed at Sandicott that faded as he took in his friend's appearance. "I would have preferred different circumstances."

"Going to the palace won't accomplish anything," Rett said. "No one will listen if the king isn't there, and Ridge and I can't get near the place without being clapped in irons."

"It wouldn't work, regardless," Kronath replied, and his face took on a shrewd expression. Ridge recalled that both Kronath and Sandicott had been generals for King Kristoph's father. "Too many people in the way. Even if you weren't wanted men," he added with a raised brow directed at the two Shadows, "we have no idea who inside the palace is indebted to Makary, or who his spies are. You can be certain that Makary would find a way to head you off. If he's the danger you say he is, he certainly has people placed to keep any suspicions from reaching the king's ears. The conspiracy may well reach the king's top council."

"They've certainly been the loudest at writing off Makary as nothing more than a short-lived fashion for empty-headed nobles," Sandicott grumbled.

"What would you have us do?" Ridge demanded.

"I believe you need to beard the lion in his den," Kronath said with a devious smile. "Imagine if Cael makes a back-from-the-dead appearance at the party at Bleakscarp. You can accuse the traitors in front of him, and it's going to difficult for anyone to gainsay you."

"And you think that's *less* dangerous than going to the palace?" Ridge challenged.

Kronath tolerated his insolence. "He'll have the two of you watching his back. I'll be there with you, to corroborate, and my guards will be present as well. And I can reach out quietly to some of the other nobles whom I know don't like Makary to test their support." He held up a hand as Ridge opened his mouth to protest. "I said, 'quietly.' I'm not going to tell them what's going on. Give me a little credit. I've won a war or two."

Sandicott remained adamant about staying on with Kronath. Ridge and Rett, after making sure that Kronath's home was well guarded, slipped out in the wee hours of the morning to go back to their new lodgings.

They were exhausted but jumpy from the adrenaline-fueled escape from Bleakscarp. After all the talk of traitors and betrayal, Ridge could barely keep himself from glancing over his shoulder, and he kept a knife in his hand. Kronath's certainty that the Witch Lord had spies and informants deep within the palace unnerved him, reinforcing his inherent distrust of everyone except Rett and Henri.

Rett looked equally haggard and uneasy. They said little on the way back, and without needing to ask, made a circuit of the block and a check of the front and rear of the decrepit lodging house that provided their new hiding place. Now that he saw it again, Ridge felt glad Sandicott had stayed with Kronath. He could not imagine bringing one of the lords of the kingdom to such a rathole.

The smell of cooked cabbage and the sound of a heated argument hit them as they came in. One tenant family had the two rooms downstairs, while Henri had secured the rooms above for them. In this neighborhood, no one paid much attention to their neighbors.

They stepped over the trip wire on the third riser from the top, a thin, strong piece of thread that could send a careless intruder tumbling, or at least jangle the bell attached to the trap as a warning.

They made sure to let their steps be heard as they approached, wary of taking Henri or Lorella by surprise. Ridge gave the coded knock, and the door opened to reveal both of the room's occupants ready for trouble. Henri held a wicked knife, and Lorella had a white-knuckled grip on a small axe.

Ridge grinned. "Easy. Just us." He and Rett stepped inside and closed the door. For good measure, Rett hesitated with his hand over the latch, concentrating. Ridge opened his Sight, just enough to sense a ripple of energy and figured Rett had added a magical safeguard.

"Where's your houseguest?" Henri asked, noting Sandicott's absence.

"Stayed with Kronath, which probably isn't a bad idea," Ridge said, stripping off his coat and hanging it near the door as Rett did the same.

"And you trust him?" Henri's flinty gaze revealed his skepticism.

"Sandicott does, and we weren't going to argue him out of it," Ridge replied.

Lorella motioned them toward a rickety table which held some bread and cheese and put a bucket of ale and two more tankards on the table.

"Eat. Drink. We've got news, and you can tell us yours," she said.

"News?" Ridge asked.

She nodded. "While you hobnobbed with nobility, I was talking to dead people. Oliver and his ghost servants are back in Bleakscarp, ready for revenge. They put quite a fright into Sandicott's wife and son. But good for us, the idiots don't know what to do about rampaging ghosts."

"So they're still willing to help?" Rett sipped his ale and reached for a piece of bread.

"More than ever. I think they enjoyed the fight." Lorella managed a tired smile. "Even more importantly, they're feeding me information. Apparently, Sandicott's son and wife came up with the story that the two of you attacked the manor to kill Sandicott, and they only barely fought you off."

Ridge swore. "So we're in more trouble now than we were before."

"Probably," Rett replied over a mouthful of food. "Let's hope Caralin was right, for all the good it'll do us."

"It explained the broken dishes, and provides even more of an excuse for Lord Sandicott to be 'indisposed' during the party," Lorella continued. "But in the meantime, they're frantic to find him. Oliver believes they're terrified that he'll expose them, and they've become even bolder about their plans."

Just as Ridge was about to launch into a recap of Kronath's plan, Rett gasped, then doubled over and pressed his hands to his head. Ridge ignored Lorella's puzzled expression and knelt beside his partner.

"Vision?"

"Like in the caravan," Rett grated, his voice tight with pain, cords straining in his neck as he tensed. "Sofen is sending someone to us."

Ridge gripped Rett by the forearms to steady him, afraid he would otherwise slide bonelessly from the couch. Henri hurried to pour him some whiskey and pressed a cup into Rett's hand. Ridge steadied the cup as he lifted it to Rett's mouth. Rett's whole form shook with the effort.

"That's it? Can't he just knock?"

The tripwire jangled the bell; then they heard a muffled curse before a quiet rap came at the door. Henri moved to answer, with a knife concealed behind his back. A boy who looked about twelve summers old stood in the hallway.

"Sofen said I have to talk to you," he said, and from his tone and stance, Ridge got the impression the visitor didn't agree.

"Come in," Henri said, standing aside, and then peering out into the hallway and looking both ways. "Were you followed?"

The boy rolled his eyes. "Give me some credit. I didn't make it this far being stupid, now did I?" He had the heavy accent of the waterfront poor. The way Ridge remembered Rett sounding when he first came to the orphanage, and for many years after.

"What's your name?" Ridge asked as Lorella made room for the boy to sit next to her on the bench. Henri checked at each window to assure no one lurked in the shadows, then went to bring some meat and cheese for their visitor.

"Hans." He had a wiry, underfed look, with a heart-shaped face and delicate features. From the size of his hands and feet, he had not yet hit his growth spurt, and a prominent Adam's apple bobbed in his skinny neck. Someone had cropped his dark hair so close he was nearly shorn bald, and Ridge wondered if it was to keep down lice.

"Why did Sofen want you to come, Hans?" Ridge wanted to reassure himself that Rett had recovered from the sending, and wondered what in the name of the Pit required putting Rett through the pain of telepathic contact.

"He figured out how to contact the others," Hans replied.

"Back up," Rett said, blinking back his headache. "How do you and Sofen know each other?"

Hans eyed Rett for a moment, head tilted and eyes narrowing. "You've got a touch of it," he said and shifted his attention to Ridge. "Less, but still some." He stared at Lorella a little longer. "Strong, but different." His gaze barely flitted to Henri. "Nothing."

"Looks can be deceiving, young man," Henri replied with an enigmatic smile.

Hans returned his attention to Rett. "We knew each other before he got taken. On the streets. I ran faster. They got him, and there were too many of them for me to fight," he added, a flush of shame coloring his cheeks.

"Sometimes it can't be helped," Rett replied, letting a bit of the wharf accent color his voice for the first time in years. "If you'd have fought, they'd have nipped you along with the rest of them."

Ridge saw the guilt ease in the boy's pinched features. "Maybe," Hans allowed. He paused. "He wants me to tell you that he figured out how to contact the ones who got sold. He thinks he can find them." His light blue eyes fixed Ridge with an implacable look. "He thinks you can help them," he added accusingly, gaze flickering to include Rett in his indictment.

"Where are they?" Rett asked. Henri brought parchment and pen to the table.

Hans seemed to focus on a spot just over Rett's shoulder, as his eyes glazed and he slipped into a trance. Speaking in a toneless voice, as if he were repeating what others told him, he named a dozen of the nobles and aristocrats, matching a captive child to each.

"Damn," Lorella muttered. "Those are some pretty important people."

"And they're aligning against King Kristoph," Henri replied quietly.

Hans came back to himself, shaking off the sending more easily than Rett ever had. That point obviously hadn't been lost on Rett, who shrugged away a moment's irritation. Ridge wondered why anything beyond using his Sight nearly brought Rett to his knees in pain but left Hans and Sofen unaffected. He resolved to ask his partner, once they were finished saving the kingdom.

"That's all very important," Rett said, as Hans looked around uncertainly to see how his news had been received. "You may help us save the king's life."

"Truly?" Hans stared at Rett, eyes wide.

Rett nodded solemnly. "Truly. Was there anything else Sofen wanted to tell us?"

Hans thought for a moment. "Yes. He says there's one of us in the place you're planning to go. The child—Sunny—can see things before they happen. She says 'don't go to the maze.'" Hans gave them a self-conscious smile. "I have no idea what that means."

"Neither do we, but it's important. We'll figure it out," Ridge assured him. They waited in silence as Hans wolfed his food.

"Do you need a place to go? It's not safe out there."

Hans gave a sharp laugh. "When's it ever been safe, mate? Never for folks like us. I'll be all right," he assured them. "Been on my own this long."

His face suddenly paled. "Shit. It's Sunny. She says—they're coming."

"How in the name of the Pit did they find us?" Rett protested.

"Grab everything you can't do without," Ridge said, standing. "We need to get out. Now."

Hans moved for the door, and Rett clamped a hand on his shoulder. "It's too dangerous. We'll get you out. Stick with us. Please."

For a moment, Hans looked as if he meant to argue. Then he

relented, nodding in agreement. Ridge thought he suddenly looked his age, young and scared despite his abilities and his street savvy.

"Come on," Rett urged, grabbing a few things around the sparsely furnished room. Henri packed supplies from their makeshift larder. It took only moments to pack since they had never really unpacked from the previous move.

Noise in the street outside told them the telepath's warning had been just in time.

"This way," Henri said, shoving aside one of the beds to reveal a trap door with a carpet nailed to it. "It's the reason I took this room," he said as he hauled open the door and his lantern showed stairs descending. "Certainly wasn't for the pleasant neighborhood."

Rett led the way, lantern in one hand, knife in the other. Lorella followed, then Hans, and Henri with another lantern and his knife at the ready. Ridge went last, lingering to pull the trap door and its camouflaging rug closed over their heads. Just as he yanked it shut, he heard the outer door splinter and voices shouting. He rushed to descend the steps.

"Hurry," he urged. "No guarantee they won't figure out where we went." He looked to Henri. "Where does this come out?" If his gut was right, they had descended below street level.

"Some of the old tenants were a bit dodgy," Henri replied with a smile. "It goes inside the wall, down to the old cellars. The basements run all throughout the city." Henri looked as if he relished the adventure.

"Hold up." Lorella lifted a hand, stopping in place. She closed her eyes, concentrating. Overhead, Ridge heard thumps, crashes, and cursing.

"Our rooms were haunted?" Rett asked, staring up as if he expected the roof to come crashing down.

Lorella opened her eyes and relaxed. "The whole city's haunted. You just have to know where to look." She dusted her hands together. "That should slow them down."

They moved through the narrow passageway until it opened into a low-ceilinged room that smelled of damp and disuse. Rett carved a

wider path with his knife, hacking through cobwebs that hung heavy
with dust and the dried husks of dead insects. Rats squeaked and hurried out of their way.

"Allow me." Henri moved into the lead, with Rett right behind
him, weapons at the ready. "I followed this to the end once, a year or
so ago when I took the lease." Ridge once again thanked their lucky
stars for their unpredictable valet. They picked their way through
rooms that had become the domain of wild animals, vermin, and
squatters. Lorella seemed unperturbed by the refuse and dirt, though
she was definitely on edge about something.

"Ghosts," she murmured. "All around us. Not sure of us. They
don't like being disturbed."

"And we don't like being hunted," Ridge replied. "Can we call a
truce?"

"Can you tell them we mean no harm?" Rett asked, with a glare at
Ridge. "And we'll be gone soon."

"They aren't the trusting type," the medium replied. Hans looked
from one side to the other, as if expecting a ghostly horde to materi-
alize. A cold breeze stirred the dust and fluttered the spider webs, making the dried insect carapaces skitter across the stone floor.

The temperature around Ridge plummeted, and unseen hands
shoved him hard enough that he stumbled. An icy force pushed him.
"Shit! What was that for?" Ridge gave a muted groan as another ghost
hit him hard enough to send him reeling. "Tell them to leave us alone!"
he called in a harsh whisper to Lorella as fists pummeled him.

Hans bit back a yelp as the ghosts yanked at his tunic to pull him
out of the way. Henri switched out his steel knife for an iron one, and
turned, brandishing both lantern and weapon.

"Everyone calm down!" Lorella commanded in a low growl. Ridge
and Rett froze, both now gripping iron knives from their belts. Hans's
eyes were wide. The cellar remained freezing cold, but the breeze
stopped, and the ghostly attacks ceased.

Lorella turned slowly in a circle as if addressing unruly children
gathered around her. "We are just passing through," she said to her
invisible audience. "We mean no harm. Bad people are chasing us, and

they'll kill us if we're caught. Please, let us pass. The men behind us are guards—bad guards. Take out your anger on them, if you need someone to hit."

For a moment, they all stood in silence. Then, the air warmed just enough to notice, and Ridge felt a sluggish cold breeze waft pass. "Are they gone?" he asked.

Lorella nodded. "They've moved toward where we came in, so if anyone follows, the guards will have a tough time of it."

"Thank you," Rett said, as Henri and Hans ventured back toward the group. "You're mighty helpful to have around."

To Ridge's relief, they faced no more ghostly opposition as they picked their way through the old cellars. Just making their way through the rooms posed enough of a challenge, forcing them to carefully maneuver around abandoned crates and barrels, broken bottles, and places where some of the ceiling had collapsed. The bones of small animals and a few emaciated human skeletons made it clear that plenty of creatures had crawled down here to die. He breathed a sigh of relief when they finally found a door that led into a back street.

"There are several other exits," Henri said in a low voice. "One of the things I liked about this location. Pity it didn't last."

"If it saves our asses just once, it's worth it," Ridge replied.

Henri opened the door cautiously, with Ridge and Rett right behind him, steel knives once again in hand. A few stone steps led up to the street. Women with baskets full of produce and bread from the marketplace vied for space with vendors and their pushcarts. Stray dogs darted around their legs, and children screeched to one another above the buzz of conversation.

They pulled their cloaks up to hide their faces. Henri took the lead, winding through the crowded alleys as if it were nothing more than a routine errand, and trusting Ridge and Rett to keep an eye out to make sure they were not being followed. Lorella and Hans remained alert, scanning for threat with their extra senses.

Despite their apparent safety, Henri took a circuitous route that frequently doubled back or looped around. No one else should have innocently kept the same route, making it that much easier to notice persistent "fellow travelers." To Ridge's relief, they made it without incident to their next bolt hole, a modest two-room lodging over an abandoned lacemaker's shop.

Henri led the way, quickly closing the shutters to avoid drawing attention to their lanterns. Rett lit a few more candles to help them get their bearings, while Ridge bent to start a fire in the fireplace to warm them from the bone-chilling cold.

"I'll bring the horses over in the morning," Henri said, setting his packs down and moving to the larder to ready a pot of tea and dig out some of the rations he had stocked for them a few weeks before.

"What now?" Hans blurted. He had remained silent throughout their escape when Ridge figured the odds were good he would try to bolt. Now, he shifted from one foot to the other, clearly uneasy.

"Now we plan," Lorella said, gently guiding him to a seat on the small couch near the fire. A thin film of dust covered everything, but for the most part, the rooms were ready to use. Their emergency hideouts duplicated enough necessities and a few comforts so that they could remain for as long as needed. Extra clothing, bedding, weapons, supplies, and long-lasting food and medicine, as well as a few bottles of whiskey, ensured they could pick up without much lost time. Most of their bolt holes were inside the main city, but Henri had secured them a few farther out in the countryside, in case the situation became truly dire.

"We'll need to look reasonably respectable if we're going to confront Sandicott's son at a party for the king," Ridge said, dusting off his hands as he got a fire blazing. "Rett and I will have to go back to Kronath's to work out the details."

Rett turned to Hans. "We need everything that the child prisoner at Bleakscarp can tell you," he said. "Even if it seems too small to matter. Anything Sofen passes along, too."

"Can I ever go home?" Hans's belligerence drained away to leave a tired, frightened boy.

"Where is home?" Rett asked gently.

"No place this nice," Hans admitted. "But I've got a brother and some others who depend on me. I make sure they eat, and I scare away bad people. I can't just leave them alone."

"The big event is two nights from now," Rett replied, with a wan smile of encouragement. "How safe it is after that depends on how that goes." He sighed. "As long as the Witch Lord and his followers have their eye on causing problems, anyone with your kind of abilities isn't going to be safe."

Hans nodded. "We're used to dodging the guards and the pick-pockets and the men who like to rough us up. We know not to let the monks know what we can do. But no one ever wanted to snatch us before."

Ridge felt for the boy. He had heard enough of Rett's tales of what it was like on the street to have a little insight, though his partner knew the hardship first-hand. He wished he could offer sanctuary with Lady Sally Anne, but even she couldn't take in every urchin from Caralocia, regardless of their talents.

"Let me work on that problem," Henri said as if he could read Ridge's mind. "I'll need to go out tomorrow for some fresh supplies and to get word of what's being said. I may have a few more resources I can bring to bear to make certain his friends are safe, if he will tell me how to find them." Hans hesitated, then nodded.

Ridge grinned at Henri. "Thanks. Don't know what we'd do without you," he replied. "But right now, we've got to save the king." Ridge shook his head and gave a disbelieving chuckle. "Two dishonored assassins, a valet, a medium, a clairvoyant urchin, and a drugged noble. By the gods, the odds are against us!"

Rett looked up at him. "You know better," he said quietly. "You've got to bet against the odds to win big."

CHAPTER FIFTEEN

"This might be the single most stupid thing we've ever done," Rett muttered under his breath as the large carriage pulled up to the main entrance at Bleakscarp.

"Probably not," Ridge replied. "But it's likely near the top of the list."

They sat in a luxurious carriage, accompanied by Lord Sandicott and Lord Kronath. Kronath kept a brooding silence that Rett couldn't decipher, and he spent part of the ride trying to figure out whether Kronath was worried about their chances, or merely angry at the Witch Lord's overreach.

Several days of rest and food, plus fresh clothing, a shave, and a haircut had done wonders for Sandicott, who managed to look imposing and dangerous instead of like a sick old man. Both nobles were resplendent in expensive brocade and silks, which stood out all the more compared to the plain, functional black worn by Ridge and Rett.

"Here we go," Ridge murmured as the carriage turned into the long lane approaching Bleakscarp.

Tonight, the manor hardly lived up to its name. Lanterns lit every window, candles in slitted pots lined the carriageway, and large bonfires dotted the grounds. The flag of Landria flew proudly from the highest tower, and the king's coach sat in a place of honor where all could see that His Majesty was an honored guest.

"Looks like they've got a full house," Rett observed.

"All the better," Kronath broke his silence. "More eyes to see the treachery unmasked."

"I'm ready to be done with this." Sandicott held himself stiff-spined like an old soldier, and his eyes glinted with anger, but Rett could see a trace of sadness and bitterness in his features.

"Are they expecting you to bring a guest, Lord Kronath?" Ridge asked.

A smile spread across Kronath's features. "Oh, yes. I told them I'd be bringing someone with me. I'm looking forward to this."

"I'm not pleased that neither of you is armed," Rett said.

"Can't bear weapons in the presence of the king unless you're a Shadow," Sandicott replied.

Rett didn't look at Ridge, but he could guess his partner's thoughts. *Are we still Shadows? Be a shitty time to find out we've been discharged.*

Ridge fidgeted on the seat beside him. Rett knew that Ridge had chanced another coded note, sent by urchin messenger, to warn Burke of the danger, since he was likely to be on hand personally to guard the king. He had not expected the warning to dissuade Kristoph from attending the dinner. But Burke's response when he saw them would say everything about how far he trusted his two wayward Shadows.

Henri had brought a second carriage, which was parked down the road a discreet distance away. He headed to make contact with his informant in the household.

Hans and Lorella slipped around to the other side of the manor, intent on freeing the prisoner, a child Hans called "Sunny."

Rett wished his companions luck. As the carriage pulled up at the manor's entrance, he hoped that luck held for them as well.

Kronath alighted first. Fawning servants rushed to greet him as he
ascended the steps. Sandicott followed a few paces behind, wrapped
in a cloak with the hood drawn up and his head bowed to hide his face.
Ridge and Rett followed, with cloaks that not only hid their identities
but also the weapons sheathed all over their bodies. Tonight, circumstances forced them to rely on knives, since swords, bows, and the
matchlock would not suit the close quarters of the Sandicott manor
and posed too great a threat to King Kristoph. Still, Rett lamented
having neither sword nor gun. Sandicott had not known how exactly
how his wife and son planned to kill the king, and despite Lorella's and
Hans's best efforts, neither the spirits nor the clairvoyant had been
able to find out. Lorella suspected that the Witch Lord might have
gifted his conspirators with amulets to make them more difficult to
read.

Forcing their hand with Sandicott's arrival might push the traitors
to desperate measures. Rett and Ridge were counting on Burke seeing
to the king's safety, since dealing with the accusations and their aftermath was likely to plunge them all into danger.

Rett's heartbeat sped up as they reached the top of the sweeping
stone steps leading into Bleakscarp's grand entranceway.

A chandelier blazed with hundreds of candles, their light reflected
from huge gold-framed mirrors that lined the foyer's walls. In one of
the nearby rooms, a string quartet played, and the music carried even
above the hum of conversation. In the center of the foyer, Lady Elsibet Sandicott and her son, Greorg, welcomed guests.

Rett only had seconds to form an impression. Lady Sandicott
looked at least a decade younger than her husband, with upswept dark
hair pinned with jeweled clips that matched the cascade of gems in the
necklace at her throat. Her gown showed her figure to good advantage,
a burgundy silk that played up her coloring. Although she chatted an-
imatedly with each guest who entered, the warmth never reached her
eyes, leaving her pretty in a hard way.

Greorg Sandicott stood a few steps to the right of his mother,
shaking hands and greeting their visitors, though his gaze often darted

away, and his hunched, stiff posture told Rett the man's mind was on other matters. He had expected a man plotting the murder of his father and the death of king would be older and felt surprised to discover Greorg to be only in his late twenties. The set of his jaw and the pressed line of his lips suggested a man used to getting what he wanted, who felt entitled to want everything.

"Lord Kronath! So delighted to see you again," Lady Sandicott gushed. Kronath removed his cloak and handed it off to the waiting servants, but Rett saw him palm a dagger as he did so.

"I wouldn't have missed tonight for anything," Kronath said in a booming voice that cut through the music and voices. "I take it the king has already arrived?"

Lady Sandicott's smile broadened. "Most certainly. His Majesty has just gotten settled in the main salon. I'll be glad to show you the way."

"And your husband? How is his health?" Kronath inquired, his tone solicitous.

Lady Sandicott managed to look downcast. "I'm sorry to say that he's not well at all," she said, as her son took a step closer, putting his arm around her shoulder for support. The gesture not only looked like playacting, but she actually flinched at Greorg's touch, making Rett wonder which one of them would eventually poison the other. "He's taken to his bed, unable to join us even for His Majesty's dinner."

"His poor health must be a weight on your mind," Kronath commiserated. "Have the doctors any hope?"

Lady Sandicott shook her head miserably. "None. It's so hard to see him waste away. I would give anything to see him restored."

"Would you? Let's see." Lord Sandicott raised his head, letting the cloak fall behind him. Ridge and Rett moved as one, tossing their cloaks at the servants to stall their interference, and stepping up to stand just behind Lord Sandicott, knives in hand as a warning.

Lady Sandicott paled. "You—you're not supposed to be here!"

Greorg froze, and where his mother radiated panic, cold rage animated his features. "I knew you wouldn't stay gone."

"I accuse you!" Sandicott's voice rose, loud enough that conversation stopped. "You poisoned me. Tried to kill me. And you are plotting violence against the king!"

"You've gone mad," Greorg retorted. "How did you leave your room? You're imagining things," he added, raising his voice as well to carry to the audience slowly gathering to find out the source of the commotion.

Rett saw several black-clad figures move closer as well. Burke and Caralin were among them, and some other Shadows whose estimation of Ridge and him were iffy at best. He saw Ridge stiffen and knew his partner had seen the threat out of the corner of his eye, but Ridge kept his focus on the drama playing out in the foyer, edging up so that he could easily throw himself between Sandicott and his wife if need be.

"Let me through!" King Kristoph's baritone sounded from the next room, and the crowd parted for the monarch.

"Sandicott? I was told you were too ill to join us."

"Lies, my liege," Sandicott said, remembering even in his anger to bow. "My wife and son have been poisoning me. They want to claim my lands and swear their allegiance to the Witch Lord."

"He's gone mad," Greorg countered. "It's the fever talking, Your Majesty. Our loyalty—"

"I can tell you everything," Sandicott said, taking another step so that he stood in front of the king, with his back to the still open door.

A shot rang out. A spray of blood and flesh splattered across the foyer. Ridge dove for the king, knocking him to the ground and covering him with his body. Sandicott sank to the floor, bloody. Greorg and his mother bolted in the opposite direction, plowing past servants and throwing furniture behind them to slow Rett's pursuit.

Rett sincerely hoped Ridge intended to follow, since he had no desire to try to catch Greorg and his mother by himself. "Stop them!" he shouted, but the servants, long conditioned to obedience to the lady of the manor, moved out of the way without thought.

Behind him, Rett could hear Burke already issuing orders to find the shooter. That freed Ridge and Rett to go after the traitors.

Rett dodged around the shocked servants and plunged down the

back corridor after the fleeing conspirators. Some of the servants, act-
ing in misguided loyalty, tried to stop him. He threw them out of the
way, nearly trampling one very determined young man who clung to
one ankle until Rett managed to kick free.

He burst from the servants' entrance and onto the wide, raised
back piazza. Two bonfires at its edge lit the start of the path that led
down to the garden. Torches on posts marked the approach to a maze
made of boxwood hedges that stood taller than a man, although a vel-
vet cord blocked off the entrance to the labyrinth.

"With you!" Ridge called from behind him, just as Greorg turned
and hurled something back toward them. It landed in one of the bonfires, which exploded a second later, hurling burning brands in every
direction.

"Didn't Sunny warn us not to go into the maze?" Rett huffed.

"If we stopped doing everything that was a bad idea, we'd never
do anything," Ridge replied. "Don't see that we have a choice about
it."

"Here we go!" Ridge yelled, never slowing. Together, Ridge and
Rett leaped from the piazza, cursing loudly as they flung themselves
over the flames. They landed in the gravel of the garden path and
rolled, patting themselves down where the flames had licked the edge
of their clothing and singed their hair.

Shoulder to shoulder, they ran after Greorg and Elsibet, gravel
crunching beneath their boots. Elsibet struggled to keep up the pace,
even with her skirts caught up in her arms. She kicked off her shoes
with their heels and slippery soles, and ran barefoot, stumbling when
the stones tore at her feet.

"Greorg!" she cried, reaching for her son, grasping at his arm.

Greorg eyed the two assassins closing the distance and tore loose
from her grip, then shoved Elsibet toward Ridge and Rett as he took
off toward the darkness of the maze.

"Nice," Rett muttered under his breath. "Keep going! I'll catch
up!"

Elsibet, once she realized that Greorg had left her behind, scrambled back to her feet and set out across the lawn. Rett caught up, his

long legs more than a match for her heavy skirts and bleeding feet. He grabbed her arm, and Elsibet wheeled on him, clawing at his face with her free hand.

"Let me go!" she shrieked. Her elaborately piled hair had started to come down from its pins, strands falling in her eyes. She kicked at his shins and tried to knee him in the groin, but Rett easily kept out of her way. He doubted hand-to-hand combat had been part of the upbringing of a noblewoman.

Rett jerked her wrist, and she cried out as he spun her around so that her arm wrenched behind her back. She tried again to kick him, and he swept her feet out from under her, controlling her fall and pinning her face-down on the lawn.

"You are charged with plotting the murder of your husband, and of the king," Rett said, surprised his voice sounded so steady given how hard his heart hammered. "I don't have a warrant for your execution—more's the pity—so you'll be restrained until you can stand trial for your crimes."

"You've ruined everything!" Elsibet screamed, anger contorting her features. Rett ripped away strips of cloth from the hem of her gown to bind her wrists and ankles.

"You can't just leave me here!" Even bound, she bucked and kicked.

"I'll be back for you," Rett assured her. "But first, I need to help catch your murdering spawn."

The maze had already swallowed up Ridge and Greorg, and Rett slowed as he reached the first branch in the labyrinth. His gut told him Greorg led them there for a reason because at face value the maze was a dead end. Sunny's warning suggested caution, and if Greorg took to the maze as his last refuge, Rett did not doubt traps awaited them. Rett stretched out his Sight, searching for Greorg, and sensed his presence close by. Then again, looking up at the man-high wall of thick shrubbery, Greorg could be on the other side of the hedge, and if he stuck to the maze, it might take Rett half a candlemark to get to him.

Rett added a bit of magic to his Sight, searching for Ridge. He found the familiar answering hum of power, and honed in on that, setting off at a jog.

Before long, he had Ridge in sight. "How did you know—" Ridge started to ask and broke off at the raised eyebrow in response. "Oh. You can do that?"

"Apparently so."

"We need to talk about that later. Could be handy if you can teach me how." Ridge put his hands on his hips. "You can sense him, too?" he asked, keeping his voice low.

Rett nodded. "Yeah. You can't?"

"I could see him when I came into the maze, and then lost him. So I was just about to try the Sight when you caught up."

"Why do you think he came in here, of all the places to run?" Rett asked as he and Ridge made their way forward with caution.

"Get enough guards, we can search the whole thing," Ridge thought aloud. "So he's either got an escape route or traps set—or both."

"I'm betting on both."

Now more than ever, Rett wished for his sword. Plunging a sword blade through the hedge reached a lot farther than his long knife, though at least in the relatively close quarters of the maze, the smaller weapon would not be so easily snagged.

"The girl they're holding told Hans we should avoid the maze," Rett pointed out.

"So of course, we ran right in."

"Story of our lives."

Rett ran the possibilities through his mind as they advanced carefully, far more slowly than he wanted to go, but paying heed to caution. *How long had Greorg planned an emergency exit?* he wondered. *Did Greorg always plan to lead pursuers into the maze, or was this a last-minute improvisation put together once he and his mother realized that Lord Sandicott had escaped?*

The answers mattered because they determined whether Greorg had months to set traps in the maze, or only a few days. Either way, the "surprises" would be dangerous, but a rushed, spur-of-the-moment set-up might be easier to defeat than one made even more lethal with the chance to test and perfect the traps.

The farther into the maze they traveled, the darker it got, despite the full moon overhead. Ridge started to move forward when Rett caught his arm and pulled him back.

"Look," Rett warned, and Ridge saw the candlelight glint on a thin line of spun silk that spanned the corridor like a spider web.

"That's not—"

Rett broke off a length of the nearby boxwood and swiped it downward, catching it in the thread and drawing it toward the ground.

Two blades popped out, one from each side, roughly on level with a man's head. Ridge's eyes widened.

"Shit. All right. Point made."

Ridge ripped a piece free from the bush next to him, giving them both something to poke with. Around the next turn, he found another trap, similarly constructed, only at ankle-height with blades that could have easily hamstrung a pursuer.

"Can you tell where he is?" Ridge asked quietly.

Rett paused, concentrating. "I don't think he's reached the center yet. Maybe he forgot where he put all his traps. I wouldn't think even he could just clear this at a dead run."

Caltrops littered the next stretch, sized to slow down men, not horses. The many-pronged steel stars covered the ground, requiring Ridge and Rett to sweep them away from step to step to avoid having the sharp points rip through the soles of their boots. Some were secured into the dirt, requiring the two assassins to step carefully. The dim light made it difficult, and more than once Ridge and Rett barely avoided a nasty injury that would have left one of them lamed.

Rett's Sight could keep them from taking wrong turns and going down blind alleys. He could not, however, anticipate obstacles and traps. So while they did not lose time on dead ends, their progress in the right direction seemed to come painfully slow.

"I'm going to kill that bastard twice for making us chase him in here," Ridge muttered as another turn revealed the next gambit. A net of knotted rope had been strung tightly suspended just inches off the ground, too wide to jump, and woven too openly to cross atop. That left them to choose between trying to dislodge the iron spikes that held it in place, sawing through the sturdy rope, or picking their way carefully through and trying not to fall on their faces.

"How in the name of the gods did he get across here?" Rett grumbled.

"Slowly, unless he knows a secret entrance," Ridge replied, opting to tiptoe through the net and hope for the best. "He knows what to expect, and if there's a trick to beating it, he's already got it mastered."

Rett caught his foot and nearly went sprawling, but he managed to make it across. At the sight of a *cheval de frise* blocking the entrance to the next turn, he let out a string of profanities.

Upright crossed boards studded with nails and cobbled together to serve as man-sized caltrops closed off the pathway. Rett frowned, noting where something had been dragged in the dirt.

"Look," he said, pointing. Ridge hung back as Rett investigated, realizing that Greorg would have had to move the barrier himself to pass by. Some effort pushed the blockade apart far enough for them to pass, a victory that still cost them time and awarded the advantage to their quarry.

Rett's Sight told him Greorg was close, just through the next hedgerow. He eyed the bushes, wondering whether he and Ridge could hack their way through fast enough to catch up to Greorg. The whiz of something flying overhead and the unexpected flicker of flame pulled him out of his thoughts.

"Drop!" Ridge yelled a second before the bomb hit. The *cheval de frise* blocked their escape, and the explosion crowded them up against the sharp edges of the barricade, spewing shards of its pottery vessel and splashes of hot oil. Gunpowder's acrid tang filled the air.

Just as Rett raised his head, another bomb came sailing over the hedge. He and Ridge curled into tight balls, putting their backs to the explosions. Their cloaks and clothing provided some protection, but Rett winced as pain lanced through him when sharp bits tore through unprotected skin.

Rett crawled back between the two halves of the barricade, dragging Ridge with him as a third bomb hit closer to where they had just been sheltered. While none of the explosives packed much of a punch from a few feet away, Rett had no desire to find out what a direct hit might do.

"Now what?" Ridge grated.

Rett reached out with his Sight, pushing hard to make a connection with Hans. He sent mental images of the attack and the impression of needing help. Ridge shook him by the shoulders, and he came back to himself with a gasp.

"You all right?"

Rett managed a wan smile. "Just sending a distress call."

Ridge gave him a look. "Hans?"

"Worth a try."

One more bomb lit up the maze; then everything went quiet. Ridge slowly rose. "I'm done with this shit," he muttered, "let's change the rules." He raised his knife and hacked into the dense, woody hedge-row. Rett joined him, and several minutes later, they emerged in the next corridor, bloodied with scratches and covered in bits of box-wood.

"Why do I stink like cat piss?" Ridge said, sniffing at his clothing.

"That's the boxwood. It's even worse when it rains," Rett said. To no one's surprise, Greorg had vanished.

"Cutting our way through isn't going to get us anywhere fast," Ridge admitted, looking ruefully at where they had chopped through the maze. "And we're easy pickings when we're stuck in the middle."

"It was worth a try."

"We've got to be close to the center," Ridge said as they ran through the next two turns unopposed.

"Might be a hidden way down into the caves there, like where we brought Sandicott out," Rett mused. "If so, Greorg's going to want to make sure we don't follow him down. Easier to fight us here than down in the caves."

No sooner had he spoken, than a loud boom sounded close by, and something tore through the hedgerow, barely missing Ridge's arm.

"Hand cannon!" Ridge hissed, grabbing Rett and pulling him

down and forward. They crawled, keeping to the far side of the corridor, trying to put distance between themselves and where Greorg reckoned them to be.

Another shot came minutes later, and Rett thanked the stars the unwieldy weapons took time to reload. This time, the lead ball burst through the shrubbery lower, at knee height. It would have crippled a standing man and might have killed one of them had the bullet hit them in the torso as they crawled.

"He sure didn't have that hand cannon when he ran from the house," Ridge muttered.

"He must have left supplies for himself along the route," Rett returned.

They stood and started to run when a third shot fired. This one came at an angle, shooting down the corridor toward where Greorg guessed they might be. Ridge missed it by a couple of strides, but the bullet tore into Rett's leg, and he went down hard.

Rett clamped his hands over the wound and felt blood leaking between his fingers. He hissed in pain. Ridge knelt beside him, prying his hands away to see the wound, mouth set in a hard line. "Maybe I'll kill him three times," Ridge murmured, ripping away the tattered remains of Rett's pant leg and tying it as a makeshift bandage.

"Wait here," Ridge said, starting to rise.

Rett grabbed his arm and yanked him back down. "You're not going without me." He gritted his teeth and gripped Ridge's shoulder hard, forcing himself to his feet by sheer willpower. "Come on. I get to kill him at least once."

The still air turned suddenly cold enough for Rett to see his breath. The wind picked up, a biting chill out of nowhere. Rett smiled. "Thank you," he whispered. "Bring him to us. Keep him out of the center."

A gust tore past them into the maze, unhampered by the dense boxwood or Greorg's traps. Ridge got a shoulder under Rett's arm, and together they made their way forward, keeping their knives in hand, ready to settle the score.

Down the next corridor, they found the hand cannon, abandoned and out of ammunition. "Come on," Ridge urged. "I think he's running out of tricks."

Rett set his jaw and forced himself to keep up. Blood leaked from the bandage on his thigh, and he felt light-headed. Still, he'd been lucky the shot hadn't hit bone. If it had shattered his knee, he'd have probably lost the leg. As it was, he bet it went all the way through the meat of his thigh, and the pain was intense but far less than facing the surgeon's saw.

The wind howled through the maze, kicking up dust and debris, yet the direction of the gusts rushed toward the center, toward Greorg. "Look!" Rett said, pointing. Between the moonlight and the torches that ringed the maze, the sky was not completely dark. A maelstrom twisted up from a spot a few turns of the maze away, and Rett grinned despite his pain.

"Lorella's rounded up some ghosts for us," he murmured. "Let's go. They'll herd him to us." The chance for a win and the opportunity to vindicate themselves gave him the strength to ignore his pain and hobble on.

A man's scream sounded from the depths of the maze. The wind's howl had changed to something far more chilling. Rett heard disembodied voices, calling Sandicott's name, keening and screeching, and they drove Greorg like the baying of hounds.

Together, Ridge and Rett prepared to make their stand as the ghosts pursued Greorg, forcing him toward them. They took up positions blocking the corridor, knives ready. Rett's nose twitched, trying to make out an odd smell. In the other portions of the maze, the scent of boxwood was strong, but now, the new smell overpowered it. Then he looked down at their feet and the stretch of gravel between them and the next corner. The ground looked wet, darker than it should have been, and Rett realized what he smelled, with a sick knot in his stomach.

"Ridge—"

"He's coming!" Ridge cut him off before Rett could sound the warning.

Running footsteps pounded closer. Somewhere in the maze,

Greorg had lit a lantern, and the light swung crazily as he ran. As soon as Greorg cleared the corner, Ridge let two throwing knives fly in quick succession. One pegged Greorg in the left shoulder, while the other struck him in the thigh.

"Greorg Sandicott—you are charged with high treason against King Kristoph. An open warrant on traitors calls for your immediate execution. Agree to cooperate and tell us all you know about the Witch Lord, and you may receive mercy," Ridge read out the warrant, a third knife already in hand. If Sandicott refused, the blade would find his heart. At this distance, Ridge wouldn't miss.

"Go to the Pit," Greorg snarled. He raised the lantern over his head and smashed it a few feet ahead of where he stood.

"Get back!" Rett yelled. "The path is soaked in oil!"

Even as he spoke, the flames from the broken lantern licked at the oil, turning into a sheet of fire that spread rapidly. "If the bushes burn—" Rett warned.

"I'll be back," Ridge said, and ran forward at full speed, leaping into the air and nearly clearing the flames. He came down on the other side on top of Greorg, and through the smoke and fire, Rett could make out the two men battling.

Ridge had training, but Greorg's courage came from desperation. Maybe he feared the executioner, or perhaps he dreaded the Witch Lord more. Greorg tore loose of Ridge's grip and flung himself into the fire, where the flames roared the highest.

"Ridge—get out of there!" Rett shouted, watching in horror as Greorg's clothing caught fire and he spread his arms wide, welcoming the consuming flames. Fire crackled at the base of the hedge, and the woody branches began to smoke. In his current condition, Rett knew he'd never make it through the maze and back to the entrance before the whole thing became a bonfire.

Ridge hurled himself at the untouched bushes a few feet back from the flames, tearing his way through with his knife and his hands. "I'm coming!"

The fire licked at the boxwood, catching quickly in the thin, dry shrubs. Rett hobbled away from the flames, and his leg nearly gave out on him. If he didn't collapse from the injury, the blood loss would get him long before he staggered out of the maze.

Ridge ripped his way through the thick wall of bushes, worse for the wear. One eye had begun to purple from Greorg's punch, and his face and hands were bloody with deep scratches from the unforgiving boxwood.

"Go on," Rett said, coughing at the rising smoke. "I won't make it. Get out. Clear our names with the king."

"Screw that," Ridge said, slipping under Rett's shoulder again and sliding one arm around his waist. "I'm not leaving you behind."

"I'm just going to hold you back, and the fire's spreading fast."

"Call your ghost friends," Ridge ordered. "They helped get us into this mess. They can find a way to get us out of it."

Rett closed his eyes once more, calling on his waning power. He knew he was nearly spent, both of energy and magic. If this didn't work—

He felt the flutter of spirits and in the distance, the touch of another power, maybe Hans, possibly Lorella. Perhaps even the prisoner, Sunny. He didn't care, so long as help came.

Please. Help us. We'll burn.

The cold wind struck up once more, rushing past them into the thick, twisting walls of boxwood. The ghosts ripped a wide opening in the next wall of shrubbery, and the noise of breaking wood and roots being pulled from the ground sounded like an earthquake. By the time the ghosts reached the next concentric corridor, they chose a new tactic and flattened a path through one hedgerow and then the next, mowing down the sturdy old bushes as if they were saplings, plowing through until the wide lawn opened up beyond.

Rett felt the heat of the flames on his back, and he and Ridge wasted no time, moving as fast as they dared over the fallen boxwood, picking through the tangle of branches that pulled at their clothing and snared their feet.

"Hang on," Ridge said, and before Rett could protest, he was slung over his partner's shoulder, hanging head down. "Shut up. It's this or bake."

Ridge managed to increase his pace, even carrying Rett. From where he hung, Rett watched the flames overtaking the rest of the maze as the fire spread quickly through the tall labyrinth walls.

"Shit! Ridge, he's still coming after us!" Rett warned, watching in horror as a burning man stumbled after them, shrieking and flailing.

"Gonna have to catch us first," Ridge grated, his voice hoarse with smoke.

Each step jolted Rett's bleeding leg, and he gritted his teeth, trying not to pass out from the pain. He looked up to see Greorg almost within arm's length. Ridge stepped wrong and went down on one knee, nearly toppling Rett from his grip.

Greorg loomed behind them, his hair and clothes aflame, skin charred and beginning to slough from his body. He stretched out an arm, blackened fingers clawing to get a grip on Rett's jacket and pull them back into the inferno.

Rett slashed at the burning figure with his knife, feeling the skin blister on his hand and his face redden with the heat. The blade cut through Greorg's wrist, and with a final cry of pain and fury, Greorg fell back into the maze that had become his pyre.

Ridge pushed to his feet, staggering forward until at last, they reached the grassy expanse that led up to the back of the manor. With a final grunt, he tipped Rett from his shoulder. Rett's knees nearly buckled, but he managed to stand. Flames rose from the maze high into the sky, as the outer rings caught fire and the flattened swath sent sparks into the dry lawn.

"Breckenridge! Kennard!" Four figures clad in black rose from cover, surrounding them. With a weary glance at Rett, Ridge lifted his hands in surrender. Rett did the same, letting his weapon fall.

"I should beat your asses and leave you for the crows." Burke stepped up; jaw set, eyes blazing, and arms crossed as if he awaited a confession.

"Does it count that we saved the king's life?" Ridge asked, managing a hopeful expression.

Burke scowled. "Unfortunately, yes."

Rett's breath caught in his throat. "Yes?" he asked, his smoke-clogged throat making the word almost a squeak.

Burke's eyebrow rose at the sound. "I'm going to pretend I didn't hear that," he said. "We're here for a rescue, not an arrest. What in the name of the Dark Ones were you thinking, running off like that?"

"I was thinking that Greorg would get away," Ridge replied, his usual confidence returning.

"What about Sandicott?" Rett gasped, remembering. "Someone shot him—or were they aiming for the king?"

Burke grinned. "Either way, there's a cell in the dungeon waiting. Caralin caught the marksman before he got far. Damn, she can run. Don't imagine he ever saw her coming, either. All the other guests are sequestered in the mansion, so none of them could run off and warn anyone else if they were in on the plot."

"Lady Elsibet—" Ridge began, realizing that the noblewoman they had tied up and left on the lawn was nowhere to be seen.

"She's inside. Where you need to be. King's orders."

Ridge and Rett exchanged a glance, and Rett felt his stomach tighten. Despite Burke's assurance that the Shadows had come to protect them, being brought before the king was no small occurrence under the best of circumstances. Bloodied and scorched, reeking of smoke and covered with twigs and leaves, and with Rett barely standing, they could hardly present a worse impression.

"Well then, by all means, lead the way," Ridge replied, but Rett could hear the nervousness beneath Ridge's cocky facade.

Chapter Sixteen

Ridge had seen King Kristoph at a distance many times. Sometimes that had been when his duty as a Shadow meant protecting the king amidst the crowd at a celebration or royal proclamation. Once or twice, he and Rett had helped keep order in a crowd of hundreds, instead of thousands, at a ball or reception in the palace.

Facing the king in a parlor and being the focus of his attention was something else entirely.

Ridge side-eyed Rett and saw his partner chewing his lip worriedly as they waited outside the room for Burke to return and present them. "I bet King Kristoph changes his socks like everyone else," Ridge murmured in an attempt to ease the tension.

Rett managed a grateful half-smile, but the worry did not leave his eyes. "Think they'll let us share a cell?"

Ridge smirked. "With the way you snore? We'll be lucky they don't drop us in a well and be done with us." His gut twisted, despite his attempts to sound unconcerned. Burke and the other Shadows might have been sent to back them up, but that didn't mean all was forgiven. Even though he had tried to keep Burke informed—with the intent of begging forgiveness later—their leader had a reputation for biding his time and holding a grudge. Going rogue very well might be an unforgivable offense.

Blood stained Rett's pant leg where he had been shot. Burke had given him an elixir for the pain and bound up the wound, but Rett still limped and looked pale, as if he might faint if forced to stand too long.

"His Majesty will see you now," Burke said, opening the door. As they passed by him, he caught Ridge's eye. "Don't muck this up."

Ridge squared his shoulders and lifted his chin, as much to encourage Rett as for his own morale. They had done what experience deemed necessary to protect king and kingdom. He might be forced to apologize, but he wouldn't repent one bit.

Kristoph sat at one end of the parlor, in the largest, most throne-like chair available. To his right, Lord Sandicott looked hard used, with a blood-soaked bandage wrapped around his shoulder, but for all that he had recently endured, he seemed to be holding up surprisingly well. Lady Sandicott, still bound hand and foot and now gagged, had been deposited on a chair against the wall, guarded by two Shadows. While Ridge and Rett had been in the maze, apparently the rest of the dinner guests had been sent elsewhere, likely taken upstairs for questioning. To Ridge's relief, Henri and Lorella were nowhere to be seen, and neither were Sunny and Hans.

"So you're the Shadows responsible." King Kristoph's voice was as big and booming as one might suspect given the look of him. He stood a few inches taller even than Ridge, with broad shoulders and powerful arms, a giant of a man, battle-forged and serious. Though only in his late fourth decade, gray flecked his dark blond hair and his full beard. Unreadable gray eyes regarded Ridge and Rett, and Ridge resisted the urge to either bolt from the room or kneel and beg for pardon.

"That all depends, Your Majesty," Rett mustered up enough breath to respond. "Responsible for what?" Ridge's partner could hardly put weight on his injured leg and barely escaped a lethal fire, but he stood at attention and answered his monarch with a steady voice.

Kristoph regarded Ridge and Rett in silence for so long that Ridge felt cold sweat bead on his back. "I've had reports of you from some of my nobles," the king said after an uncomfortably long pause. "Lord Rondin did not speak favorably."

"We can explain, Your Majesty," Ridge began. Kristoph held up a hand and Ridge's mouth snapped shut.

"Duke Barton, on the other hand, attested that you foiled a plot by his brother to involve him in treasonous affairs without his knowledge. And Lord Sandicott informs me that the two of you saved his life and mine." Those gray eyes seemed to see through Ridge down to the bone.

"Given the testimony Lord Sandicott provided—and what we have gained under duress from Lady Sandicott—it would appear you have uncovered information of great importance. I'd like to hear it."

Ridge swallowed hard and cleared his throat, finding his mouth dry and his breath shallow. "It's a bit of a long tale, Your Majesty."

"I have all evening, since the dinner—and my assassination—have been called off."

Rett gave a slight nod, and Ridge took a deep breath. "The crux of it is, the Witch Lord is more dangerous than many have assumed. We've been gathering evidence to prove that he is instigating rebellion against the throne and gaining the support of nobles who find his ideas enticing."

"Go on."

Ridge licked his lips, doing his best to avoid throwing up from the nervous clench of his stomach. He could taste bile in the back of his throat. "Very well," he said, wondering if he was signing both their warrants and launched into the whole, sordid story.

Kristoph listened intently, and the further into the details Ridge got, the darker the king's expression grew, mouth set and brows furrowed. Rett nodded from time to time in silent support. Ridge left out anything about their Sight or Rett's magic, but could not completely omit Lorella's role or that of the clairvoyant children. A glance in

Burke's direction suggested their leader was distinctly unhappy to be hearing most of the information for the first time.

"...and that's how we ended up chasing Greorg into the maze, Your Majesty," Ridge finished, wishing he dared wipe the moisture from his sweaty palms.

"About that," the king said, studying Ridge and Rett curiously. "I'm told your exit from the maze was hardly customary. Your fellow Shadows attested to seeing, and I quote, 'the hedge ripped apart as if by two strong, invisible hands and then flattened like the sweep of a god's arm.'"

"Quite poetic, Your Majesty," Ridge replied. "But we had nothing to do with it. Not really. The ghosts had a bone to pick with Greorg, and they got their chance. We were just lucky it cleared the way for us to get out." What he said was true...and what he didn't say wouldn't be noticed by anyone but Rett.

"Ghosts?"

"Old houses like this are often haunted, Your Majesty. Apparently, some ghosts are loyal even after death." He thought about Oliver and the ghosts at Duke Barton's home and wondered who all the nameless spirits had been who came to their rescue in the maze, and how they owed their loyalty to the lord of the manor.

Kristoph's eyes narrowed as if he suspected there was more to the tale, but he did not press. "Your accusations are most disturbing," he said. "It would seem that Yefim Makary bears more scrutiny, as do those who flock to his teachings." He frowned once more. "About these children—"

Ridge had omitted any mention of such a child in Sandicott's household, and he hoped the lord had remembered their plan not to mention Hans or Sunny. "The children we rescued from the caravan are under the protection of Lady Sally Anne at Harrowmont," he replied. "She's been most gracious and has offered them a permanent home with her." As they spoke, Henri and Lorella should have been on their way to Harrowmont to add Sunny to those in Lady Sally Anne's care, while Hans insisted on returning to help his brother and the other urchins he protected.

"I see. And the others you were not able to recover?"

"Still being held prisoner but we have discovered which of the nobles purchased them," Ridge replied. He saw a flare of anger in Kristoph's eyes and knew that regardless of what the king thought of children with magical abilities, he despised slavers.

"I'll want that list as soon as you return to the city."

Ridge inclined his head in acknowledgment. "Of course, Your Majesty."

"And these children…is this something for the monks to handle?"

Ridge drew a long breath. He had anticipated the question, and while he did not want to lie to the king, at the same time, he had no intention of putting the children at risk for abilities that had already caused them so much hardship. "Makary's promises are built on lies. It would be like him to concoct a story about seers and fortune tellers, and then kidnap regular children and pass them off as something they weren't, Your Highness."

Kristoph's expression suggested he was not entirely persuaded on the matter, but he let it rest. "I will see that any children enslaved be freed and any nobles found to be involved in such matters will be punished. It appears that the crown owes you and your partner a debt, in spite of somewhat…irregular…methods."

Ridge blushed in spite of himself. "Thank you, Your Majesty," he replied, and Rett murmured the same.

"If you have no more to recount, you are dismissed," Kristoph continued. "My physician will tend your leg." He paused. "I will leave the handling of those…irregularities…to Burke, with the note that your monarch is deeply grateful, and wishes to acknowledge the courage and personal risk necessary to uncover traitors to the crown."

Ridge almost choked when he saw a hint of a smile touch Kristoph's mouth and the barest wink.

Burke bustled them out before Ridge could put his foot in his mouth, leading them into the kitchen where he sent a servant to fetch the king's physician. He pulled out two chairs from the table and glowered at his wayward assassins. "Sit."

Ridge and Rett did as they were told. From the way Rett winced,

Ridge knew his partner was in pain and probably light-headed from his injury. Burke seemed to notice as well because he spoke to a kitchen maid who returned with a glass of whiskey for Rett. He pointedly did not offer the same to Ridge.

"When we're back in the city, I want you to go over your story again," Burke said evenly, with an expression that let Ridge know they were not off the hook. "Just in case there are details you remember that might have been omitted in the excitement of the evening."

Ridge had no intention of telling Burke more about either the children or the magic that had enabled them to track down the culprits. He hoped to keep Lorella out of the story as much as possible, for her safety. The less Burke knew, the less he would have reason to worry. The way Ridge looked at it, withholding troublesome information was a kindness.

"What's going to happen to Lady Sandicott?" Rett asked. Ridge could hear the strain in his voice.

"She'll stand trial for treason, with her husband testifying against her," Burke replied, stepping out of the way as a balding man with a fringe of gray hair strode into the room and started ordering the servants to fetch him supplies. "It's going to be an utter mess."

Burke retreated to let the physician look at Rett's wound. Despite his bluster, the doctor's examination proved thorough, and he treated the injury proficiently.

"Stay off that leg for a couple of weeks," the physician ordered as he stood, glowering first at Rett and then at Burke, who had the good sense to hold up a hand in appeasement.

"Whatever the doctor orders," Burke replied.

"Ruddy soldiers. Think they're invincible," the man groused. "Think they've got to prove they're tough. That's a load of shit. If you bleed, you need to heal—same as everyone else. Am I making myself clear?"

Rett hid a smile at a tirade that was obviously aimed at Burke. "Completely, sir."

"Good. Change the dressings, keep it clean, and use the salve I'll give you, and if infection doesn't set in—and you don't push too hard—you should be good as new."

Rett and Ridge thanked the physician, who bustled out. Burke looked ruffled by the doctor's rant.

"Don't think that means you can lounge around, being useless," Burke cautioned. "There's plenty you can do without needing to stand. Cleaning swords. Research. Interviewing informants. I'll come up with a list for you."

"Happy to oblige," Rett replied. Ridge heard the sincerity in his partner's voice. After the close call they'd had in the maze, he suspected Rett felt grateful—and a touch guilty—enough to do whatever penance Burke demanded.

"And you're not automatically forgiven, just because of His Majesty's gratitude," Burke said, glaring at Ridge. "Your definition of 'leeway' and mine apparently need to be reconciled."

Ridge managed to look appropriately abashed. "Understood."

"Do you think this will make the Witch Lord back off?" Rett asked, perhaps figuring that his injury would win him a little forbearance.

"Honestly?" Burke asked. "No. I don't think men like Makary give up that easily. They're in it for the long slog, because the prize is so rich. Revolutions have casualties. There are plenty of loyal nobles, but there are always enough aristocrats who've got their noses out of joint over one imagined slight or another. I think Makary's a devious bastard, and he'll regroup and come at us from a different direction."

Burke gave them an evil smile. "Which is one way you're going to make this up to me. By training the rest of the Shadows on what you've learned about the Witch Lord, and—once Kennard here is fully healed—doing extra training sessions to make sure you and your fellow assassins are in peak condition."

Burke glared at Ridge as if daring him to object, but Ridge just managed a rueful half-smile. "Thank you. Sir."

For a moment, Burke stared at him, assessing the sincerity of his too-easy surrender, then muttered an expletive under his breath. "You're both going to be the death of me. I'll see you back in the city. Sandicott agreed to allow you to stay the night here. Report for duty in the morning." With that, he left them in the kitchen and headed back to the rest of the team.

"Could have gone worse," Ridge said.

Rett glared at him. "Absolutely. We could have been beheaded, tossed into an oubliette, drawn and quartered, hanged, or just banished."

"As I said," Ridge replied, refusing to take the bait. "Come on. If we're not needed here, let's get some rest, before Burke changes his mind."

EPILOGUE

"Son of a bitch." Ridge and Rett stood across the street from the burned-out remains of their most recent haven. Little remained beyond charred support beams and wreckage. While the flames had died down, smoke still rose from the ashes.

"Someone set this after what happened at Bleakscarp," Rett said, jaw tight with anger. "Makary must have had someone inside Sandicott's household, or someone at the dinner who rode straight to give him the news. There'd be no other way he'd have heard about it and had time to send someone to burn the place down before we got back."

"Maybe he wasn't trying to do it before we came home," Ridge mused. "Maybe he intended for us to be there when it burned. I don't think he likes us."

"How many places do you have set up that we haven't used?" Rett asked Henri, who had just returned from taking the children to Harrowmont. Henri stood beside them in the early morning cold, staring at the burned-out husk.

"In the city? Three. At this rate, I'll need to set up a whole new set of apartments before long. Good thing they're under false names. People might think we attract bad luck," Henri replied.

"And they'd be right," Rett said. Ridge accepted the setback with his usual aplomb; something Rett had learned long ago had more to do with fatalism rather than serenity. Ridge had always been that way, from the time they were in the orphanage, accepting whatever blows fell with resignation as if it were to be expected and somehow deserved, and then soldiering on.

Fuck that. Rett had never held much with acceptance, and he sure as blazes didn't believe they deserved the hand they'd been dealt. The lessons of the streets had etched themselves in Rett's bones and scratched their laws into his soul. Loyalty to those he claimed as family and vengeance against those who dared to threaten them. And right now, standing in a cold drizzling rain, his leg throbbing with Greorg's bullet wound, and their comfortable lodging gone up in flames, the fight against the Witch Lord became personal.

"I'm going to get that bastard," Rett muttered.

"And I'll be beside you all the way," Ridge replied. "But right now, the rain is running down the inside of my shirt, I'm cold and hungry, and I still smell like smoke. I want dry clothes, a hot meal, and a warm bed, and our gods-damned house is gone!"

"Follow me." Ever-unflappable, Henri led them to the stable where their horses were boarded, settled up with the stable master, and headed back into the city. Even Ridge's grumbled imprecations seemed to have no effect on their squire's calm demeanor. Rett had no idea how the man managed, especially since he had to contend with the two of them, on top of their circumstances.

Henri's route doubled back on itself several times, necessarily circuitous despite the miserable rain in case anyone followed them. Finally, when Ridge's silence had grown worrisome, and Rett's temper neared its breaking point, Henri stopped in front of a brick building.

The tall, narrow building had once been something official, though it now stood abandoned and in disrepair. The bottom windows had been nailed up with boards.

"This way," Henri said, leading them around back. They tethered their horses to a post and followed Henri up the rear steps after he unlocked a suspiciously new padlock on the door. Rett's limp slowed him, but he waved off any help. Despite the outer appearances, the inside looked solid and in surprisingly good shape.

A door at the top of the steps opened into a space with two medium-sized rooms and a third small area that could serve for larder and storage. Henri had provisioned it and their other bolt holes some time ago, with duplicate supplies and essentials. One room had a fireplace and held three cots and a trunk that was doubtless filled with clothing as well as basic weapons. The second room had chairs, a table, and a small couch. Rett snorted in amusement when he saw that the table held a deck of cards and a full bottle of whiskey. In the small room, Rett glimpsed jugs, jars, and tins of supplies on the shelves that lined the walls.

"I like it," Ridge said, stepping inside. Despite a thin layer of dust, the room had a cozy feel. "Just the right size and the building is brick, so maybe it won't burn as easily."

"Certainly my hope," Henri replied.

Rett took a deep breath, trying to let go of his anger at the Witch Lord, at least for now. He clapped a hand on Henri's shoulder. "Nice job," he said, moving past Henri to rearrange the shutters to allow more light, as Ridge stacked wood in the fireplace to start a fire. Henri looked quite pleased with himself as he hung up his cloak, shook off the last drops of water that clung to his shoes, and went to see what he could concoct for breakfast from the provisions in the storage room.

"Once we're settled, I'll see about fetching water and getting some eggs, cheese, and the like from the carts in the market a few streets over," Henri said. "Maybe a chicken for the pot." He looked at Rett's wounded leg and pursed his lips. "Definitely a chicken for soup. Speeds healing."

Rett chuckled. "I think that's more for a fever than a gunshot."

Henri shrugged, nonplussed. "Good for what ails you."

Ridge sat back with a satisfied grin as the fire began to blaze, lighting the room and immediately driving back the worst of the chill. He wiped his hands on his pants as he stood, and swiped his sleeve across the table as he pulled out a chair. "Change your clothing and sit down," Ridge ordered, with a look at Rett. Henri came back a few minutes later with cups and poured them all a measure of whiskey as Ridge and Rett changed out of their soaked garments. At some point in readying the room, Henri had managed to procure dry clothes for himself as well.

Too sore and tired to argue, Rett complied and fidgeted with the cards as he thought. "What now?"

Ridge shrugged. "You heal. We track who the winners and losers are with the Witch Lord, and try to figure out his next move."

"Where's Lorella?" Rett looked to Henri.

He smiled. "Lady Sally Anne offered her sanctuary, and Lorella decided to take her up on it, for now. Duke Barton's children have moved on, and she's afraid—rightly so, in my opinion—that after what happened at Bleakscarp and elsewhere, she's too visible for her own good. Thought she might be of use at Harrowmont, helping the children learn to handle their abilities."

Rett thought about how it had been for him and Ridge, struggling to learn to control what they didn't understand and at the same time, terrified of the consequences of discovery. "I'm sure she'll be an asset."

"I suspect that after what we told the king, he'll be taking a long look at the docks, which should put a crimp in the opium trade—and the smuggled weapons," Ridge mused.

"We probably didn't make any friends with the caravan masters, either," Rett said with a sigh. "Especially the ones who were enslaving and selling the children."

"I had a talk with Master Hans," Henri said, clearing his throat. "He refused to go to Harrowmont because he wanted to get back to his brother and friends here in the city. But since he was one of the…feral…urchins and knew others who might also be at risk, he agreed to work with us. After things settle down, he'll help us relocate any of the children with abilities he can persuade to go to Lady Sally Anne's."

"And she's all right with this?" Rett asked, eyebrows rising.

Henri chuckled. "I believe the good lady is actually enjoying herself—as are the women to whom she provides sanctuary. The urchins may find themselves quite soundly mothered."

What Rett remembered of his time on the streets before the orphanage was cold, hunger, and danger. He wouldn't wish that on anyone, let alone a child. When Ridge nudged him gently with an elbow, Rett realized he'd been silent too long. From the look in Ridge's eyes, his partner guessed where his thoughts had gone.

"They'll be safe," Ridge said. "And better than the monks—they won't have to hide who they are and what they can do. Together, they can figure it out. And they've got Lorella to help. It'll be a good thing."

Rett nodded, finding his throat too tight to speak.

Ridge looked up at a sudden thought. "What about the ghosts at Bleakscarp? Much as I appreciated the rescue, all that anger could be dangerous if it weren't being directed at murdering, traitorous scum."

"When Lorella comes back, she's offered to intervene—if Lord Sandicott agrees," Henri said. "We had plenty of time to talk on the carriage ride to Harrowmont."

"How bad do you think we'll have it when we report for duty?" Rett asked, taking a slug of his whiskey.

Ridge shrugged. "Burke'll make us pay—kinda has to, as an example. On the other hand, Kristoph made his feelings pretty clear. So, more than a warning; less than an execution."

Rett glared at him. "That's the best you can do?"

The fire had already warmed up the new rooms and cast a cozy glow. A kettle began to boil on the hearth, and next to it, a cauldron with onions and dried beans would become a warm soup in a few hours. They were mostly undamaged, King Kristoph was alive and grateful, and Burke didn't seem inclined to make them overly miserable. They'd beat back the Witch Lord, and while Rett felt sure they hadn't seen the last of Yefim Makary, they'd have breathing room to regroup.

Hard experience had taught him to appreciate whatever good moments life tossed his way since storms would surely follow.

"Yeah, I think that for now, I'll take it. Not too shabby, compared to the alternatives." Ridge grinned. "Let's have a little more of that whiskey, and enjoy what we've got while we can."

Watch for Ridge, Rett, and Henri to return in Sellsword's Oath, Book 2 in the Assassins of Landria series.

AFTERWORD

Assassin's Honor is epic fantasy without the epic length, offering a lighter experience for readers who like a rousing medieval adventure but want something a little shorter, with fewer point of view characters and interweaving plot threads, something more like a movie than a TV mini-series. My goal was to give you all of the excitement and action of a 'big fat fantasy' with less of the wrist strain. If you know a friend who gave up reading thick tomes because life keeps them too busy, this is for them—please spread the word!

I think of this series as Butch and Sundance if they were medieval assassins, a buddy-flick with some funny moments to counter the darker threads, an adventure that doesn't take itself too seriously. Rett and Ridge will be back for more in Sellsword's Oath.

ABOUT THE AUTHOR

Gail Z. Martin is the author of *Vengeance*, the sequel to *Scourge* in her Darkhurst epic fantasy series, and *Assassin's Honor* in the new Assassins of Landria series. *Tangled Web* is the newest novel in the urban fantasy series that includes both *Deadly Curiosities* and *Vendetta* and two collections, *Trifles and Folly* and *Trifles and Folly 2*, set in Charleston, SC. *Shadow and Flame* is the fourth book in the Ascendant Kingdoms Saga and *The Shadowed Path* and *The Dark Road* are in the Jonmarc Vahanian Adventures series. Co-authored with Larry N. Martin are *Iron and Blood*, the first novel in the Jake Desmet Adventures series and the Storm and Fury collection; and the Spells, Salt, & Steel: New Templars series (Mark Wojcik, monster hunter). Under her urban fantasy MM paranormal romance pen name of Morgan Brice, *Witchbane* and *Badlands* are the newest releases.

She is also the author of *Ice Forged*, *Reign of Ash*, and *War of Shadows* in The Ascendant Kingdoms Saga, The Chronicles of The Necromancer series (*The Summoner*, *The Blood King*, *Dark Haven*, *Dark Lady's*

Chosen) and The Fallen Kings Cycle (*The Sworn, The Dread*).

Gail's work has appeared in over 35 US/UK anthologies. Newest anthologies include: The Weird Wild West, Alien Artifacts, Cinched: Imagination Unbound, Gaslight and Grimm, Baker Street Irregulars, Journeys, Hath no Fury, and Afterpunk: Steampunk Tales of the Afterlife.

Find out more at www.GailZMartin.com, at DisquietingVisions.com, on Goodreads https://www.goodreads.com/GailZMartin, and free excerpts on Wattpad http://wattpad.com/GailZMartin. Join Gail's newsletter and get free excerpts at http://eepurl.com/dd5XLj

Also by Gail Z. Martin

Deadly Curiosities
Deadly Curiosities
Vendetta
Tangled Web
Trifles and Folly
Trifles and Folly 2

Darkhurst
Scourge
Vengeance

Ascendant Kingdoms
Ice Forged
Reign of Ash
War of Shadows
Shadow and Flame

Chronicles of the Necromancer / Fallen Kings Cycle
The Summoner
The Blood King
Dark Haven
Dark Lady's Chosen
The Sworn
The Dread
The Shadowed Path
The Dark Road

Other books by Gail Z. Martin and Larry N. Martin

Jake Desmet Adventures
Iron & Blood
Storm & Fury

Spells, Salt, & Steel: New Templars

49638317R00140

Made in the USA
Columbia, SC
25 January 2019